SHOULD HAVE KNOWN BETTER

Also by Grace Octavia

Take Her Man

His First Wife

Something She Can Feel

Playing Hard to Get

Published by Dafina books

SHOULD HAVE KNOWN BETTER

GRACE OCTAVIA

Dafina Books

Kensington Publishing Corp.
http://www.kensingtonbooks.com

DAFINA BOOKS are published by

Kensington Publishing Corp.
119 West 40th Street
New York, NY 10018

All Kensington titles, imprints and distributed lines are available at special quantity discounts for bulk purchases for sales promotions, premiums, fund-raising, and educational or institutional use. Special book excerpts or customized printings can also be created to fit specific needs. For details, write or phone the office of the Kensington Special Sales Manager: Kensington Publishing Corp. 119 West 40th Street, New York, NY 10018. Attn: Special Sales Department. Phone 1-800-221-2647.

Dafina and the Dafina logo Reg. U.S. Pat. & TM Off.

ISBN-13: 978-0-7582-6537-1
ISBN-10: 0-7582-6537-9

First trade paperback printing: November 2011

10 9 8 7 6 5 4 3 2 1

Printed in the United States of America

To all of the happily divorced women who have approached me at book signings and said,
"You need to tell my story!"
Hell hath no fury!

Acknowledgments

This isn't my story or one I even knew how to tell. But at some point, it seemed that everywhere I went, I was meeting women who were divorced and/or divorcing, and they wanted me to share their stories. They were angry. They were heartbroken. They were in pieces and wanted the world to know what it was like to go through something so terrible it threatened to ruin the very fabric of who they once thought they were. They'd lost control of the car and threatened to drive off of the bridge. I had to tell the story, they said. Now, that was a tall order. I write comedy. I write about love and squabbles. Not real pain. Not true pain. And who really wanted to read about that stuff anyway? But then, at a book club meeting for *Something She Can Feel*, I met a woman who changed my mind about my inability to write about such a sad topic. She said divorce was the best thing that ever happened to her. No—she said her marriage, the breakup of it, and then the eventual divorce were the best thing that ever happened to her, because it showed her who she really was—a boring librarian. She laughed, filled her glass up with more wine, and we both listened as other women in the club sipped and shared similar stories. Soon, we were all laughing at late-night trips to some man's new apartment, what it was like having a crush at forty, and feeling like you could lose your mind if you have to go to court to see the man you hate just one more time. I looked around and realized that the book club was less about reading and more about talking about these kinds of things. It was a safe haven. A safe place. And no doubt a way for these women to work through their pain. And, yes, most of them had joined the group during or after their divorce. From this, I came up with the idea for the Hell Hath No Fury House in this book and from there, the story behind this book was born.

It's all advice and all comfort for women who have been there and done that and now say they "should've known better."

I want to acknowledge every reader, male or female, who has been through this kind of trauma and allowed me to be with you along the way. As a reader, you allow me to speak to you, mirror you and make a play out of something that is very real in your life. It's humbling, and I don't take the responsibility lightly.

To the book clubs, virtual and actual, thank you for your support, free wine and consistent lists of my hits and misses (really). I firmly believe you all are the hidden support groups for women around the world. Ladies, if you are reading this and you don't belong to a group—find one. They're so much fun.

To my agent and confidant, Tracy Sherrod, thanks for your continued friendship and belief in my work.

To Mercedes Fernandez, my editor and sounding board, thanks for giving me phone time and trying to help me be on time!

I love all of you! Thank you so much.

Fire

I never really believed in God. Not a god. Not "the God" that you probably believe in. I know that must sound peculiar coming from a preacher's daughter. But, you know, I just never had a reason to honestly think someone or something other than myself would show up to save me when the whole universe was crashing in and burning me to bits. And that's what God is—what you really say He is—a savior. Some big hand to hold you together when you're a pile of hot ash. And I'd been there before. My son has autism. Mild autism. When he was three years old, he stopped saying, "Mama." Just stopped one day and then a man with a gray beard in a white jacket told me that he had a disease I could hardly pronounce. There was no cure. There was no cause. They couldn't say where it came from. "It came from me," I cried and sobbed in the bathtub with my hands resting over my vagina. The water was boiling all around me and turning to lava, scorching me alive. I didn't think any god would come then. And no god came. I got myself out of that fire. I fought to save my son. I was the only one there.

That wasn't the god the good Reverend Herbert George II talked about on the pulpit every Sunday at First Salvation Church of God in southwest Atlanta. No. Sitting there in the first row beside my mother in one of her lavender suits with sparkly lilac rhinestones around the collar, I listened as my father talked about a god who saved and fixed and came "just in the nick of time"! That "on time" god. Right?

I always knew it was a lie. It couldn't be true.

Nothing my daddy ever said was true.

The good Reverend Herbert George II killed my mother every day. But "Thou shall not kill"? God should've put something more direct in that chapter of his good book. Like don't kick your wife so hard in the stomach that she can't have any more babies.

There was no God.

I didn't expect it. I didn't see.

But that's just all what I believed then, how I understood things before I'd been on the earth for thirty-three years and ended up locked in a bathroom, once again, blaming myself for losing everything I loved.

I was so angry, the fire within me was burning up, the world crashing in.

I was about to kill somebody.

Either myself. Or my husband. Or my best friend. Or maybe, all of us.

And not figuratively. Seriously. The gun was on the floor; I was running out of the energy to save myself.

I cried. I felt like no one would ever hear me, but I cried out for the name I'd heard my mother scream so many times. My God. The heat in me boiled out of my mouth so fast that I lurched forward to my knees.

"God," I cried. "God, help me!"

1

The second fire started on a regular day.

Summer was coming and the teenagers in the library were getting restless. The new Georgia heat was making people crazy. Not to mention it was Friday, and that brought with it a particular kind of recklessness.

"And get this, girl." Sharika, my coworker at the triple-wide barn-sized library flicked her pink and yellow airbrushed fingernail tips in my face for some kind of dramatic buildup. "She up and killed herself. Just did. Shot herself in the head . . . or maybe the stomach." The air conditioner clicked on and hummed, making her get louder. "In the stomach!"

She paused and looked at me for a second, her dark brown face in a tight frown beneath the harsh halogen lights that hung over the help desk. She was thirty, short, and probably fifty pounds overweight, but you'd never know it by how she carried herself, switching and always with one hand on a poked-out hip. She was funny in a way that women like her just could be. The kind where her high self-esteem was to hide low self-esteem. But smart. She could recite classes in the Dewey decimal system like poems. Had a quick temper though.

"Isn't that some shit? She killed herself," she said and a hand went to her hip.

Behind her, I could see a cheerleader and her boyfriend padding rather suspiciously down the hallway toward the bathroom.

I nodded at Sharika and made a mental note to look after them in a few minutes. When I'd selected library science as my major in graduate school, I never imagined I'd end up chasing hot teens out of the slender bathroom stalls of a tiny satellite library. But then again, I don't really recall what I *did* imagine I'd be doing here.

"Now that's a damn shame. Killed herself over that man. Fuck that!" Sharika went on. "Won't catch me killing myself over some fool. I have too much to live for."

"Shssh!" I warned, elbowing her. "Somebody might hear you up here cursing."

She rolled her eyes and looked around the half-full, square-shaped reading room where we were both librarians. Four long, wooden tables, which had been donated to our location when the main library downtown underwent renovations, made a large square in the middle of our dwindling and aged stacks of books. It was 3:33 in the afternoon and, besides us, the only other adults in the library were Mrs. Harris from the seniors romance book reading club and Mr. Lawrence, the neighborhood misfit. For hours, we watched as the hot teens took turns trying to sneak off to the bathroom and back stacks for secret rendezvous, Mr. Lawrence pretended to look for jobs in an upside-down, week-old newspaper that no longer carried a classifieds section, and Mrs. Harris faked reading *Their Eyes Were Watching God* as she secretly spied on Mr. Lawrence.

"You don't think these two old folks cuss?" Sharika shot, her backwoods Augusta drawl purposely positioned to bite at every syllable she uttered. "Please, they could and would cuss both of us under a bus. Don't sleep on old people! They'll cut you first and cuss you last!"

Sharika giggled at her joke and I couldn't help but smile. She was crazy, but so right. Reverend Herbert George II had had a way with words, too, especially when he'd had some drinks in him.

"But really." Sharika swiveled her seat around to mine. "I just feel so bad for her. Why would she do that? Kill herself for some man? They were divorced already. It was time to move on."

"How long were they married?"

"Twenty years."

"And you said there was another woman?"

"Yeah, apparently he'd just gotten engaged to some tramp . . . some whore. And how she found out: stumbling on their wedding registry at Target?!? At Target?"

"Why did she look up his name?" I asked the obvious question, trying to seem a little concerned with Sharika's tale. Every day with her had a new story. And sometimes it was hard to tell if the story was based on real life or a book. She told both just the same. And if you missed a step, she'd happily start right back up again. It was important to feign some kind of attention.

"You're missing the point," she announced.

"Which *is*?"

"Which *is* that there's no reason to kill yourself for a man. I don't care who he married or who he left you for. There's just no reason. Life goes on. Shit, she could've found a better man . . . and the way things are going today, she might've been able *to get a better woman*!" She pulled a few wispy strands of her blond bangs from her eyes, and I considered for the third time that day that maybe someday someone who really loved Sharika would tell her that blond just didn't work for her. My skin is two shades lighter than hers and the most diversity I see in hair dye is jet black and just black. She calls me a "Plain Jane," but at least I'm not a grown woman walking around with blond bangs. I wear my hair cut at the ears and curled under: early Michelle Obama style. I know it gets . . . regular . . . but it's functional. And my husband couldn't care less about things like that.

"Is this one of your friends?" I got up from my seat at the mock mahogany counter and placed a stack of returned movies on Sharika's reshelf cart.

"Dawn, I told you this is from the book I read last night," Sharika answered. "Have you been listening to me? God, I just feel so sorry for the woman. Like for feeling so down that she thought the only way out was suicide. That's awful. And how did everybody miss it? Her friends? Her family? No one knew she was about to put a gun to her head? I've never been that caught up and I don't plan on getting there either."

"Oh, come on! You're speaking like a single woman who's never been in love," I said. "After having been married for twelve years, I can kind of understand her—the character. This woman wasn't just caught up. She was in love and she lost it. That can be devastating for anyone. I don't support suicide, but nothing will make you contemplate catching the first bus out of here like heartbreak. I know that. Ask any of those fools jumping off the Golden Gate Bridge."

I slid the last book from our return bin onto Sharika's cart and she jumped up from her seat to tug it away.

"Again," she said, playfully cutting her eyes at me. "I ain't been nowhere near such a bus, and I don't plan on getting directions."

"You get back to me when you finally fall in love," I replied. "When you find a man you love and he breaks your heart, you get back to me about that bus."

I sat and watched Sharika attempt to walk away, readjusting her too-tight yellow skirt as it rode up with each step. When she first came to the library, after the last co-librarian—a white woman from Athens who'd burst into tears one day when one of the teens called her a cracker—quit quite expectedly, I thought little of Sharika. She seemed too flashy and too loud to really be interested in being a librarian. But after just days of working beside her, I saw that Sharika, who was just three years younger than me, might have been more qualified for the job than me. While "business" and "acumen" and "customer" and "service" were words that seldom came together in her mind, she was a voracious reader who coveted knowledge from words like soap-opera fans do the story lines of their favorite characters. She was one of those people who could read *Giovanni's Room* in one evening and come back to work the next day talking about it as if it were the most interesting thing she'd ever read. The most interesting thing about that, though, was that she was always doubting her skills. She'd been talking about going back to school for her doctorate in library science for years, but she could find every excuse in the world not to: the programs were racist, the best ones were too far away . . . But I thought she was just scared of something. Of someone seeing what I saw every day and not being able to look past it to see who she really was. Yeah, she needed some polish, but the passion was there already.

I clicked on my computer screen and looked at my desktop photo, a picture I'd taken with my husband during a camping trip to DeSoto Falls a month before. His head leaned into mine. I was peeking over at his silhouette and smiling. I could see the sun setting in his sunglasses. Reginald had taken the picture with his cell phone, and since I still hadn't picked up the prints we ordered from our digital camera, this was the only shot I had. He kept begging me to go to Target to get them, but I never had time.

Except for the hot teenagers, hours in our little library were unpredictable. Sometimes they were unacceptably slow since the only thing to do was watch people argue over computer terminals and fall asleep as they pretended to read a book about screenplay writing or starting a marijuana garden. And other times, time ticked like a bomb as the drama of simply having different kinds of people crammed into the only remaining library in Augusta's poorest neighborhood promised full frontal action: a lovesick girl might discover her boyfriend making out with his ex-girlfriend in the reference section; Mr. Lawrence might decide to take a long afternoon nap and snore so loudly that it sounded like a demon was about to climb out of his mouth.

"So, you think she should've killed herself?" Sharika asked as we ushered the last few stragglers out of the library before closing.

"No. I didn't say that," I said. "I just pointed out that I know how hurt she must've been. Love is an amazing thing. And when you've been married for a long time, divorce is like . . . it's like failing at what everyone said will be the most major thing you do in your life. So you don't want to let go."

"Then why are so many people getting divorced?"

"Lack of focus. Forgetting what they signed up for. It can be any number of things," I answered, helping her stack a few books people had left on a table onto her cart. I pulled the keys to the front door from the pea green cardigan I kept at my desk for afternoons when the air-conditioning in the library got a little nippy. "I'll lock up out front," I added before leaving Sharika to tidy the rest of the floor.

On my way to the front door, I decided to check out the bathroom to make sure none of the teens had been left behind; we'd unknowingly locked a couple in the library for the night once before. When I went to pull the swinging door, it flew out quicker than I'd expected and I could tell someone was pushing from the other side.

"Oh, shi—" I groaned, feeling the corner of the door scrape the top of my penny loafer. I looked down at the damage and was ready to scold the fast cheerleader and her boyfriend with the short, raggedy dreadlocks that I'd seen sneaking off earlier, but when I looked up, instead there was Mrs. Harris standing in the doorway. "I'm so sorry," I apologized, embarrassed that I'd almost cursed in front of her. "I didn't know you were in here. We've closed. You can come back in the morning at—" I stopped myself, noticing that Mrs. Harris hadn't said a word and she looked even more surprised than I did. "Is everything OK?"

"Sure, honey," she said, her voice more sweet than usual. She flashed a bright smile, but didn't move and held the door only half opened. Her shirt was misbuttoned.

After a second, I tried to push the door open, but she held it steady.

"Are you sure everything is OK?" I asked again.

Her smile quickly dissipated.

I pushed the door again, this time with much more force, and it swung back so hard, it should've slammed against the wall inside of the bathroom, but it stopped short.

"Ouch," a male's voice cried.

With equal surprise and concern, I stepped into the bathroom to see who was behind the door.

"Mr. Lawrence?" I looked from him to Mrs. Harris and back. His shirt was completely unbuttoned. "You two?"

"No, no, not *that*, honey," Mrs. Harris tried to reassure me with her smile.

"Not *that*? What do you mean, Maggie?" Mr. Lawrence asked.

"I mean, it's not what she's thinking," she answered.

"The hell it's not," Mr. Lawrence said. "It's *everything* she's thinking!"

"Chuck!" Mrs. Harris looked down and suddenly desired to rebutton her shirt.

"Look, I don't really care what *it* is," I said sternly, "as long as it doesn't happen in the library. You two are too old for this."

"I know," Mrs. Harris agreed shamefully. Her shoulders sank and she went and stood beside Mr. Lawrence as if they were teenagers.

"I mean, do I need to take away your bathroom privileges like I do some of the kids from the school?" I asked.

"No," they answered together.

"Good," I said and it was all I could offer in such an off situation. There were no parents to call. They were the *grandparents*.

I rushed home, ready to tell my husband all about the senior bathroom tryst. Reginald was raised in Augusta and Mrs. Harris had been his third-grade teacher. He'd never believe she was canoodling in the bathroom with Mr. Lawrence. But my rush was put to rest when I turned onto our street. I could see through the rosebushes on the corner that his rusty green work truck wasn't parked in the driveway, and I hardly needed to stop to read the note on the front door to find him. He'd taken the twins to the park.

The other thing the doctor with the gray beard in the white coat couldn't tell me about my son's autism was why his twin sister hadn't gotten it and if she ever would. He told me to keep a diary and bring her back in six months. Seven years later and my daughter, Cheyenne, was still OK. But really we'd all been affected by autism.

"Here you are," I said, finding Reginald sitting on the end of a bench of a long row of babysitting, BlackBerry-holding dads.

Reginald was a big man. He came from big Southern people, and had muscular, broad shoulders and the kind of lacquered black skin that made him stand out—even in a room full of black people.

"Oh, hey," he said dryly before clicking his phone closed, and I could tell in just those two words that it had been a bad day.

I looked out over the muddle of bright playground equipment. Kids were everywhere, screaming and pulling. I saw my daughter's red shirt at the top of a jungle gym. It was a three-walled clubhouse where she and her girlfriends, too old to continue to enjoy the sand and slides and too young to sneak off to the bathrooms, kept court.

"Where's R. J.?" I asked.

"Sandbox," Reginald said, pointing his phone in the direction of a sea of babies and toddlers and preschoolers scooping sand into pails. In the middle of the tide was a ten-year-old in a dark blue hoodie. His head hung low.

"He had a bad day?" I asked to confirm.

Reginald got up without speaking and walked me halfway to the sandbox.

"The school called me to get him early," he told me. "I had to cancel two jobs."

"Oh, babe, I'm sorry," I said, feeling a little pinch in my gut.

"I really need you to get off early so you can get them from school," he said. "It's killing me. Especially now that it's about to be summer. More light equals more hours and more grass to cut."

"What am I supposed to do?" I said this with a straight face as I waved at the mother of one of Cheyenne's friends. "I can't ask Sharika to close the library by herself. She already opens alone so I can get the kids to school."

"Just do something," Reginald commanded. He came in closer so the woman couldn't hear him. "And stop making it seem like I'm the bad guy. I'm just trying to get us ahead a little. I'm starting to feel like I can't do anything big because I'm so busy dealing with all of this stuff." He gestured to the sandbox.

"Stuff? You mean our kids?"

"You know I don't mean it like that. I just need you to have my back. That's all I'm saying. We can't get what I want us to have if you don't support it. Is that so bad? Is it so bad that I want more for my family?"

"I never said it was bad," I said. "You're just starting to sound a little different."

Reginald wasn't a particularly argumentative husband, not like some I knew, but we'd had this argument before. The truth was that Reginald never wanted me to work in the first place. His mother had never worked. His grandmothers had never worked. When we first got married, I was OK with it. Not working? Most of my friends were buried in work and dying to find a man who wanted to take care of them. I stayed home and took care of his parents and tried to make their house—which we'd moved into when we'd gotten married—our own. But then I got bored. Going to graduate school was something I started online when I was pregnant and on bed rest. I picked what I thought was the easiest major, and when I graduated I convinced Reginald to agree to me working so we would have health insurance as he built his lawn care business. Unfortunately, getting that job at the library meant that Reginald had to pick up the twins from school every day. They were ten, but R. J. wasn't allowed on the bus because of his meltdowns.

"His teacher said he wouldn't speak all day," Reginald said. "She realized at lunch that a red marker was missing from her desk. Another kid said R. J. had taken it. He admitted that he had it, but wouldn't give it back."

"Did you get it back from him?"

"I've been on calls all afternoon, Dawn. Come on; don't do that."

"I wasn't doing anything. I'll get it."

We stood there and watched Reginald Jr. push his hands into the cool sand and leave them buried there for a time. Kids half his size ran in tight circles around his space in the sandbox.

"When we got in the car," Reginald went on, "he just kept saying, 'park—255—' "

"Means Drive. 255 Means Drive," I added, walking toward R. J. "His favorite place. The park."

"Hey, Mama's honey bunny." I inched in slowly on R. J.'s right side.

He didn't respond. He kept his wide, brown eyes buttoned to the sand between his legs, but I could see my reflection in the corner of his eye. I squatted beside him. This kind of detachment was typical when he'd had a new experience or was being confronted with a series of things he'd rather not face. He could see me, but he was pretending he couldn't.

"How was school?" I asked, dusting a few stray grains of sand from the red sweatpants he was wearing.

R. J. looked up from the sand and over at the benches where Reginald had been sitting. While he was Reginald's "Jr.," he followed his sister in looking like me. All three of us had my father's bushy eyebrows that would turn into a unibrow with a month of no grooming, my mother's brown eyes, and teeth that were perfect without the aid of braces. He had his father's size though. Had always been the biggest kid in his class. The doctors warned us that as he grew, the more difficult it would be for us to control his meltdowns.

"Bad day, huh?"

R. J. pushed his hands farther down into the sand.

"Well, you know what Mama says about bad days." I paused to give him a chance to respond, but he didn't. "Don't focus on what happened, focus on what you will do next." I slid my hand into the sand beside R. J.'s and clutched it.

He looked at me as if he'd seen me someplace before.

"So what are we going to focus on now?" I asked.

R. J. looked from me to his left hand that was still buried in the sand.

"What, precious? You want Mama to hold your other hand."

I slid my hand into the other sandy grave and tried to clutch his hand, only it was balled up. I tried to force it open, but R. J. quickly released his grasp and slid into my hand what felt like a stick. I pulled my hand out of the sand.

"A red marker?" I held it up.

"Trouble," R. J. said affirmatively. "I'm going to get in trouble." He nodded and looked at his father, who'd come up behind me.

"Oh, sweetie. It's not trouble. You just have to give it back and apologize. Can you do that?"

R. J. nodded again.

"You can't take things that don't belong to you. Do you understand that?"

"Yes, Mama," he said.

"Now, let's get your sister."

Whenever a day came, and there were many of those days, when we had to manage the negative outcomes of R. J.'s autism, it was nearly certain that we'd have to handle Cheyenne's attitude.

In my brief stint writing diaries about her, I wrote of a baby who was always trying to climb away from me—and that was before she could really climb. The doctors later concluded that she'd likely never develop autism, but I knew something else was brewing. The more I pulled her to me, the more she pushed away. And soon, I just let her go. She taught herself how to walk.

By the time I lassoed her away from her friends and into the car, she was promising to hate me forever and swore a life of eternal silence before telling her brother to stop looking at her "with his stupid bug eyes."

It was getting dark outside. Reginald had driven ahead of us in his truck. I looked at the twins in the rearview mirror.

"Stop being mean, Cheyenne," I said, deciding to crush the prospects of a fight by making R. J. recall everything they'd done in school that day. Cheyenne rolled her eyes at the travesty of discussion and seemed to push her back so hard into the seat that it was clear that she wanted to disappear.

"Oh, I almost forgot," Reginald started coolly after dinner. "I listened to the messages on the machine when I got in. Sasha called."

The house was just getting quiet. The twins were in their bedrooms. I was washing the dishes. Reginald sat at the kitchen table looking over receipts.

"Sasha? You mean from Spelman Sasha?"

The old faucet spat out a rush of overheated water and it nearly burned my hands.

"Yeah. The one with the, you know, television voice, like, 'Hey, Dawnie, this is Sasha Bellamy—' " He'd contorted his voice into a nasal know-it-all inflection, the one he preferred to use when he was making fun of certain people of a certain class. " 'I'm in Augusta. I wanted to stop by your place tomorrow. I have some free time. Maybe I can stay for the weekend. Spend some time with you and the kids. Can't wait to see you, soror. Give me a call.

Awesome!' " He flashed a cheerleader's smile and then pretended to vomit.

I slapped him with the dish towel.

" 'Awesome!' " he repeated robotically.

"She said she's coming here?" I asked, tossing the towel onto the counter. "*She* wants to come to *our* house?"

"It's all on the machine. Listen to it. I left it on there."

"She's coming here tomorrow?" I looked around the kitchen. Down at my chipped fingernails. "But this place is a mess. Why didn't you tell me about the message earlier when we got in?"

"I'm telling you now. I figured that since she's *your friend*, she'd follow up by *calling you* on your cell phone," he said smugly.

I rushed over to my purse hanging on one of the chairs and pulled out my cell phone. I clicked it on.

"You know I can't keep this thing on at work," I said. I had a text. It was Sasha saying everything she'd left on the machine. She planned to be at my house at noon. She'd come to town for the same conference.

"What's the big deal anyway, Dawn? Isn't she your special sorority sister—your *soror*?" Reginald joked sarcastically.

"I can't believe this." I tried to ignore his crack. "I wonder why she's coming here."

I walked over to a little magnetic mirror on the refrigerator. My edges were gray. I had so many split ends my hair wouldn't hold a curl.

Reginald, even in his sarcasm, was right about Sasha being my special friend. She'd been the only best friend I'd ever had. She'd been my roommate at Spelman. We pledged Alpha together. We shared secrets in the dark, whispered dreams into each other's ears. And so far, she was making good on all of hers. Sasha Bellamy had gone from being a flamboyant country girl from North Carolina to Ms. CNN, queen of the black liberal female voice. America saw her every night on television. But I hadn't seen her in person in nine years. We kind of lost touch when I left Atlanta.

"I'm so unprepared. Maybe I should just call her and tell her not to come. We could meet for lunch."

"Great idea. That's the direction I was going in," Reginald said quickly.

"Oh, wouldn't you love that?" I snapped. "You probably waited so late to tell me so I'd have no choice but to cancel."

Reginald hated CNN. He called it fake news for rich liberals. And he especially hated Sasha's show, which was taped at the national headquarters in downtown Atlanta. He called it "The Wannabe Watch." Needless to say, he wasn't exactly fond of Sasha. But Sasha also wasn't fond of him. They'd met when I started dating Reginald my sophomore year of college. Reginald thought she was bourgeoisie and stuck up and Sasha thought Reginald, who wasn't a student in any of the schools in the Atlanta University Center and worked at Spelman cutting the grass and cleaning up flower beds, was a bum preying on college girls.

"I'm just saying, no sense having people in the house who are going to cause a bunch of chaos," Reginald said.

" 'Cause a bunch of chaos'? You don't even really know her."

"She's a tramp."

"Don't say that. That's a bunch of old gossip."

"So, you're saying she didn't sleep with half of the frat boys at Morehouse?"

"She was in relationships with some of those guys. Plus, that was a million years ago."

"OK. I'm sorry. You're right. She *was* a tramp," he said. "Things could be different with her now, because we all know tramps change," he laughed.

"We've all grown up and changed," I said. "And you know she has some issues with men."

"Her issues weren't with men. They were with herself. Sasha can hardly take her eyes off of herself long enough to keep a man."

I looked in the refrigerator. There was nothing but leftovers.

Not even an apple. I'd need to go grocery shopping. I closed the door and looked back into the mirror. The thin hairs between my eyebrows were connecting.

"And if *we've* all grown up, then what's the problem?" Reginald asked. "Why are you even thinking about what you need to do around here? You have two kids. She should understand." He looked up from his little stack of crumpled papers and at me like I was Cheyenne complaining about not being able to go to the mall with her friends. "Do you really care what that woman says about"—he looked around the room—"anything?"

I didn't respond.

He leaned back in the chair, pushing it onto its back legs, and exhaled exaggeratedly.

"Yeah, you've all *grown up*!" he said. "I'll never understand your people."

I walked out of the kitchen quietly. There was nothing to say. Reginald was ready to pounce into one of his favorite topics and he would've loved for me to get aggravated and call Sasha to tell her not to come. That, of course, was something that had occurred to me, but then I was more afraid of how that snub would look than my bummy, aged house and battered hair.

Five little bottles stared at me from the bottom of my bathroom sink. Hair sheen. Hair grease. Hair dye. Hair glue. Hair remover. I removed the last bottle and dabbed a little pink glob onto the hair between my eyebrows. There was no way I could dye my hair and still have enough time to clean the house, get the twins washed and in the bed, and somehow lose thirty pounds. I looked down at my hips. It was the years, not the babies, that had them spreading the way they had. For years, I'd tried to blame the twins, but once they'd started walking and talking and I'd passed the weight I was on the scale the morning I'd gone into labor, I knew it was me. And I was OK with that. I was even OK with my husband having more toiletries than me. I'd never been a particularly gorgeous woman and the sheer work it took to keep the charade going was exhausting. Nails and hair appointments. The gym and the clothes. Did this match that and was it riding up too high on my thighs? I had no time for it. I had a family to run and a husband to keep happy. Reginald never seemed to care how I looked; in fact, he was annoyed when I spent too much time on myself.

"Look, I'm sorry I didn't tell you when I heard the message," Reginald said, standing in the doorway of the bathroom. I was leaning over the sink, wiping the hair remover from my forehead. "I just hate to see how these people always get to you. I mean, if anything, you should be proud of what you have. Yeah, Sasha is on television every night, but does she have a husband? Does she have a family?"

I just looked at him.

"Exactly. Money doesn't equal happiness. That's why I hate those fake-ass Atlanta people who support that status bullshit. I—"

"I know," I said, stopping him. "I just need to get myself together—"

"Don't worry about it." Reginald perked up suddenly. "I can get the kids to bed. Give you some time."

"Really?"

"Yeah."

"No, I'll get R. J. He needs to read his—"

"Dawn, I have it," Reginald said. He pointed to the open door beneath the sink. "As you were."

After responding to Sasha's text saying I was happy to hear from her and giving her my address, I dyed my hair and sat in the living room under the dryer watching a prerecorded edition of her show. She was smiling at some handsome Indian doctor, talking about free health care and black women who suffered from fibroids. She held a pen that looked heavy and expensive in her hand and nodded as the doctor spoke. She looked so beautiful and smart and all I could think about was all of the years that had gone by and how much things had changed since we'd pledged Alpha together and sworn to never lose touch.

I finished folding a pile of clothes that had been sitting on the ottoman in the living room for two weeks and replayed the episode.

2

Reginald made good on his promise to help. He even woke up early to cut the grass and prune the little rosebushes that edged the walkway to the front door. His parents had bought the house in the late '60s. It was a humble little ranch they'd purchased outright with his father's veteran's benefits. Time took its toll on the house though. Wherever something could sag or chip, it did. We never had enough money for repairs—nothing beyond patch-ups. But it was comfortable and it was ours. It was home. Yet I knew it could never compare to whatever Sasha's place looked like in Atlanta.

The clock ticked closer to the time Sasha was supposed to arrive. I finished poofing the pillows in the living room, organizing the fruit in the fruit bowl (I'd gone to the supermarket at 2:00 a.m.), and wrestling with Cheyenne's hair. I got everyone into the living room for a meeting.

I lined them up and inspected kneecaps and clothing, and reviewed my expectations for the afternoon. No sports. No arguing. No fighting. No Internet. No yelling. No friends over. Everyone was to be on their best behavior. I felt silly for saying these things, but I knew my family. Reginald didn't want Sasha there in the first place. Cheyenne was annoyed just to be annoyed. R. J. was already finding it hard to understand why his usual Saturday routine of going to the park had been disturbed.

I noticed a riotous hair between his eyebrows and slicked it down with a finger I'd wet with my spit.

"Yuck!" Cheyenne groaned as R. J. winced. "That's nasty."

"Cheyenne!" I called.

Reginald unbuttoned the top button of the shirt I'd laid out for him on the bed.

"Reginald!"

Now Cheyenne was scratching at her stockings.

"Can I take these off now?" she groaned. "It's too hot for stupid stockings."

R. J. rubbed his forehead and the long hair went back into a riot.

Reginald unbuttoned another button and looked at his watch for the third time.

"It's getting late," he said. "You sure she's still coming?"

My arms at my sides, my hands in fists, I was completely annoyed. This was getting impossible.

"Everybody!" I shouted. "Listen, you are all going to have to focus. Just for me. Just for a minute. I told you my friend is coming and I need you all to act right; just for a little while."

"Why, Mama? Why do we have to act right?" R. J. asked.

I looked from R. J. to Reginald, who shrugged his shoulders.

"It's getting late, sweetie," he said. "Maybe we should let the kids go outside and call them back when she gets here."

"They'll get dirty and Cheyenne's hair will—" My list of grievances was interrupted by the sound of a car pulling onto the gravel in our driveway. The kids ran to the window.

A car door slammed. Reginald and I went to open the front door. There was a limousine idling behind the green pickup. The driver was out and preparing to open the back door.

"A limo," Cheyenne gushed, pushing past me to get outside.

Her brother trailed behind her.

Two kids from around the corner were outside sitting on their bikes in the middle of the street. I thought to tell them to get out of the road, but then my eyes followed theirs and stopped on a brown hand with long, shiny red nails, holding onto the outstretched arm of the driver. There was a hush as it seemed that everyone, including me, had forgotten that we'd known exactly who was getting out of the back of that car. Our little crowd waited. Another kid stopped short on his bike. One fell.

My throat swelled.

Sasha's head of blond curls popped out from behind the door and everyone gasped—or was it just me?

"Dawn!" she yelled, breaking the hush over the scene, pushing past the driver and meeting me halfway up the walkway. She took these deliberate long strides in her black heels. She had on a red wrap dress and sparkling diamond earrings I could see into from three feet away. I was happy now that I'd made everyone overdress for the visit. My gray slacks and charcoal blouse seemed just enough standing in front of Sasha.

I'd watched the taped version of her interview with the cute Indian doctor five times before I'd finished drying my hair. I swear this woman walking toward me looked thinner and younger and even more beautiful than what I'd seen. Yeah, she'd grown up from being twenty-one to thirty-three, but the beauty she'd had when we were young had matured into this dramatic parade of perfection. Seeing her floating toward me like Miss America, I whispered what I was sure most people thought when they saw her in person. "She's somebody."

Sasha threw herself heavily into my arms, wrapping hers around my neck and squeezing tightly. She smelled so sweet, so unmistakably feminine. So not like me.

We rocked back and forth. I could see Cheyenne and R. J. standing behind her.

"I can't believe it's you," she squealed, tightening her grip. "My college roomie!"

"Sasha!" I said, still shaking in her tight embrace.

She let loose and backed up a bit, cupping my face in her hands. She was crying and smiling.

"It's been too long!" She pulled me back into her arms and rocked some more.

Cheyenne's eyes narrowed suspiciously on her back.

While I flashed Cheyenne a warning look, I was also a little put off by Sasha's tearful greeting. It seemed so sincere, and so heartfelt. In her moist eyes, I saw a friend who'd missed me. Though I'd missed her, too, maybe my nerves or surprise that she was visiting stopped me from fully feeling the moment. I told myself to let go. I wiped one of her tears and kissed her on the cheek.

"It has been too long," I said, looking into Sasha's eyes.

I felt Reginald's hand on my shoulder.

"Hello, Sasha," he said.

"Oh, Reginald," she said. "You look great."

She grabbed him and pulled him to her the same way she'd done me.

The kids laughed and pointed at the baffled look on Reginald's face behind her back.

I sharpened my eyes on Cheyenne again and they stopped quickly.

"And Sasha," I said, lightly tugging Sasha's arm off of Reginald's neck. "These are the twins; I don't think you've seen them since their christening in Atlanta."

She turned around and crouched down seemingly expecting to greet two little toddlers, but Cheyenne and R. J. towered above her.

"Oh, my goodness," she hollered, pulling them down to her. "You two are so big! I can't believe how you've grown!" There was more crying and rocking.

Reginald hustled over to the driver to get her bags.

"Come on; get inside," I said. "I'm sure you're tired from your conference."

"Super tired," she said, looking up at the house. "Oh, what a quaint little cottage."

I'd hardly planned what we would do during Sasha's visit beyond showing her my herb garden and offering her an apple from the fruit bowl. But by the time the sun was setting, I realized that none of that was necessary anyway. She had a story. I had a story. I had to know. She had to know. And we kept asking whatever happened to this person and that person. Where is she now? What is he doing? We giggled and gossiped like we were back in our dorm room. And, oh, it was so refreshing. Just having company for me. You know? So much of what we'd done in our house was for Reginald. For the kids. And right then I found myself playing with my hair. I told Sasha I liked her perfume. She pulled the bottle out of her purse and sprayed a dash on my wrist.

"I spray it everywhere," she said, stashing it back into her purse at the dinner table.

We laughed, but everyone else just sat in their chairs lazily and rolled their eyes. Cheyenne fingered a meatball on her plate of spaghetti. I would've snapped at her, but she was the only one of them who was still showing signs of life. R. J. and Reginald were completely worn out by our conversation.

After surviving a series of Sasha's questions about what it was like having a twin, R. J. was avoiding eye contact with Sasha. And Reginald only broke his stare to give me a look of disapproval about something Sasha had said.

"So what's it like being a big television star?" Reginald asked rather randomly.

"It's wonderful," Sasha answered. "I get to travel the world, meet interesting people"—she looked at Cheyenne and smiled—"learn new things. I couldn't have asked for a better career."

"It can't be all good—must have some downsides," Reginald pushed and I managed a half-pleasant smile, afraid of where he might be going with his questions. I knew Sasha could feel the tiny tension, too, and was hoping she'd back down quickly, give him what he wanted, so she could get back to talking to me.

"I can't say anything bad about the industry at this point. Of course, I have to work hard—go up against the big boys on bad days—but who doesn't have to do that?" She looked over at me for agreement and I nodded.

"Actually, at the library, my coworker Sharika and I always have to try to—" I offered, but Reginald quickly cut in.

"I don't bow down to any big boys," he said. "I have my own business. I'm my own man. That's how it is when you work for yourself."

"Well, of course, I wouldn't mind running my own business, but I couldn't exactly open my own television network and have the same outreach that I do at CNN."

"Bob Johnson did," Reginald pointed out.

"Bob Johnson? He sold his soul to Viacom. Sold our soul. You can't compare that," Sasha said.

"Who's Bob Johnson?" Cheyenne asked after finally eating her meatball.

"The founder of BET," I replied.

"The man went out there and made something happen for himself. He didn't depend on white folks for anything," Reginald said.

"OK," I interjected. "Enough of the grown people talk. You two are boring the kids." I reached over and rubbed R. J.'s back.

"The kids need to hear this," Reginald said. "They need to know all about their mother's friend who works at CNN. What it's like being on top. Nothing wrong with a little spirited conversation. Right, Sasha?"

"Of course not," Sasha agreed. "Do you two ever watch the show?"

"Once in a while," I said quickly. "I loved the piece you did about black women serving in Iraq last Thanksgiving. It was so touching."

"Oh, you saw that? I so loved working on that feature. I used every favor I ever had to get on that base. Those women were so courageous."

"So what brings you to Augusta?" Reginald asked abruptly. "Must be hard to get time away."

"Well, as I told Dawn, I've been at a journalism conference in downtown Augusta for the last three days and I figured I had to stop through to see you guys before I headed back to Atlanta. I'm actually on a two-week vacation."

"And you came to little old Augusta?" Reginald asked. "I'd think someone like you would go to France or Paris."

"Paris *is* in France, Daddy," Cheyenne snarled. "If she goes to Paris, she's been to France."

Reginald didn't even look at her.

"Wow, that was so smart of you, sweetheart," Sasha said. "What school are they at, Dawn? Westminster? Episcopal Day? Augusta Prep?"

"Oh, no; we don't have them in private school," I answered. "We just can't do it right now."

"What? Are you serious?" she pushed, waving off the bread basket as I tried to pass it along. "You simply can't trust your children's education in the public school system. I did a special on it. I'd put them in private school. What, it's only about $18K a year per kid."

"Yeah, Reginald and I have considered switching them over," I said, avoiding Reginald's eyes. "But the public schools here aren't so bad."

"Don't believe the hype," Sasha said. "Look up the numbers."

To this, I smiled and lifted the bread basket again. "Anyone need more bread?" I asked.

This sort of conversation was what I wanted to avoid. Reginald's distaste for what he called "you people" the other day was actually a pure disdain for upper-class blacks who enjoyed being . . . upper-class blacks. A self-proclaimed country boy, who exalted the simple life his war-veteran father had provided for his family, Reginald found this sort pompous and ridiculous. He said they were blinded by their desires to be white and measure up in the eyes of the white American dream.

They all refused the bread and passed the basket around quickly.

When it landed back in front of me, I jumped up just as Reginald was about to say something.

"OK, dinner's done," I said. "Let's clear the table."

The plates were half empty and no one had touched the bowl of carrots I'd roasted, but I grabbed the bowl of spaghetti from the center of the table.

"We're done?" R. J. asked.

"Yes, baby," I said. "Now, clear your plate and go and wash your hands. We're getting ready for bed."

I smiled pleasantly and walked swiftly into the kitchen, snagging Reginald's shoulder to signal for him to follow me.

"Be nice," I said once we were in the kitchen. "Just be nice to her. Please!"

"I'm trying, but she's a—"

A curse was interrupted when Cheyenne handed him the bowl of carrots and disappeared back into the dining room.

"She's just different," I said. "She has different views than yours. And that's OK."

"I'm not a child," Reginald said. "I know people see things differently, but that woman is just a—"

"Here, Daddy." R. J. stopped his father this time, handing him the basket of bread.

Reginald took it and handed it to me.

"Look, I just need you to make it through dessert," I said once R. J. left.

"Dessert? You just said dinner was over!"

"For the kids. I got some tiramisu and dessert wine for us," I said. "I thought it would be nice."

"Tira—what? And you don't even drink. Can't you two do that without me?"

"That will be odd," I tried. "Come on. It'll just be like fifteen minutes. Have one little bit and then you can go to bed."

Reginald looked at me.

"Please. Just be nice. Only a little while longer."

"OK," he said firmly. "But if she starts acting crazy again, I'm going to let her have it. I hate people like that. You know it."

"I know, babe," I said, handing him the marbled tiramisu I'd stashed in the back of the refrigerator so the kids couldn't see it.

As I expected, Reginald was much better after he'd had something sweet to eat. While he scoffed at our sweet dessert wine, his third beer had him at ease and I actually saw him smiling at Sasha.

"So, how are the men in Atlanta?" I asked Sasha as she was in the middle of a speech about how hard it was being a single woman working in entertainment. Her red lipstick had faded a little and her hair was pulled back into a ponytail. "I know they're all falling madly in love with you."

"Love? Hardly." Sasha answered. "The ones who aren't homosexual are self-sexual—"

"What's that?" I asked.

"Self-obsessed. You know, the ones who work out seven times a week, get mani-pedis, and only date women who look good in pictures with them?"

"Oh, you mean the new metrosexuals?"

Sasha and I laughed as Reginald looked on confused.

"What, you don't know any men like that?" Sasha asked him.

"Afraid I don't."

"And that's a good thing," I said, patting him on the back.

"Then there are the married men who are dating," Sasha went on, "and the dating men who never want to get married."

"Come on; it can't be that bad," I insisted.

Sasha sat back and twisted the fork in what was left of her tiramisu.

"No, there are some bright spots . . . there was Derrick . . . We even got as far as picking out an engagement ring."

"See, that's promising." I winked at Sasha.

"Yeah, it *was* very promising. Until I realized I was paying for the ring myself. That joker had five kids and five baby mamas—all of whom were deep into him for back child support!"

Reginald was the only one who laughed then.

"Five?" I repeated.

"Five!" she confirmed. "Well, I only knew about two at first—and you can't hate a thirty-five-year-old man for having two kids—but then it seemed like every time we had a heart-to-heart his heart needed to open up about another kid. I was in too deep to kick him to the curb. But then, I realized he was broke. That was it for me."

Reginald looked at me.

"Then there was Arthur. He was a painter."

"Oh, an artist!" I perked up.

"Um . . . negative. He painted houses. He was more broke than Derrick, but I'd just turned thirty-three. I was feeling bad about being single and took a chance. He was good to me. Moved in. Painted my whole house—outside and inside."

"Resourceful!" I tried, cutting a second slice of tiramisu for Reginald's empty plate.

"Yeah, but then he painted my neighbors' house and slept with them, too."

Reginald kicked me under the table.

"Who knew he could fuck two lesbians?" Sasha added.

"Lesbians? Well, be glad you got rid of him. He sounds like a jerk."

"Or the luckiest man in the world," Reginald mumbled and I kicked him back harder. "Ouch!"

"Well, I took him back. I figured moving would fix that little ditty. But then he slept with my assistant."

"He was a womanizer!" I said.

"No, girl; my assistant was a man," Sasha revealed, crumbling to the table in defeat and bouncing her head against the wood.

"That's awful," I said, reassuring Sasha by rubbing her hand from across the table. "I can't believe he was a . . . a gay man who also slept with lesbians."

"And painted houses," Reginald added before I kicked him again.

"No need to feel sorry for me." Sasha straightened up in her seat and exhaled. "I'm in counseling now and I realize that I've been picking the jerks. I need to make better decisions for myself."

"That's right, girl," I said. "There are good men out there."

"Exactly! Look at Reginald," she said. "He's a good guy. Husband. Father. Who would've thought you two would've lasted this long? It's been . . . what . . . twelve years since Spelman. Who would've thought you'd still be together?"

I looked at Reginald with a soft smile.

Sasha had been there when Reginald was outside of our dorm giving his little speeches about the ailments of the black upper class. I felt sorry for him. I stopped. I thought his ideas were silly, easily disproved, but I was impressed by his belief in the things he was saying. Most of the men I knew only meant what they said for a time, when they were in public, when people were watching. But in Reginald's eyes, I saw sincerity. When Sasha tried to pull me past him, saying he was just an angry lawn-mower man, I thought I saw someone who loved his people and really wanted what was best. When he finally asked me out, I said yes.

"Who *wouldn't* think we'd still be together?" Reginald asked though he knew exactly what Sasha meant. And any answer she could give would simply indulge him in confirming all of the things he'd always thought about her and "you people" back then.

"I'm just saying, Dawn was seven years younger than you. She was a Spelman girl. There were Alpha brothers across the street at Morehouse just dying to get with our Dawn."

I laughed, but quickly straightened my face when I saw how Reginald was looking at me.

"No, they weren't," I said, brushing her off.

"Oh yes, they were!" she insisted.

"Well, she made a good choice," Reginald interjected. "Seeing as how they're all gay and have five baby mamas and want their women to pay for stuff and all—Dawn doesn't have to worry about that stuff. She has a good man. Don't you, babe?"

"Yes, babe," I said.

"Your house is paid for. You don't have to work. And while your kids aren't in private schools, they live in a great community and never have to wonder where their next meal is coming from. You have everything a woman could want."

He smiled and pinched my cheek.

The door to the guest room where Sasha was staying was ajar.

A spare quilt wrapped neatly over my arm, I pushed the door open a little.

"I brought you an extra blanket," I started before peeking inside and seeing Sasha bent over her suitcase in nothing but a red thong. "Oh, I'm sorry!" I stepped back out quickly and shut the door, embarrassed at my intrusion.

"Oh, it's OK. Come on in," Sasha called from inside of the room.

I pushed the door back open, sure Sasha had taken the few seconds alone to put on a T-shirt or robe, but there she was, standing in front of her suitcase looking as if she'd just stepped out of a Victoria's Secret thong photo shoot.

I rubbed my hand against the unpredictable patterns of the quilt my grandmother had made before she died, pulling it against my cotton nightgown. I couldn't think of anything to say.

Sasha was almost naked. I couldn't remember ever looking like that in my underwear.

"I'm sorry for pushing in. We don't really have very many unlocked doors around here when we're changing clothes," I said awkwardly. "It's the kids."

"Oh, I understand." She slid on a thin red chemise she'd pulled from the suitcase.

"I brought a blanket for you. It gets cold in here at night, even with the weather changing. I thought you might need it."

"Thanks, soror; always looking out for me." Sasha came over and took the blanket before kissing me on the cheek. "Stay and chat me up for a bit. I know I won't be able to sleep after all that debating."

"I'm sorry," I said, stepping into the room. "Reginald just gets so caught up . . . and then he goes on and on—"

Sasha had placed red cinnamon-scented candles all around the room. She had jazz playing on her laptop.

"It's no biggie. He's fine."

"You travel with candles?"

"Yes," Sasha said. "And wine!" She pulled a bottle of red wine from her suitcase and bounced onto the bed laughing.

"I guess that's a fine way to travel."

"Please, I stay in so many hotels for work, I have to try to make my own space. And when that doesn't work"—she paused and held up the expensive-looking bottle of wine—"I drink." She got up and gathered a glass and bottle opener from the nightstand.

"Oh, it can't be that bad, Ms. CNN. You're a household name. Everyone knows who you are. And it must look great in your bank account."

"Yeah, I worked for all of that. I sacrificed a lot," she said, opening the bottle. "News is hard on you and being a black woman in the business is even worse."

"How so?" I sat down on the bed.

"People just expect you to be a hard-nosed bitch. So you try not to be. And then they run over you, and then you have to be a crazy bitch just to get what you want. Anderson Cooper says he wants a certain shot, he gets it. I say I want a shot, they ask my producer. I say, fuck the producer. He wouldn't have a job if it wasn't for me."

"But there are way more black people working in television . . . at least more than there were when we were growing up. What about A. J. Holmes? I love that brother's work. He can't be like all of the other good old boys," I said, bringing up a black reporter who did special segments on CNN. He was probably one of the most handsome men on television. He looked more like a model than a news reporter. I snuck to watch him in the bedroom on Sunday mornings when Reginald was in the living room watching football.

"He's actually pretty cool," Sasha said. "Fine as all get-out."

"Don't I know!"

"But he's still one of the boys. And when it comes down to it, he'll side with them."

She poured a glass of wine and tried to hand it to me.

"Oh no, I can't," I said, feeling the weight of the wine I'd already had at dinner.

"I insist, soror," she said. "Take a load off!" She held the glass of wine out right in front of my eyes.

I reached for it.

"But what will you drink out of?" I asked. "Let me go into the kitchen and get another glass."

"No, no," she said. "I have the bottle."

Thirty minutes later and the guest room had become a dorm room at Manley Hall. Lying in the bed beside Sasha, my head felt so heavy, but I just couldn't stop laughing.

"And that girl, you know the dark-skinned pretty one who refused to pledge with us . . . What was her name?" Sasha went on after sharing what I was sure was an embellished tale of a classmate who was caught making out with one of her students behind a high school in Phoenix. It wouldn't have been so unbelievable had the student not been a girl who the police first thought was a boy. Turns out the girl was on the football team. Now the news was about a classmate who'd just gotten a divorce. "What was her name?"

"Black Barbie?" I answered. "You mean Black Barbie? Marcy's best friend?"

"Yes . . . Kerry. That was her name. Kerry Jackson."

"I remember her well. We took biology together over at Morehouse when Spelman didn't have the class. She was so pretty. God, it was hard just walking into the classroom behind her," I said, recalling how it seemed like some kind of R&B music video whenever Kerry was near. Her long, jet black hair, normally parted down the middle, would blow in an invisible breeze that always missed me, and boys would look on and grin like she was a piece of chocolate candy. She never budged though. Never gave them any attention.

"You know she married that fine-ass Alpha frat brother Jamison. Well, apparently he was having an affair with some woman his mother hooked him up with from her church!" Sasha gushed.

"That's madness," I said, again thinking Sasha was just talking dramatics. "Impossible. Who would cheat on someone like Kerry? She came from a good family and everything." I looked over at Sasha. What she didn't know was that my mother had been Kerry's mother's maid for the past fifteen years, and I'd already known about the divorce.

"I know she had a *good* family," Sasha said and I could hear the wine in her slurred voice. "And she was pretty to be so dark. You know what I mean?"

"Please, I almost couldn't pledge because I was darker than the bricks outside of Manley."

"Anyway," Sasha said, frowning. "Kerry took Jamison's trifling ass back and he did it again. Flew out to California and got shacked up with the woman he'd cheated with. Got her pregnant. He was so whipped he almost lost his business."

"Rake It Up?" I said.

"Yeah, a million-dollar lawn care service she helped build. I wish a Negro would try that with me!"

"Yeah, I've been meaning to hook Reginald up with him," I said, thinking of Reginald's sagging business list. The recession had many of his once-loyal clients cutting their own lawns now. He had to go corporate with his list or he'd be shut out. It was my biggest concern. But mentioning corporate to Reginald was like asking him to sell his soul.

"He's thinking of expanding?"

"We're considering some things," I lied. "It's just so damn hard to get him inspired. He's gotten all caught up in his white and black thing and then there's the uppity Negro thing." I sat up. "I just want him to see that there's more to life than . . . Augusta!"

We both laughed.

"Well, you know what to do!"

"What?"

"Put that thang on him!" Sasha squirmed around in the bed like she was having sex.

"Oh . . . *that thang* hasn't been happening up in here in some time," I admitted and I was surprised I'd let that come out of my mouth. I hadn't told anyone about our sometimes sour sex life. Months could go by. As long as Reginald had *Sports Center* on at night, he wouldn't touch me.

"Are you kidding me?" Sasha eyes got wide. "You better handle that thing in there. His fine, chocolate, big ol', hay-bale tossing, slave-looking ass!"

Sasha and I laughed so hard, we bumped heads.

"It's not that I don't want to," I said. "I love having sex. But he gets tired and bored sometimes, so we just wait until the spirit moves him."

"The who moves what?" Sasha asked. "And when does that happen?"

"Like two times a month," I claimed solidly. "Maybe three."

"Well, have you tried other things? Like toys and movies . . . a threesome?"

"Oh, no, he'd never do that!" I laughed at the idea.

"But you would?" Sasha looked into my eyes.

"Well, I'd consider it . . . I guess if he wanted to," I spat, nervous in her stare. "You've done that?"

She winked at me flirtatiously

"What? Have you?" I pushed.

"Dawn, it's like an appetizer in Atlanta," she confessed indirectly.

"Really?"

"A second girl in bed means a second date."

"Wow," I said. "But where's the commitment in that? If he's so busy having sex with other people, how do you know if he enjoys sex with you?" I was a little embarrassed that I was so ignorant about this. I couldn't imagine that Reginald would want something like that. We'd never even discussed it.

"I don't really care," Sasha answered dismissively. "As long as he's having sex and still with me, it's all good."

"But aren't you looking for love? For a good man? Do you think a good man will want all of that?"

"Any man would."

"I'm serious."

"Please, the time for pressure and convincing dudes to settle down with me is over," Sasha said. "The next fool who rolls up in me without a condom will thereby be known as 'Baby Daddy.' "

She laughed, but I could only offer a slight and uncomfortable giggle. Something in her voice was just too serious.

"You're joking, right?" I asked. "What about what you said at dinner? About therapy?"

"Dawn, I'm ready to be a mother. And if I can't get a ring by spring, I'll get a father by fall."

"But don't you think he has a right to know? Like, are you gonna tell the guy your plan?"

"Look, I don't want to sound like some kind of evil sociopath. I am all for disclosure, but the truth is that men like Reginald are gone," Sasha explained. "They just don't want to get married anymore. They want to play around. They want to love you. But the responsibility that comes with marriage just isn't something they desire. I get that. But I need to do what's best for me. I'm not getting any younger." She flicked at her breasts as some sort of example, but they looked pretty firm and high to me. "Implants," she whispered.

I looked at her boobs again with my mouth aghast.

"Really?" I mouthed.

"Really," she mouthed back.

I shook my head and forced myself to look away from her breasts.

"But what about the ones who are marrying?"

"Please; they're either weak and depending on the woman for whatever reason, on the down low and hoping to hide, or expectant fathers—let's hope mine is the latter," Sasha joked.

"Sounds like you have it all figured out," I resigned.

"I'm not expecting anything from anyone. I make enough to support me and my child. He can dip if he wants."

Short on rational things to say, I smiled and replied, "Well, I'm sure looking like you do, you'll find one to stay in no time." I tossed one of the blond curls hanging lazily from Sasha's head back behind her ear.

"Oh, yes, Blondy catches them every time," Sasha said.

"Blondy?"

"Yeah, my wig. Men love it." She pulled the wig off and showed off a head of tight black nappy curls that hardly stretched beyond the tips of her ears.

I actually gasped, remembering how many times I'd looked at

and studied and envied those curls when I saw Sasha on television.

"It's a wig?" I quizzed, amazed. "A wig?"

"Yes, a lacefront. Cost me $7,000. Some white girl in Cali cut off all of her hair for me."

"That's a lot of money." I fingered the thing on the bed between us. It looked something like a blond Yorkie or cocker spaniel.

"And well worth it," Sasha said. "If a nice car is a chick magnet, Blondy is a dick magnet."

I don't know when I decided to go back to my bedroom after sharing my grandmother's quilt and two bottles of dark red wine with Sasha, but I did. My feet were ripened watermelons. My head was a pumpkin ready to be plucked from a patch. Everything on me felt heavy and weighted. And every step I took beyond the last brought me closer to sleeping on the cold hallway tile—funny how cold floors look so comforting when you're inebriated.

I nearly fell into the bedroom door instead of pushing it open with my hand. What was right in front of me wasn't quite as close as I'd thought and when I tried to straighten up and consider that maybe the doorknob was farther away, it was two inches closer.

"Ouch," I groaned, hitting my hand against the space above the doorknob and then cracking my forehead on the wood when I tried to console my aching thumb. "Shit!"

Embarrassed by the sound of myself cursing so loudly in the middle of the night, I looked around for witnesses and then laughed at my suspicions.

"Who's out here, Dawn?" I joked with myself. "No one! No . . . one!"

I finally managed to get ahold of the doorknob and attempted to sober up before walking into the bedroom.

"Get it together, Dawn," I scolded myself firmly before turning the knob and opening the bedroom door just a little to see if Reginald was still asleep.

In a flash, I saw that the bedroom was dark, but the television was on. I didn't look directly at the screen. It was hanging on the door beside the wall. But I heard Sasha's voice and saw the colorful lights patterned on the bed.

Beneath the mosaic reflecting onto our comforter, I saw Reginald's eyes wide open. The comforter was up to his neck. Something that looked like a teepee was erected near his midsection. I was quiet for a second, listening to Sasha's voice and watching the top of the teepee rise and settle.

I thought to say something; I don't really recall what it was, but just the idea of shaping my drunken thoughts into a sentence made me stumble and fall into the cracked doorway.

Reginald was obviously surprised and he shot up quickly like the bed had turned to fire.

"Dawn!" he yelled like I wasn't supposed to be walking into my own bedroom. He jumped right out of the bed.

"What are you doing?" I asked in a haze. I stepped in to see the television. It was another taped episode of Sasha's show. She smiled brightly into my bedroom with a purple halter top that showed a line to her cleavage.

"Just watching the news," Reginald offered.

"Sasha's show?" I said. "We never watch that." I made my way to the bed and just tossed my whole self onto it without digging into the covers.

Reginald was still standing where he'd landed. His gym shorts were hanging low at his knees.

"What? Why are you looking at me?" he asked.

"What? I always look at you."

"You're drunk."

"No," I said and even in that one syllable I managed a slur. My head on the pillow, I watched as Reginald straightened his shorts and sat back down on the bed. "Why did you get up if you were going to sit back down?"

"Why do you keep asking me questions?" He sounded highly annoyed.

"I was just wondering—"

"You're drunk." He clicked the television off and in the darkness my mind began to spin.

I reached out for him.

"Why did you turn off the television?" I asked.

"Dawn, you're drunk," he repeated.

I reached farther and then moved my body toward his. "You wanna do something nasty?"

Reginald turned to me. After my eyes adjusted to the darkness, I saw his eyes.

I slid my hand into his pants and he pulled it out quickly.

"Dawn, I'm tired and you're drunk," he said. He dropped my hand, as if it were diseased, back onto my side of the bed.

I groaned and tried to settle into the idea of sleep. Flashes of red silk and candles and wine spilling from a bottle swam in my head.

"Be nice to Sasha," I said with the last light breath I had in me.

"I said I'd try," Reginald said. "That's all I can promise."

When someone hasn't had more than one or two alcoholic beverages at a time in three years, it's usually best to take it easy when stepping back into the league of libation. Had I considered this logical concept, I wouldn't have had the four extra glasses of wine I'd shared with Sasha before returning to bed with Reginald. But the jokes and old memories and sex talk was flying and, well, who was counting? Who? Eight hours later, and I was. My head had an invisible ax in it and it was still spinning after I'd lifted it enough from the pillows to see that the sun was bright in the sky outside of my bedroom window. The room was quiet.

"Reg—" I tried calling Reginald but it came out as a little

spurt. I lifted my head a little more and it felt like a television. "Owwww." My face fell back into the pillows.

I heard the bedroom door open and I turned, sure it was Reginald.

"Honey, my head is—" I looked and Sasha was standing in the doorway fully dressed and in heels. She quickened toward the bed dramatically.

"You OK?" she asked. "We heard you scream or something."

"Oh, my head . . ." I complained, but really my senses were now divided between my headache and Sasha's perfect appearance. She sat down beside me on the bed and I saw that she was wearing eyelashes.

"Hangover? Oh no, girl. That's too bad!" she purred before giggling.

Her blond wig was back in place. I looked for glue or a stitch of thread. Nothing. It looked like that hair was growing right out of her head. She was wearing blush and diamond earrings again. Different ones.

Something sharp rumbled through my stomach and I closed my eyes to stop from vomiting.

"What time is it?" I asked after catching my breath. I wiped my mouth and discovered that a wad of saliva was dangling from my chin.

I used what little energy I had to try to rearrange my twisted nightgown.

Sasha frowned sadly and leaned over to rub my leg. As her hand moved, I saw the muscles beneath her breasts perk up. She was wearing a red tank top with a low, low neckline.

"A bit after noon."

"After noon?!?" I tried to get up, but a head spin and kick through my stomach sent me back to the pillow to hold my head.

"Yeah, you overslept. But just like old times, I had your back." Sasha kissed me on the cheek and I could see that the cotton tank top she was wearing was perfectly ironed—so were the jeans!

"Where is everyone?" I asked. "The kids must be starving."

"They're in the kitchen eating a little brunch. Want some coffee or something? I know you don't want to get out of bed yet. I can bring it in to you."

"Brunch? Reginald cooked?" I tried to get up again, but I hardly made it past an inch.

"No. I did. Got up before everyone else. Just made some eggs . . . and bacon . . . and grits . . . a little French toast, potatoes, a quiche, homemade biscuits." Sasha paused.

"All of that?"

"And orange juice—fresh squeezed after I went to the supermarket. Do you mind that I drove your car? Thank God for GPS!"

"It's no problem. I just feel so bad you had to get up and do all of that. You're my guest and . . . I don't know why I'm so hungover."

"Well, you don't really drink. You can't just jump back in."

"That's true," I agreed. "Wait, how do you know that?"

"Know what?"

"—That I don't drink." I'd never been a big drinker really, but right after college when I left Atlanta with Reggie, I found that I was drinking every night. Just a little to ease the tension of being a new bride in a new city. But then, at one point, it was every day. I was concerned. Reggie laughed. He said it was OK. I'd get used to the alcohol. I'd be able to handle it like everyone else. But soon I was on my knees every night in front of the toilet and when I'd nearly gotten caught drunk driving at a police checkpoint one Saturday night, I stopped. I didn't drink alcohol unless it was at a party or festive occasion. I decided that's what last night was. But it'd never hit me like that before."

"Reggie told me you weren't big on drinking. He said you slowed down a long time ago."

"Oh . . . He told you that?" I said. Hearing my husband's nickname, one he'd hardly ever used since his father, who everyone called Reggie, passed away, was odd. Suddenly, I wondered where he was.

"I was talking to him this morning. I got up pretty early. I just assumed you guys would be going to church."

"Oh, we don't really do church too much. It's just not our thing—"

"But you were raised in the church. Your dad was a pastor. Have you lost your walk with the Lord, child?" she asked jokingly. "You know us good Southern girls can't miss a Sunday service . . . not with all the fine men there."

"No . . . Reginald never liked the church," I offered as an excuse. "He sees religion as a sign of weakness. And with the kids . . . It's too much. R. J. can be a handful."

"Oh no; he's the most precious thing ever. So sweet," Sasha said. "I read to him this morning—Reggie and me."

"Read to R. J.?" I eyeballed Sasha. Most mornings, before I sent R. J. to the bathroom to wash up, I read a short book to calm him. It was initially a suggestion from his therapist, but over time, it just became our morning "Mommy and R. J." thing. As the sun rose and the sounds outside of his window came to life, we'd read the books of his early childhood. *Goodnight Moon* was his favorite. He said he liked reading it in the morning because it was when the moon was really going to sleep. He never let anyone else read to him in his room. Most days, without that book, he'd start his day off on a wrong and declining note. "You must be joking. R. J. won't let anyone but me read to him—and especially not his father. Something about the sound of his voice."

"I know, Reggie told me as we watched the sun rise. But it was the craziest thing—I suggested that I start reading and Reggie take over after that. It worked. We read *Goodnight Moon*. It was the most precious thing. That boy is amazing."

"Yeah, I know," I agreed before remembering something Sasha had just said that bothered me more than the idea of her reading to R. J. "What did you say at first?"

"What? What do you mean? About the book?"

"No. Before that."

"About reading?"

"Before that."

"Talking to Reginald?"

"When?"

"Sunrise?" Sasha said blankly. "Yeah, we watched the sun rise together on the porch. I got up early."

My pains went into a quick remission and I was up out of the bed and in my slippers.

"Reginald?" I hollered, dashing down the hallway toward the kitchen. "Reginald?"

"Oh, Dawn, you don't need to get up. I can bring you a plate. I have your back." Sasha came up rushing behind me.

"Reginald, you watched the—" I stopped speaking instantly when I turned into the small kitchen to see my family happily laughing around the table, clean and fully dressed as they ate. R. J. was laughing. I could actually hear R. J. laughing.

"Honey"—Reginald pulled out a seat between him and R. J.—"We have this seat saved for you."

Before the empty chair there was a full place setting of my father's mother's antique china and a table full of steamy food. It literally looked like a picture from a catalog.

"Yeah, Mama," Cheyenne joined in, pointing at the chair with Reginald. "We saved you a seat."

"Oh," I said, not quite sure of how to respond to such a gesture from Cheyenne. I sat down. "What were you guys laughing about?" I asked.

Sasha sat in the chair on Reginald's other side, between him and Cheyenne.

"Just a joke Sasha told us about sperm—" Reginald answered.

"Sperm?" I cut him off, afraid of what he was about to repeat in front of the kids. "I hope it wasn't too—"

"Sperm *whales*, darling." Reginald looked at me as if something was wrong and I realized that I was wearing only a thin nightgown.

I crossed my arms over my breasts to cover my protruding and sagging nipples.

"Say the joke again, Ms. Sasha," Cheyenne cheered, squirming in giggling ecstasy in her seat.

"Yeah, Sasha," Reginald added. "Say it for Dawn."

"Not again," Sasha said humbly.

"Please," they begged together—even R. J.

"OK. We can hear the joke again," Sasha said. "But Reggie, you tell it this time."

"Me?" Reginald pointed to his chest meekly.

"Yeah, Daddy, tell it," Cheyenne agreed.

"Daddy!" R. J. affirmed.

"But I just heard it!" Reginald stalled.

"I said it three times!" Sasha pinched Reginald's arm playfully and he winced.

"OK. OK," Reginald said, pretending to be convinced by the pressure. "I'll do it if Dawn wants to hear it."

"Do you, Mama?" R. J. asked, linking arms with me.

"Sure, baby," I said. "Of course I want to hear the joke." I looked at Reginald, but I could see Sasha on his other side smiling adoringly at him as she patted Cheyenne on the back.

"Well, there was this lady sperm whale named Trixy and she couldn't read," Reginald started and they all laughed.

The rest of the joke was so absurd that I couldn't possibly keep up or remember it. After thirty seconds of Trixy, I was just nodding along and spying at my family around the table. They were laughing after nearly every word and R. J. even smiled at his sister. When it was over, Cheyenne was laughing hysterically and leaning into Sasha's shoulder. I laughed, too, but I knew that no one was convinced that I'd gotten the joke. My head was aching. The room was spinning. I didn't want to hear another joke about anything.

After I nearly vomited when a spoonful of Sasha's eggs were scooped onto my plate, Sasha insisted that I return to bed and shuffled me down the hallway with a cup of coffee in her hand.

"You can stay in here all day if you like," she said, tucking me back into the bed. "I can handle them."

"I'll be better in a second. I just need a little nap." I sighed. I wanted to fight my illness, but my head was getting heavy again and I wanted to sleep so badly. I knew it must've been the hangover causing this, but I really felt ill. Sasha chalked it up to age.

"We'll be fine. Get some rest." She poofed the pillow behind me one more time and headed toward the door where she turned off the light. "You deserve a break."

As I drifted into a dream of slimy eggs and Trixy the sperm whale, I promised myself that I wouldn't sleep too long. I'd just get an extra hour and then get up to clean the house. I had to get the kids' stuff ready for school on Monday and cook dinner. Sasha would probably be leaving early to get back to Atlanta and I wanted to spend a little time with her. Sixty minutes would be enough. It would be two o'clock. I'd need to rush to get the house in order. I agreed to and promised myself this much, but when I finally lifted my head again and looked at my cell phone, it was after five o'clock.

"What?" I sat up quickly and looked around the room like I had to be dreaming. How could I have slept for four more hours?

I hurried to the bathroom, drank nearly half a bottle of Pepto-Bismol, and popped two Advil. My face looked sunken and shriveled in the mirror. I thought of taking a shower, but I was almost sure the weight of the water would wash me down the drain. That's how ragged I felt.

I was happy to find Reginald was alone in the living room with the kids. They were sitting on the couch watching a basketball game. I didn't know where Sasha was, but the idea of my house being back to normal was calming. Nothing had really happened or went wrong, but I was getting more tired and my lingering hangover was beginning to make me feel agitated. I decided that it wasn't her. She hadn't done anything wrong. I just wanted to be alone with my family.

"I should've known you guys would be in here doing the sports thing," I said, smiling at my little crew doing their usual Sunday evening routine. Reginald was far from being the most attentive father, but the kids' desire to be around him and the reality that watching television presented an activity where he didn't have to really do anything, made Sunday sports an easy pick. "Where's Sasha?"

Someone scored and no one could take their eyes off of the television. R. J. pointed toward the kitchen.

Before I could see Sasha, I heard her talking. She said that something was wonderful. I walked into the kitchen. The refrigerator door was open. She appeared from behind it and smiled at me. She pointed at my baby blue jogging suit and gave a thumbs-up as she continued her conversation. She closed the door with her foot and carried a head of lettuce to the counter as if she'd been cooking in my kitchen for years.

"That's great, Joe," she said. Her voice was sweeter and more sultry than usual. "You can leave the tickets at Will Call. But, like I said, I'm not sure I'll be back in Atlanta by then. Still taking care of my soror!" She sighed at me sympathetically.

I walked to the counter where she was standing. There was lasagna cooling on the stove. I reached for the lettuce, but Sasha pulled away, shook her head.

"Love it, darling," she said. "Smooches." She hung up the phone and looked at me.

"I can't believe you cooked dinner," I said. "I can't have you make a salad, too. I can do that."

"Nonsense. You need your rest."

"No, you need your rest. Don't you have to get back to Atlanta?"

"I'm in no rush. I've been enjoying myself so much. I could get used to Augusta."

"But what about that phone call? Sounds like you have a hot date."

"Date? Oh, no." Sasha laughed. "That was just Joe Johnson. He plays for the Hawks. A good friend of mine. I did a feature on his charity. He leaves me tickets sometimes."

"Tickets?" Reginald asked, appearing in the kitchen suddenly to switch out his beer. He tossed an empty bottle into the trash and went to the refrigerator. "Tickets for what?"

"The Hawks game tonight," Sasha revealed.

"You have tickets for the game?" Reginald looked up from the refrigerator.

"Yeah, my friend Joe left them for me."

"Joe Johnson?"

She nodded.

"Joe Johnson left you a ticket for tonight's game?" Reginald let the refrigerator door swing closed without getting a beer.

"Floor seats," Sasha said.

"And you're not going?"

"Well, it's three tickets and I don't have anyone to take, plus I'm here with you guys, so I'll miss this go 'round."

"Are you pulling my leg?" Reginald pleaded. "You can't just not go. It's the damn play-offs. You have to go."

"But I don't have anybody to go with," Sasha said helplessly. She perked up and her eyes widened on Reginald and me. "Wait, would you guys like to go?"

At the same time, Reginald and I gave two different answers.

Me: "No. I'm too tired and I have too much to do around here."

Reginald: "Of course. I haven't been to a game in years."

"Honey, we can't," I said to Reginald.

"Why?" he asked.

"It's Sunday . . . and we have to get ready for the week." Suddenly, I sounded like I was ninety years old.

"Oh, no," Sasha said. "That's too bad. It's fine though. Bad timing. We'd have to be there in like two hours anyway to make tip-off."

"We could still use the tickets," Reginald said. "It will only take two hours to get to Atlanta from here—less than that if I drive. I can be ready in ten minutes and—"

"I could go with you," Sasha volunteered. "And then I wouldn't need to call a driver. You could just drop me off at home."

"Well, OK!" Reginald nodded along like this was the best plan he'd ever heard.

I could feel myself frowning at the scene.

"OK," Sasha said. "But what about the third ticket?" She looked off as if she was thinking. "Wait, didn't you say you haven't been to a game in a while? Has R. J. ever been to one? We could take him."

"No, there's no way he could handle all of those people," I said. "It would be overwhelming and he has school—and Cheyenne will be crushed, too." I turned to Reginald. "You know she likes watching basketball with you just as much as R. J. does."

"I know she does, but maybe it's time for me to spend some time with just R. J. for a change. He should come with me," Reginald said, like this had been his idea. "Spend some time with his old dad. I remember when my father used to take me to games when I was a kid. I loved it. Cheyenne will be OK."

I so didn't want Reginald to go all the way into Atlanta—with Sasha, and with R. J.—but no reason I could gather made any sense after Reginald brought up his father. And now the idea of him doing anything constructive with R. J. was a little attractive. There was just the thing about Sasha going. But, I felt some relief knowing he was dropping Sasha off. Then I could get things back to normal. I felt bad thinking about the only company I'd had from undergrad in years that way, but something was just bothering me.

Reginald forgot all about the beer. Within what seemed like minutes, he was outside on the front steps in his Hawks jersey with R. J. at his side in a smaller one. I stood in the doorway holding a bag of cut-up squares of lasagna.

"Eat these," I said. "No sense spending money on those vendors at the game."

Reginald took the bag.

"Tell Cheyenne I said I'll bring her something nice," he said.

"I will."

"See you in a bit." He kissed me lightly on the cheek before running to the car like the roads to Atlanta would evaporate at any moment. He'd already packed all of Sasha's bags into the trunk. The plan was to drop her off after the game and be home by midnight.

R. J. waved from the window and I blew him a kiss.

"Let's not make this our last good-bye," Sasha whined. She tossed her big, heavy designer purse over her arm. She was also wearing a Hawks jersey. Later, as I lay in bed and watched the news alone, I'd think of how odd it was for her to have the jersey in her bag not knowing she'd be going to a game and all. She hugged me tightly. "I want to see you more."

"Me, too," I said.

"It's been so nice being here—with your family. I really enjoyed it."

"We enjoyed it, too."

"I insist that you come visit me in Atlanta. And I'll come visit you again. And—"

Reginald honked the horn. We looked at the car. He pointed at his watch.

"Don't worry," I said, laughing at Reginald's anxiousness. "We'll keep in touch."

"Dawn, I want you to know that all of that old stuff from the past, it's in the past," she said. "I love your family. We were all wrong. You made a great decision marrying Reggie. You guys have the perfect life. Everything a girl could want."

"You think so?" I said.

"You have it all." She looked into my eyes. "Maybe I'll be as lucky as you one day."

The minutes after Sasha left with Reginald and R. J. went by slowly and without any form of exclamation. The house was silent. Nothingness pushed its way through the hallways the way it does at a funeral home before a family has come to grieve some lost love. I walked through the empty rooms, fixing and reorganizing, putting away and tucking, reminding myself that Sasha was right: my life was great. It wasn't perfect, but it was good. And I was so glad she could see it. I needed her to see. I know that sounds petty or childish, but I'd been living for too long with the idea that everyone thought I'd messed up my life and now everyone would know that I was doing fine. Hey, I wasn't some Spelman alum interviewing people on CNN, but I had a good life of my own. I had a husband and two children. A home. It was no fantasy, but it was mine.

I found one of R. J.'s battered action figures in the dining room and went to take it to his room. As I neared the end of the hallway where the room was just across from Cheyenne's room, I remembered that she was there in the house with me. She'd been so quiet since Reginald told her that she couldn't go to the game. I expected some big fight. Some big show—while she pushed me away when she didn't have a use for me, she tended to cling to her father—but there was nothing. She'd stomped off to her room and closed the door.

I set the action figure on R. J.'s bed and tiptoed to Cheyenne's door. I pressed my ear against it. There was silence. I stepped back and looked at the door. I wasn't in the mood at all to fight with Cheyenne. If she was handling her anger with her father by being silent, I wanted to leave her alone and just hope she'd come out of her funk a little happier than she'd been before it appeared.

I stood there and looked at a group of floating pastel balloons Cheyenne had painted on the door a few months ago. I was about to walk away, but then I stopped myself. Maybe, I thought, maybe we could just have a good time. Just me and her. We could talk or watch a movie together until Reginald and R. J. got back.

I knocked. There was no answer. I knocked again and then I opened the door slowly.

The lights were on in the room. Cheyenne sat on the floor in the middle of a little purple carpet she'd set in front of her bed. Everything in the room was purple—picture frames, stuffed animals, a comforter set, and curtains.

She was playing one of her handheld video games and didn't look up at me.

I knocked on the inside of the door.

"Chey, what are you up to?"

"Nothing." Her voice was flat and tight.

"Nothing?" I repeated, walking into the room. "Doesn't look like nothing to me." I sat on the bed. A purple canopy stretched over the frame.

"Well, if it's not nothing, what is it?" she asked.

"Looks like one of your games. Nintendo?"

She laughed. "No. Playstation." It had been a setup.

She clicked the game off and chucked it onto the bed.

"It's so boring," she said, getting up from the floor. "I hate it here." She went and flopped into a furry purple beanbag she'd gotten for Christmas.

"It's not that bad," I said. "I'm here."

She stared at me like I was crazy. Sometimes talking to her was like going into battle.

"All R. J. is gonna talk about when he gets back is that stupid game," she went on like I'd said nothing.

"Chey, I know you wanted to go to the game, but they only had three tickets. Daddy will take you next time," I said. "Who wants to be at a funky old basketball game anyway? And with the boys? We can spend quality time together. I can play Playstation. Or we could watch a movie."

Cheyenne cut her eyes at me again and I felt it right in my throat.

"You don't know how to play my games," she said. "You play R. J.'s games."

"Come on. Let's not go down that road. You know I spend time with you. And what I do for your brother, I have to. He just needs more attention than you," I said. "You know that."

Cheyenne rolled her eyes and let the bottom of her mouth hang low to show her disgust.

"Do you want to watch a movie with me?" I asked, trying to ignore her demeanor.

"I think I'm going to go to bed," she said.

"Bed? It's so early."

"Test tomorrow." She got up from the beanbag and went to grab her bathrobe. She wrapped it over her arm like she was ten years older and looked at me. "I'm going to get into the shower."

"OK," I said. "Well"—I started getting up from the bed—"I'll be in my room if you change your mind. We can watch something scary. You like scary movies."

"Not anymore," she said. "But I'll let you know."

She turned and walked down the hall toward the bathroom. I was left standing in the middle of her room alone with my hands in my pockets. I wanted to scream for her to come back and make her talk to me. But it would only make things worse. We'd had this argument before. I wasn't a bad mother. I knew that. She knew that. I was doing what I had to do. And no matter how angry Cheyenne got with me, the fact was that R. J. was always going to need me more. He just would. And she needed to be strong enough to understand that. Another fight wasn't going to get us there.

I carried a bottle of wine to bed that night. I don't know how it got into the refrigerator, or how it got so quickly in my hand, but I hadn't been in bed alone in years. And after dealing with Reginald leaving with Sasha and Cheyenne's attitude, I needed something to ease my nerves. Everything seemed so impossibly upside down—and in two days.

"She's gone," I told myself, lying in the sheets with an emptying second glass of wine in my hand. The light from the TV crept along the blanket over my lower body in the dark room. Sasha was on the screen wearing a thin yellow sweater and huge diamond earrings. She was sitting next to a woman holding a book. The word "bliss" was on the cover.

"All women need to chase what they want," the woman said. She had blue eyes and a blue broach on her blouse to match. "They need to aggressively pursue their dreams."

"At all costs?" Sasha said, leaning into the woman and smiling the same way my family had smiled at her around the table this morning—it was expectant, taken. "No matter what? That's what you say in the book."

"Well, that's what aggression is. It's about fighting. About chasing. Women need to learn more of this. You don't hear men questioning whether or not they should go after a job because another man has it—no, they go in and they fight for their position. They chase bliss relentlessly."

"If only all women knew this," Sasha said firmly. She reached out and held the woman's hand. "Thank you for coming on the show." She looked at the camera, at me. "This has been Sasha Bellamy with a little message every woman ought to hear: chase your bliss. Good night." She smiled at me with her blush and glossy lips, and winked.

I finished my wine and poured another glass, hoping it would keep my eyes open long enough to catch Reginald coming in the door.

So when Reginald did finally get home, I was asleep alone, for four more hours. I'd stay that way. Whispers from the living room pulled me from a dream at about 3:00 a.m.

"Reginald," I called, shaking myself awake. I looked at the clock. The room was dark. I could hear laughing outside the door. Murmurs. A hush and a warning for quiet. I was about to get up, but then Reginald came creeping into the room. He slid into the door and snapped it behind him.

"Babe?" I called sleepily. I bent over and turned on my night-light beside the bed.

"I'm sorry," he whispered. "Did I wake you?"

"Yeah," I said. I tried to get up. "Where's R. J.?"

"No, no, no," Reginald said. He came over to the bed. "He's fine. He's in bed. I already put on his nightclothes and everything."

He went over to his side of the bed and sat down to take off his sneakers.

I looked at the clock again.

"It's after 3:00 a.m.," I said.

"You know," Reginald started, "I have no idea what time it is!" He laughed and I could tell that he'd been drinking. "No idea." He pulled off his socks and tossed them across the room.

"So, what happened?" I asked. "How was the game?"

Reginald got up and started removing his clothes. Even in the dull light from my lamp, I could see his tight stomach muscles, a little patch of hair over his pelvis.

"Hawks lost, but they still have a shot."

"Well, what time did it end?"

"I don't remember. Why?"

"*Because it's 3:00 a.m.,* and I know it didn't end at midnight," I asked. "So, what happened?"

Reginald looked at me as if I'd just asked him seven questions and told him to take out the garbage.

"So?" I repeated.

He looked at my nightstand where the empty bottle of wine sat beneath the lamp.

"You been drinking?" he asked.

"I'm fine. I can have a little glass of wine."

"Hum."

"What's 'hum' for?"

"I'm just surprised to see you drinking so much. It's not like you."

"Whatever, Reginald. You've clearly had your fill, too," I said. "Anyway, what happened? Why did you take so long?"

"We went by Sasha's house."

"You had to drop her off. But where does she live that it took so long?"

He got up and pulled some shorts out of the dresser beneath the television.

"No, no. It wasn't far. She just wanted us to see . . . inside." Reginald put the shorts on and got into bed.

"Inside? You went—"

"It was amazing. She has an indoor pool."

"An indoor pool?"

"Yeah . . . *in* Atlanta! She swims a lot. I guess that's how she keeps her body so tight."

"Her *what*?"

"I didn't mean it like that. You know, I mean, she has good taste. Flat screens everywhere. Leather couches. All white. And the yard out back. Must be half an acre."

"Half an acre?" I couldn't imagine just how much land that was, but I knew it must've been a lot based on how wide my husband's eyes were.

"Six bedrooms. Three-car garage. A Maserati."

"She has a Maserati? I didn't know journalists made that kind of money."

Reginald laid back contentedly on his pillow. He stretched his hands behind his head and smiled at the ceiling.

"Well, it was her father's before he died. She let me drive it."

"You drove the car?" I sat up. "What was R. J. doing?"

"He stayed at the house with Sasha. Don't worry; lil man was cool."

"I'm not worried. You know he doesn't like being left with people he doesn't know."

"I don't think Sasha is someone he doesn't know. He likes her," he said. "Anyway, I drove that car up 85 doing 100. I felt the air moving through my fingers on the steering wheel. That car is beautiful."

I could feel something in Reginald—something settled and just easy. He was happy in a new way.

"I never thought I'd say this"—he paused—"but if that's Atlanta living, it's pretty cool. And get this, the house is on Lover's Lane."

"Lover's Lane? Really?" I laughed in a show, hoping he'd jump in. He couldn't mean what he was saying. Not Reginald. He couldn't be serious. It almost sounded like he was impressed by all of these things.

"What?" he looked at me. "Why are you laughing?"

"What's 'pretty cool'? The hustle? The showboating? The 'Who's Who in Black America' parade?" I listed his common judgments of the city and city folk. "You hate that stuff."

"I know, but it's not all bad. Some good things. Hey, I'm not complaining. We actually got to go into the player's club after the game. Joe is a cool cat."

"Joe?"

"Joe Johnson. We were going to go out for drinks with some of the players, but we had R. J. with us . . . so . . . Well, Sasha said—"

"*Sasha* said?"

"Oh God! Here it comes . . ."

"Here what comes?"

"You're doing that thing. That jealous thing."

"I'm not jealous," I said. "I just think it's odd that you were referring to you and Sasha as 'us' and 'we' and you just quoted her. Like twenty-four hours ago, you hated her. And the day before that, you practically begged me to tell her not to come here."

"You asked me to get along with her. I was just being nice," he said defensively. "And she's not so bad. She's actually really smart."

I fell back into my place in the bed and folded my arms over my chest.

"Listen, Dawn, I didn't mean anything by that. She's just smart is all. She's talking about helping me expand my business. You know, get some new clients."

"Expand your business? I've been trying to get you to do that for years and you never said I was smart."

"But she has contacts. And she said that she might be able to hook me up with some folks. One of her friends, this Kerry Jackson, her husband owns a landscaping company that has the lion's share of business in Atlanta. She could hook me up with him."

"I've told you about Kerry and Jamison before. And they're divorced."

"Really?" He looked at me confused. "Anyway, look, I believe her and I think I want to try to do something. Make a move in Atlanta."

"But you said you wanted to keep the business small and personal. That you have relationships here you want to build on. That's why we moved here."

"I know what I said," Reginald said in a detached way. "But things change. It's kind of like how Sasha explained it to me in the car—you have to chase bliss relentlessly."

"Chase bliss?" I flipped through my memory, trying to recall where I'd heard that line before. I sat up again and looked at the television. "Sasha didn't say that. That's some dinky thing some woman said on her show."

"So?"

"So, it's not her advice. She got it from someone else."

Reginald looked annoyed and exhaled.

"What?" I asked after a second. "Don't look at me like that. I'm not jealous. That's not what this is. It's not about me being jealous. You're just—"

"I'm going to sleep," Reginald said abruptly. He reached past me and turned out the light before turning to face his side of the bed.

I sat there stunned. Alone, half drunk, and stunned. What was happening here? Reginald could be a nice guy, but never this nice. And certainly never this nice to one of my friends. And that was why I had so few.

I turned away from him. I'd never seen him like that. Not in over twelve years had I seen him so giddy over a thing like a nice car or front row seats at a basketball game. He usually found a way to make fun of those things. It just wasn't who he was. Yeah, he'd smile at me and the kids. Laugh at something on television, but never too much. He was a worker. A hard worker. He believed in principles and family. Work ethic and holding on. But now, his eyes were shining. And it was about none of those things.

I turned back toward him.

I looked at the deep crease in his back, how sharp and hard it was. His body was a record of how hard he worked. I'd always wanted him to have more. To be more. But I never wanted to push him. I was afraid I'd lose him.

I reached out to him. Raked my dangling index finger up the small of his back.

"I'm sorry," I whispered in his ear. "I didn't mean to ask you all of those questions. I'm happy you had a good time."

"It's fine," he said emptily.

I kissed his shoulder and opened my mouth for a quick bite

and lick. I slid my arms under his and pushed my breasts into his back.

"I love you," I said before kissing his shoulder again. I closed my eyes and wrapped my leg around his waist, pulling him back toward me. He didn't move though. And soon I noticed that his body was as heavy as it was when he was asleep.

"I'm tired," he said.

"Tired?"

"It's been a long night. I need some sleep." He readjusted himself in the bed a little.

I backed up and looked at him and I'm almost sure my eyes were completely crossed in some odd puzzlement. Reginald and I didn't have sex often, but the once in a while that we did, never once had he turned me down. Well . . . not twice.

"You sure?" I asked and I wasn't clear about how exactly crazy that sounded until Reginald turned to look at me.

"Yes, I'm sure," he said and then he turned back to his side of the bed. "Oh," he started after a pause. "Sasha's here. We're going to Phil Landon's in the morning."

"What?" I shot up again. "Sasha's where?"

"She's here. We're going to Phil Landon's tomorrow. You know, the car dealer."

"I know who Phil Landon is," I said. "But that's not what I asked. Why is she here? You were supposed to drop her off in Atlanta. That's the whole reason you went to her house."

"Damn, Dawn, you make it sound like you don't like the woman or something," Reginald said, turning back around annoyed. "Look, she knows Landon and she thinks he might have some work for me. That's all. She's hooking me up. Getting a contract like that would be amazing. Landon has ten dealerships and they all have grass. Big money. You could finally quit your job."

"I don't want to quit my job," I said.

"Don't you think it's a little late to be arguing about this?"

"Late?" I got out of the bed and put on my bathrobe.

"What are you doing?"

"You bring a woman into my house in the middle of the night and you expect me to be OK with it? No."

"She's not just some woman. She's your friend."

"Well, she should've asked me first," I said, putting on my slippers. "You should've asked me first."

"Sasha," I called sternly, pushing into the guest room without a care of what naked or ridiculous red-light scene waited inside. I was irritated beyond anything I could articulate. "Why are you—"

"Hey, baby," she called from the bed. She was sitting up, looking at a photo album I recognized immediately. It was Cheyenne and R. J.'s baby album. I hadn't seen it in months. "You still up?"

"Yeah," I answered and already my disposition was softened by what I saw. "Reginald just told me that you were here and I wanted to know—where'd you get that?"

The room was dimly lit by a lamp beside the bed. A single candle was burning on the dresser.

"It was under Cheyenne's pillow," she said. "I went in a minute ago to put a little stuffed Hawk I got for her at the game on her dresser. I went to give her a good-night kiss and there it was."

"That book was in Cheyenne's room?"

"Yeah. Come have a look." She patted on a space beside her in the bed.

"Sasha, I came in here to ask you why you—"

"Girl, you better come over here," she said, stopping me. "Look at you"—she pointed to one of the pictures and smiled—"you looked so beautiful."

My shoulders fell a little as my purpose for confronting Sasha waned. I could see my full, pregnant stomach poking out over the cover.

I went over to the bed and sat on the edge a few reluctant inches from where Sasha had suggested I sit.

She turned the book to me. Cheyenne and R. J. were bundled

up in a single bassinet at the hospital. Cheyenne's eyes were still closed. R. J.'s little hand was wide open and over his mouth.

"She didn't open her eyes for the whole first day," I said. "I asked the nurses if something was wrong and they said sometimes it just takes time. R. J. didn't cry. Not once."

"They have to be the cutest things I've ever seen," Sasha said. "You're so blessed." She handed the book to me and I flipped through some of the pages. Reginald holding R. J. up in a little Falcons jersey that hardly hung onto his shoulders. Cheyenne dressed up like an elf for their first Christmas. She slept the entire day.

"When did you find out about R. J.?" Sasha asked. "You know, about the autism. I've always wanted to ask, but I didn't want you to think—"

"It's fine," I said. "You'd be surprised how many people never ask. Never ask me anything about him or it. They try to pretend he's not there. Or not different. He is." I leaned back against the wooden headboard and told Sasha about R. J. and his autism. I told her about my nights of crying. About how sometimes R. J.'s silence could kill me. And how other times when he said just three words together and looked me in the eyes, I felt like it was all worth it.

"It must be hard," she said, "dealing with everything."

"R. J.'s autism isn't as hard as people dealing with R. J.'s autism. The looks. The comments. One day I was in the grocery store, trying to check out, and R. J. was having a meltdown. He was just hollering for his father and then Skittles, and then whatever else he could get his hands on. He was three, but so strong, and I couldn't keep him calm. Cheyenne was standing there, holding onto the cart, watching. I kept trying to keep him still and soon a crowd was watching. They were looking at us like he was some out of control toddler and I was a bad mother. One man said, 'Get it together, lady. Control your child.' " I wiped a tear from my eye and closed the book. "I felt Cheyenne disappear. She was so embarrassed. I wanted to do the same, but I had to be there. I had to fix it. And the thing about R. J. is that he can feel when I'm upset and it just makes things worse."

"You don't go out much anymore, huh?" Sasha asked.

"No. We can't. I can't."

"Whew, child," she said, wiping her own fresh tear. "I don't know about you, but I need a glass of wine."

She rolled over and got out of the bed.

"Wine? It's almost four in the morning."

"And?"

I was sleep-deprived. I was hungover. I was annoyed. I was eager to prove that I was none of these things. So, just three hours after I drank two bottles of wine with Sasha in her bedroom and cried so hard my eyes were as puffy as poached eggs, I sat at the breakfast table and stuffed three whole banana honey pancakes into my mouth. I listened to Reginald and Sasha go on about the Hawks game and Joe Johnson, and the play-offs and how cute it was to see R. J. cheering in the crowd with the other little boys. He even danced at the game. He got up on a chair and did the wave. Reginald couldn't stop laughing. R. J. wouldn't reenact the scene, so Reginald got up to demonstrate. Cheyenne held her little Hawk in her arms and smiled at her father. He'd gotten Joe Johnson to autograph a T-shirt. She'd stashed it in her book bag to take it to school.

I kept repeating how wonderful all of this was—it was all I could say without each of my symptoms being read by everyone at the table. But inside I was at war. I hated how I was feeling and I hated everyone for me feeling that way. And I can't explain how each of them became a part of that war in my mind, but I guess that was because I couldn't say what the war was. Was it about Sasha? Was it about Cheyenne? Was it about Reginald? Or R. J.? What was it? Or was there anything? Did I just need to go back to bed? Or did I need to get out of that house?

Sasha had just finished telling a joke about a penguin named Topsie who could juggle. She dropped another pancake onto my plate. I thanked her with a pleasant smile.

"Wonderful," I said.

"These are so good, Auntie Sasha," Cheyenne said, finishing her pancake.

"Thank you, baby girl," Sasha purred, reaching across the table to pinch Cheyenne's cheek and revealing a completely muscular and mysteriously tanned arm.

I rolled my eyes, but quickly changed my face to a smile when I saw Reginald looking at me.

"Yeah, it is," Reginald added firmly to spite me. "I would never have thought that honey would taste good on pancakes. It's amazing. Isn't it, Dawn?" He set his eyes on me the way I looked at Cheyenne when she wasn't behaving quite appropriately.

"Yeah, it is," I said. "Wonderful."

"Well, there's a secret ingredient," Sasha teased, batting her fake eyelashes at Reginald.

I peeked over at the microwave. 7:05 a.m. How early did Sasha have to wake up to make all of this? There was no way. She had just as much wine as me and when my alarm went off, I pressed snooze three times. I had no time to shower and skipped R. J.'s reading time only to walk out of the bedroom to find out that Sasha had read *Goodnight Moon* and prepared breakfast. She was dressed, in full makeup, and had the kids' lunches prepared.

"Can Mama get your secret?" R. J. asked.

"Sure." Sasha grinned at me. "I'd be happy to share the secret recipe with my soror."

"Thanks," I said humbly.

R. J. had a fork with a huge, rectangular piece of pancake hanging from it. Honey rolled off of its edges.

"No more, R. J.," I said. "That's enough."

R. J. continued to move the fork toward his mouth.

"You've had enough," I repeated. "There's a lot of sugar in that."

"Actually, honey is all natural, so it's OK," Sasha offered.

I kept my eyes on R. J. and repeated myself again.

He froze with the fork in his hand.

"Oh, Dawn, let him have it," Reginald said, stepping into the standoff. "He needs energy. The boy has a big day at school today. Don't you, son?"

R. J. was still frozen, but his eyes shifted from me to Reginald like a pendulum. He looked down, smiled at the last bit of food, and stuffed it quickly and barbarically into his mouth.

"Absolutely not!" I grabbed the plate from in front of him and slung it so hard, it nearly fell off of the table. "That is not how we behave at the table." I pointed a rigid finger at R. J. "You will apologize!"

R. J.'s eyes were locked on the empty space where his plate had been.

My eyes were locked on him. And I remember that I was feeling like I should stop myself. That this was too much to put him through before school. That I was overreacting. But then I was thinking I was right. And he had to learn this. He couldn't just behave however he wanted to and expect people to pick up the pieces and act like nothing was happening.

"Oh, he doesn't have to apologize to me," Sasha said. "What about you guys?"

"Mind your business," I shot back.

"Mama, can I go get—"

"Be quiet." I stopped Cheyenne from leaving the table.

In the silence, R. J. got up from his seat.

"What are you doing?" I asked.

"Leave him alone, Dawn. Let him go," Reginald said.

"What do you know about letting him go?" I asked, turning to Reginald. "He can't have too much sugar. You know that. It'll make him hyper and then he's more likely to have a seizure or a meltdown." I was nearly screaming at Reginald when I saw his eyes widen on R. J.'s seat.

I turned.

R. J. was standing on it.

"What are you doing?" I asked. He'd never done that before.

"Son, get off of the seat," Reginald called sternly.

R. J. just stood there gazing at the cheap light fixture over the table.

"I told you he couldn't have too much of that honey," I said.

"I'm sorry. I didn't know," Sasha said.

"Not you," I said. I looked back at R. J. "I'm not going to beg you to get off of that seat. You get down right now!"

"We're going to be late to school," Cheyenne said almost so softly you might not have heard her. "I have to take my T-shirt—Joe Johnson signed it."

"Get off of the chair." Reginald got up from his seat and reached for R. J.

"Don't pull him down," I said to him. "We have to talk him down."

"Talk him down?" Reginald held out a hand to R. J. "Do you see this? Do you see this? What is he doing?"

"I told you!" I said.

"Son, get down from the table," Reginald insisted.

R. J. folded his arms over his chest.

"Are you saying I don't know how to take care of him? That I'm doing something wrong?" I asked.

"He didn't say that," Sasha said.

"Because I don't recall you ever offering any advice. Any kind of solution."

"Boy!" Reginald raised his voice and it shot through my spine. "You get off of that chair or I'm going to take you down myself!"

"Don't scream at him," I said.

Cheyenne got up and ran from the table.

"He's tired from last night. You had him up all night riding around Atlanta," I said. "You knew he had school today. That was too much."

"Means Drive," R. J. said mechanically. Reginald and I stopped talking and looked at him. He covered his ears and said louder, "Means Drive. 255. 255 Means Drive."

"Shit," Reginald spat.

"255 Means Drive. 255 Means Drive!"

"I'm not dealing with this crap this morning." Reginald grabbed R. J. from the seat at the middle of his body like he was a toddler and pulled him to the floor.

"What was that in there?" I asked, nearly charging through Reginald in our bedroom after we'd gotten R. J. calm.

Sasha was in the living room returning some calls she'd written down on a long sheet of paper. Reginald and I were darting around in the bedroom, getting ready to leave the house. I told the twins to wait in their rooms until I was ready to drive them to school.

"You tell me what happened in there," Reginald suggested snidely as he pulled a tie from the closet.

"What's that supposed to mean?" I asked. "You know we don't handle him that way."

"*We?* What *we*?" he chuckled uneasily. "That's not how *you* were sounding. *You* told *me* what to do and then *you* did what *you* wanted to do. There was no *we*."

"He could've had a seizure," I said, sliding on my old penny loafers.

"He didn't."

"How do you keep snapping at me when you know I'm right?" I pleaded. "When you know he can't have all of that sugar and he was up late last night? He can't go to school like—"

"God damn! Give it up. He was fine before you started acting all crazy." Reginald pulled the tie in place beneath the collar of his shirt and stood there as if I was supposed to come and tie it, but I walked right past him and closed the closet door. "The boy was fine. And then when you got angry, he got angry." He grunted and started tying the tie himself.

"This isn't about me. It's about you not listening to me," I said. "I told you it was too much sugar and you were so busy being so nice to Sasha that you didn't—"

"Sasha? Are you serious? Are you back on that again?" He dropped the ends of the loose tie and grabbed my arm as I tried to walk past him. "You're acting like you're jealous of her. I told you this would happen."

"I am not jealous."

"Please, every five minutes you act like she's stealing your thunder just because she made some damn pancakes or told a joke. That's not acting jealous?"

"Well, what about how you're acting?" I lowered my voice. "You brought her back into this house without even asking me. Was that supposed to make me feel better?"

"I told you what that was about. I told you she said she would help me. That's all it is."

"You didn't even touch me last night."

"What are you talking about?"

"You don't want to have sex with me!"

"I'm not talking about this." He pulled off the tie and threw it onto the floor. "Where's my blue tie?"

"I know she's beautiful," I said, following close behind Reginald as he went to the closet. "I see you looking at her. She calls you Reggie."

"Who cares what she calls me?" he said like it was the most ridiculous concern in the world. "I'm not talking about this." He pulled the closet door open.

"Even in college . . . men always looked at her," I said.

"Here it is!" Reginald pulled the blue tie from the closet and put it around his neck. "Look, I'm not talking about this. I told you why she's here. She's taking me down to Landon's. That's it. She's your friend. You told me to be nice to her."

"You keep saying that," I said.

"Because it keeps being true!" Reginald walked to the mirror hanging behind our bathroom door and started following his reflection as he adjusted the tie. "Look, if you're that worried—and I don't know why—why don't you come with us?"

"I have to go to work," I said, unconsciously picking the other tie up off of the floor and flinging it onto the bed. "I have to take the kids to school."

"Well, you wouldn't have to go to work if you'd—"

"I'm not quitting my job." I went and stood behind him in the mirror.

"—if you'd call in sick." he said, looking at me through the mirror. "And stop cutting me off."

"I can't call in sick. You know I use those days in case something goes wrong with R. J."

"Well, what about when something's going right with me?"

"Don't make this about you." I went to the dresser to get my work ID badge.

"Just a minute ago it was," Reginald said, turning around with his tie still undone. "Just come if it will ease your mind. Maybe you can help or something. Sasha could show you how to network . . . you know, talk to people."

"I talk to people all of the time. It's my job!"

"I mean in business. I didn't mean it the way you're saying. Why do you keep changing my words? You do realize that you're being sensitive about everything everyone says?"

"I'm not changing your words. And I'm not being sensitive."

"Fine," he said, coming toward me. "Look, can you tie this?"

3

My husband, my college roommate, and I sat stone-faced in a row of white leather chairs along the side of Phil Landon's sleek glass desk. As we'd been the entire way over to his central dealership in downtown Augusta, we were quiet and trying hard not to look at one another. And I didn't care. I'd called in sick to come along for the ride that Reginald seemed confident would change his life, but I was in no mood to be a helping hand. I might've looked like a helping hand. I might've held a pad and pen and vowed to try to ask smart questions at smart times, but I couldn't lie to myself. I knew Sasha had heard us arguing in the bedroom. I couldn't give her the satisfaction (and didn't know why I thought she'd be satisfied) of thinking I'd had an argument with my husband. She had no business being in my house and I needed to take control of the situation. Reginald could've spoken to Landon at any time, and on his own. His father had bought three Fords from him before he died. That had to be worth something. So, what was Sasha going to do? She had the big connections and beauty, but she wasn't necessary. Reginald needed to see that. So, I wanted him to do well. But if he didn't and it was Sasha's fault . . . well, it would be her fault.

"So, when does the car come to take you back to Atlanta?" I

asked Sasha as pleasantly as I could. We were waiting for Landon to come into the office. His secretary was getting our coffee . . . and Sasha's espresso.

"Dawn, now's not the time for that," Reginald snapped.

"No, it's fine," Sasha said. "I have a driver coming later tonight."

Reginald looked at me and grimaced.

The secretary, a brunette with big green eyes and braces that revealed that she might have been twenty-two, came in juggling four coffee cups in her two hands.

Landon walked in behind her with his hands in his pockets. He looked nervous. Maybe a little tired.

"I'm sorry I'm late," he said and his voice boomed through the office in a way that articulated his confidence. "I wasn't exactly expecting to see you, Ms. Bellamy."

"And still, you came," Sasha said cheerfully, getting up to greet him. "Now, that's love."

Reginald and I followed and stood up, too.

The secretary slid the small cups onto a little table beside the desk and curtsied out the door.

"These are my friends," Sasha said, holding Landon's elbow as she ushered him toward us. "Dawn and Reginald Johnson."

"Yes, yes!" Landon said, shaking our hands. His smile was crooked, almost tense. He was a middle-aged white man with hair that was so gray it looked like it had never been any other color. His eyes were blue and his belly was too big for his shirt.

"Great to meet you," Reginald and I said.

Landon took a sip of his coffee, slid the cup back onto the saucer, and went to take a seat behind his desk. He had one of those Irish Claddagh wedding bands on his ring finger. Two teenage boys with blue eyes and hair just as gray as their father's were posed in football uniforms in photos on his desk.

"So, what exactly brings you here?" Landon asked Sasha and I swear I couldn't tell if his tone was friendly or just serviceable.

"Your favorite color, of course." Sasha crossed her legs slowly and kicked up her patent leather black stilettos for him to see.

"Black?" Landon said.

"Black coffee," she nodded at the coffee. "Black shoes." She nodded at her shoes. "And black pus—"

"Horses!" Landon said quickly before Sasha could continue. He wiped some beads of sweat from his brow.

"Yes, you love black horses, too." Sasha grinned.

I felt like I was listening to someone's phone conversation and missing pieces.

"But I don't have any black horses," Reginald said, confused.

"You said on the phone that you had business," Landon pointed out.

"Well, Mr. Landon, I own a small lawn care company. Nothing big. Just me and some fellas I pick up now and again." Reginald rambled and I could tell that he was nervous. "I been working on lawns my whole life and I was thinking maybe if you can find some work for me—"

"What he's saying is," Sasha interrupted him, "he's the best, so whomever you now have is fired. He has a five-man operation. Two trucks and the latest equipment. People will stop at Landon's just to touch the green grass."

Landon nodded.

"And buy a car," Sasha added. "So, what are you going to do?"

"Hum . . ." Landon sat back. "Tell me, are you two from Atlanta? The South?"

"I'm from Atlanta," I said.

"And I'm from Augusta," Reginald said. "My father, Reginald Johnson Senior, bought three trucks from you. Everyone called him Reggie."

"Oh, man," Landon said and suddenly his eyes met with Reginald's. Some of the nervousness I'd sensed in him earlier seemed to dissipate. "Reggie . . . Reggie Johnson. I know who you're talking about. He bought his first two pickups from my daddy when he still ran the place. Last one from me. He worked in construction. Right?"

"Yeah, that's my dad. Worked with his hands. Could make anything."

"Ain't this something. Why didn't you go into construction with him?"

"I went to college . . . and that didn't work out. Wasn't for me, so I got a job in Atlanta. That's where I met my wife here. Came home and started my business," Reginald said. "When I got in, I started small. Kept it that way. I make enough to support my family."

"Got kids?" Landon asked.

"Two."

"A son?"

"Yeah," Reginald said.

"How old?"

"Ten."

"Got a good arm on him yet? You know Georgia's gonna need a little help when Richt goes out!"

"If Richt goes!" Reginald said.

The two men laughed heartily.

"I hear ya, Captain. He got them to the grave. Go Dawgs!" Landon slapped the desk and got up to high-five Reginald.

Sasha seemed annoyed by their quick friendship.

"Look now, I think you're good people. Good country people," Landon said and I was so sure Reginald had reached his breaking point. While any other person who hadn't been raised in the South would've seen Landon's words as a straight compliment, calling another person "good country people" had become a way for white people in the rural South to passively identify other Christian or allegedly truthful white people and Christian and completely submissive black people. Reginald hated the saying and I knew he was about to find some way to spar with Landon.

"Why, thank you," Reginald said and I looked in his direction to see if he was actually his father's ghost: his drawl had suddenly become that thick.

"Now, I'll tell you what. I got two dealerships sitting far west on 20—like thirty minutes out of Atlanta. Got a contractor on them now, but his contract is up at the end of the summer. You take on those dealerships, show me what you can do, and well—we'll see about that fella's other contracts when they come up."

"You serious?" Reginald asked.

"Serious as them Dawgs beating on Tech last fall!"

"Now, I have good references," Reginald said, flustered. He snatched a folder I'd been holding on my lap and held it out to Landon over the desk.

Landon held his hand up to stop him.

"I'll take Ms. Bellamy's word," he said.

"Oh, you can always trust my word. If I say it, I mean it." Sasha crossed her legs again and kicked her shiny shoe up higher.

"Well, you've made that very clear," Landon said and once again I felt I was eavesdropping halfway through a conversation. Landon was working hard not to look at Sasha's leg.

"I guess this meeting is adjourned," Sasha said, getting up and grabbing me by the arm. "Until next time."

I felt so many things walking out of that office. I didn't understand any of Landon's actions or reactions. There was this coded exchange going on between him and Sasha, who I wasn't sure even needed to be in the meeting. Call me crazy, but all she did was flirt and show off her shoes. Really, she could've set Reginald up with Landon from Atlanta. And that got me to thinking about Sasha and the little game she played to get Reginald to go to the basketball game and then somehow finagle a way back to Augusta. The city was beautiful, but not that beautiful to return. The back and forth was outrageous. It was obvious that something was wrong. Walking beside her, I remembered all of the times she mentioned that she'd been on a two-week break. Maybe she didn't want to be alone. Maybe, unlike what Reginald had assumed, she didn't have any plans to go to Paris. She clearly didn't have a man. She probably didn't want to sit in her big old house alone all of those days. That made me feel really bad about snapping at her earlier. Maybe Reginald was right. Maybe I did feel like she was stealing my thunder and I was being sensitive about it.

In spite of all of that, the feeling of seeing my husband get something he really wanted or really needed was so fulfilling that I was willing to let it all go. I always knew he had potential and if he'd just step up and claim it, he could do anything.

He had a big grin as we walked through the parking lot. Before we got in the car, he hugged Sasha and said thank you.

Yes, I hugged her, too.

Seeing Reginald so happy erased most of the discomfort I'd been harboring about Sasha and her extended visit. The new contract was a big deal for Reginald. For us. For my family. Maybe we'd be able to afford private school after all. I had my old friend to thank for that.

I felt silly about feeling pushed aside by my family because Sasha was there. I knew my faults and now I could see clearly that I'd overreacted. Sasha was very different, but she was being good to me. Good to my family. I had to support that.

"Damn it! I chipped my nail," Sasha groaned, pulling her hands out of a sink full of murky dishwater.

"Oh, no," I said, rushing over from the stove where I was closing the lids on a few containers of leftovers from dinner. The kids were in the back getting ready for bed and Reginald was still on the phone calling everyone he knew to tell them about the Landon contract. "I told you that you didn't have to do the dishes," I added. "I can get them."

"No, I said I'd help you out around here," Sasha said. "I just wish we could put all of these dirty dishes into the dishwasher and call it done."

"Who are you telling? That would make things much easier, but R. J.'s allergies are no joke, and unfortunately, one of them includes whatever they put in the dishwashing detergent to stop it from bubbling over. I tried it once and I don't think I've ever seen so much vomit."

"That's so sad. Poor thing. And to think you've dealt with it all of these years."

" 'Dealt with it' isn't at all how I see it. I'm just a mother and that's what I do."

Reginald walked into the kitchen and slid an empty glass into the dishwater.

"Shutting the troops down!" he exclaimed proudly.

"Oh, I'll come get R. J. settled in," I said, putting the leftovers into the refrigerator.

"No, I've got it," Reginald insisted. "You, my darling"—he kissed me on the cheek—"spend time with your big-city friend before she sets out." He'd been sweet to me since we left the dealership. It seemed like nothing could really bother him now that he had that contract. He was even talking about getting a new car.

"Big-city friend?" Sasha laughed and rolled her eyes at Reginald. She stuck out her tongue to his back as he walked out of the kitchen.

"He's so silly," Sasha said.

"Yeah, he's quite the jokester today," I agreed. "I only wish you all had gotten to know him, you know, in undergrad."

"Well, times were different then. We were all different then. And the idea of one of the sorors dating the lawn-mower man was a bit much."

"He was more than a lawn-mower man." I laughed.

"I know; I'm just saying how it was talked about back then. You know? The gossip."

"People thought I was settling," I said. "But I was in love."

"We know that now, but back then, we were young and thought we had something to prove to the world."

"True, very true indeed," I said, turning to Sasha as she let the water out of the sink. "Hey, I want to thank you again—"

"You already thanked me."

"No, again. I want to thank you for coming here and helping me out. I know I haven't been the easiest host, but I appreciate it, and I hope it won't be your last visit."

"Wow," Sasha said and in her voice there was so much surprise. "You know what, I couldn't have spent my vacation in a better place! Now, I just have to find out what I'm doing with the rest of it!"

"Rest of it?"

"I'm off for the rest of the week."

"Well, you could stay here," I suggested, noticing that once again she was mentioning her vacation time. She clearly didn't want to go home for some reason. And I felt like she was just waiting for me to ask her to stay. I needed my rest, but I couldn't just throw her out—not when I knew something was wrong and she'd done so much for my family.

"In Augusta?" she said. "Nah. I already called my car. He'll be here in an hour."

"Call him back. Look, I can take off tomorrow, too," I insisted, "since I'm on a roll. And we can spend one more day together." I reached out and lifted her hand with the chipped nail. "Get our nails done. It's my treat. It's the least I can do."

"You think so?"

"I insist! We have to. Lord knows how long it's been since I've gotten a manicure and I'm sure my coworker can handle the lazy Tuesday crowd without me."

"But it won't be too much?"

I grabbed her cell phone off of the counter.

"Call the driver. No pickup tonight. We'll let him know when you're ready to go home."

Sasha's driver wasn't too happy about her canceling the call. He was already halfway to Augusta and cursed her out in Spanish . . . and French . . . and a few other words we decided were Italian as we reenacted the phone call a dozen times on the twins' old swing set in the backyard.

"I'll have you fired!" I said, impersonating the dramatic, hard-nosed tone Sasha used on the phone.

"I didn't say it like that?" Sasha hollered like we were on a school yard. She took a sip of her wine and stood up in front of her swing as if she was on a stage. "I said," she started, *"You, sir, are fired!"*

I almost spit out my wine.

"You didn't say it like that," I said. "You can't fire him and I know you didn't call him sir!" I laughed and I felt that laugh just shake through my body. My eyes were heavy, but the night was so bright around me. Even in the dark, the grass was this emerald green. The sky, oh, the sky looked like the ocean with diamonds floating all around in it. And it wasn't until I heard Sasha laughing at me that I realized that I'd said all of this aloud.

"Girl, I think you need more wine," she said, getting the bottle from a little basket we brought outside.

"I don't know," I said, feeling my body sway with the breeze . . . or the swing. "I don't want to get too drunk! The mister won't like it."

"He doesn't like it when you drink?"

"No . . ." I took a swig of the wine she'd just poured into my glass. "He doesn't like me!"

"Shhh," Sasha whispered.

As I drank, I felt two little pebbles grinding in my teeth and spit them out. I figured dirt had somehow snuck into the glass. I took another sip of the red wine and again it was a little grainy.

"What do you mean, he doesn't like you?" Sasha asked.

"We don't have sex anymore," I blurted out. "No sex. No dice. He doesn't like me. That simple!" I looked down at the glass. "Is it just me or does this wine have rocks in it?"

"It's red wine, silly," Sasha said. "That's just sediment from when they made it. It happens with expensive bottles."

"Oh," I held up the glass and saw little pieces of white flecks floating in the bottom. "Sediment!" I exclaimed and took another sip.

"Why do you think he doesn't touch you?" Sasha said, coming over and standing by my swing.

"I told you," I rattled. "Borrriinnng. I'm boring. That's it. He doesn't even look at me anymore. Not how he looks at you."

"What?" Sasha chortled a bit. "And how is that?"

"Come on; you know you're beautiful. Your eyes. Your hair. The way you hold your breasts out." I sat up in the swing and poked my breasts out, but then I had to wrap my free arm around the chain to stop from falling. "You're smart and funny. Men just love you."

I nearly dropped my glass, but Sasha steadied it in my hand.

"Ever think of spicing it up?"

"What? Like you said before? Having a threesome or something? I told you he doesn't like that kind of stuff."

"He might." Sasha put her glass down and looked up at my ocean sky smiling.

"What?" I scowled at her. "What are you saying? You really think I should do that? Like have some other woman in my bed . . . with my husband?"

"Not just some other woman. Someone you trust. Someone you . . ."

"You mean you?"

Sasha gazed at me.

"I'd do it," she said, like I'd just asked her.

"What?" My head tipped forward on that word. "I can't do that. *With you?*" I giggled, but Sasha was quiet.

"What's wrong with me?" she asked.

"Nothing . . . I just . . . A threesome? *With you?*" I looked at the house, at my dark bedroom window. "You think he'd like that? No. I couldn't do that." I sat up in the swing again in an attempt to shake off the alcohol and any prospects of anything in the conversation. "I couldn't . . . my father was a preacher . . . my . . . I'm not into women. That's crazy." I got up from the swing. "Let's go inside."

I walked away from her, slid my glass into the basket with the wine bottle, and picked up the basket. I felt Sasha following behind me to the house, but I couldn't turn around. I didn't have any reason to turn around, but I just kept reminding myself that I couldn't. I didn't want to look at her.

"You're beautiful," Sasha said when we were halfway up the path to the back door.

"Thank you," I said dismissively. I felt myself swaying and discerned that the faster I got into the house the better.

"What, are you mad at me?"

"No, I'm just trying to get inside. It's getting a little chilly out here." I stepped onto the first wooden step at the back door.

Sasha took my arm and turned me around.

"What?" I said.

She stole the basket and tossed it to the ground.

I went to grab it, for fear that the glasses would break, but before I could, she grabbed my chin and pulled my face to hers. She kissed me. Spread my lips with her tongue and pushed it into my mouth.

I pulled back, but she held my chin tightly and then wrapped her other arm around my back.

Soon, my tongue was in her mouth, too, and I felt like the ocean was falling into me. It wasn't like kissing a man. It was like kissing her. Her. Everything that she was, that I wasn't. Everything beautiful. Everything strong. Everything easy. It was a delight. And I can only say that right now. Looking back. Because then I was scared and confused by that feeling. How my whole body vibrated with hers. And as soon as I felt my own hand wrapping around her back, I snapped.

"No," I said, pulling back from her hold. "No. What are you doing?"

"You're so beautiful," Sasha said.

"I'm not a lesbian!"

"God, Dawn, will you relax?" she said lightly. "It's nothing. It's just a kiss. A little practice."

"I don't need practice," I said. "I said no." I went to open the door, but she grabbed my arm again.

"I'm not some crazy lesbian chick—you know that," she said. "I just want you to be happy. I just want to help." She paused. "I really do."

"Look, I know down in Atlanta, you all call that help, but it's not what I need in my marriage right now. I'm OK. He'll come around."

I slipped into the kitchen and finished off the bottle of wine the next morning. I needed something to face the folks at my breakfast table and forget what happened the night before. I kept complaining to myself about the weird kiss and the weird moment, but it was really all about how I felt. How that weird kiss and weird moment made me feel was just abrupt. I didn't want to look at Sasha. I didn't want to look at Reginald. I just wanted to get through breakfast, get the kids to school, and have this last moment at the nail shop with Sasha. I told myself to let it go. I didn't think she'd actually meant anything by it. I believed what she said about the kiss being "nothing" and just wanting to help. But what I felt wasn't nothing. It was a rush. And I didn't know what to do with that.

So, with the wine and the weirdness, I was in this odd kind of autopilot that next morning. I overslept again and missed R. J.'s story, only to find out that Sasha had done it again. And made pancakes . . . again. I listened to a joke about a lion named Nino Brown and laughed as Reginald tried to retell it and added in his own lines from *New Jack City.* I got the kids to school. I called into work. I got dressed and went to Sasha's room to let her know I was ready for our "girl's day." I just needed to make one stop.

"OK," she said, sliding her nude toes with red polish into a pair of heels.

I watched for a second and then snapped back to look off and away.

"Is everything OK?" Sasha asked, grabbing her purse.

"Yeah, just need to stop by the library for a minute."

"No, I mean with you. Are you OK? From last night? Because I—"

"Sasha, it's fine. I'm fine," I said, forcing myself to look into her eyes. "It's all good. I . . . I . . . I . . . I believe. I'm fine. We're good. Let's go have girl's day."

"We'll just be in here a second," I explained to Sasha, turning into the vestibule leading into the library. She was walking beside me in a perfectly wrapped purple dress. I could smell her perfume again. "I'm sure it's nothing. Probably an issue with the computers. I'll call tech support."

"I'm fine," Sasha said. "No rush."

I waved at a few familiar sleepy faces as we headed behind the help desk. Mr. Lawrence and Mrs. Harris sat on opposite ends of the main floor.

"Hello?" I called, stepping into the back office with Sasha still behind me.

We almost ran right into Sharika as she was walking out of the back office.

"Oh, I was just on my way up front," she said, her leg half wrapped around the desk where she was clearly sitting and on the Internet.

"Yeah," I said, "I rushed right over here when I got the message about the emergency. What's up? Kids run the Internet down again?"

Sharika was quiet; she pushed back on her heels and put her hands on her hips. She looked right past me and at Sasha.

"Is that the woman from the news?" Sharika asked and it was

rather off because Sasha was right near her and could hear the question.

"Oh, where are my manners? I apologize." I backed up so Sasha and Sharika could shake hands. "Sasha, this is my coworker Sharika Freeman and Sharika, this is my college roommate and soror, Sasha Bellamy—she's visiting from Atlanta."

They exchanged weak smiles and shook uneasily offered hands.

"You have that show on CNN? Comes on late at night."

"That's me," Sasha said, smiling. "You watch?"

"No. I watch A. J. Holmes."

Sasha's smile flatlined.

"You know him?" Sharika asked.

"Yes, I do."

"Sharika, what's the emergency?" I jumped in. "You said you needed me to come by."

Sharika slid her hand back onto her free hip and slowly shifted her focus from Sasha to me.

"We have an emergency," she said.

"I gathered as much, as you said that over the phone," I said anxiously. "Now, what is it? Is there something wrong with the computers?"

"No, that's not it. Much better!" Sharika led me and Sasha back out to the main desk.

We stood in the middle of the help desk area, following Sharika's eyes and looking out over the floor.

"It's them," she whispered to me. "Mr. Lawrence and Mrs. Harris." She pointed from one to the other and looked at me. "They've been at this all morning."

I looked at Mr. Lawrence sitting in his usual seat near the dying fern at the end of a row of tables. He had no old, upside-down newspaper and was just staring hard across the room at Mrs. Harris, who was pretty much doing the same back at him. He sucked his teeth at her and she rolled her eyes at him. And then they did it again.

"You two are looking at those old people?" Sasha asked and I nodded. "They sure don't look happy."

Sharika looked Sasha up and down as if she'd intruded on some private conversation. And, in Sharika's mind, Sasha was. Sometimes Sharika read about drama; other times, she created her own. She was either an actress or the ringmaster.

"So, what do you think, *Dawn*," Sharika asked. "I think they look angry about something."

"I guess so," I said. "But how is that an emergency?"

"Well, after what happened in the bathroom the other day, I don't want any drama up in here," Sharika said. "Lord only knows what those two have going down."

I watched as the pair exchanged angry glances again. A teenager sitting directly in the line of fire got nervous and moved to a different table.

"What, you think she slept with one of his friends? He stole her money? Come on, they're old. It'll pass," I said.

"But I don't want it to pass in here," Sharika said. "The county already thinks we're a joke. The last thing we need is another fight. And I was reading this book like last month about an old couple who got into a fight in an animal hospital and—"

"I don't think we have anything to worry about," I offered. "And if you really think it'll be a big deal, I'll speak to Mrs. Harris on my way out. How about that?"

"I guess that'll work," Sharika said and I turned in time to see her cutting her eyes at Sasha again.

"Wonderful. Hey, Sasha, why don't you go and wait in the car for me." I handed Sasha the car keys. "I need to check something on my computer really quickly before we go."

"That's fine." Sasha took the keys and smiled at Sharika. "Great meeting you."

"Yeah, the pleasure was all mine," Sharika said vacantly.

After Sasha walked out, I pulled Sharika by the arm into the back room.

"What was this about?" I asked.

"What do you mean?"

"What I mean is that I call in to take a personal day and you say there's an emergency and it's just Mr. Lawrence and Mrs. Harris giving crazy eyes across the room? That's not an emergency." I held up my hand signaling to a girl who'd just walked up to the counter to wait a minute until we came out. "And then, what was all of that with Sasha?"

"What did I do to Ms. Thang?"

"You weren't exactly nice to her, Sharika," I said.

She looked away.

"What? What's going on with you?" I asked.

Sharika cowered in a way I'd never expect from her. Her hands fell to her sides.

"Is something wrong?"

"It's nothing," she mumbled. "I just wanted your opinion was all. . . . I know it's probably stupid and I—"

"What is it? Spit it out!"

She looked at me and reached into her pocket.

"Here," she said, handing me a sheet of thick, white paper.

"What's this?"

The letterhead announced that the letter was from the University of Illinois.

"They accepted me," she said as I read.

"Stop it! This is the top Library and Information Science program in the country! This is great! I'm so excited for you." I was fully amazed but not surprised. She'd been talking about going back to school—and then talking about not going back to school—forever. I didn't even know she was applying. I looked up at her expecting the same excitement I was feeling about the news, but there was no expression. "Aren't you excited?"

"It's so far away," she said.

"Yeah, it is," I agreed. "And that's why we have cars and buses and trains and planes. It's kind of cold up in Illinois, but I'm sure

I can get there in the summer." I laughed and playfully whisked Sharika's arm with the paper, but she remained unmoved. "Wait a minute—you're not serious about this distance thing, are you?"

"It's *really* far." Sharika stepped back and sat on the desk. Her shoulders sank in toward her chest. "I've never lived outside of the South. Can you imagine that? *Me* outside of the South?"

"It's the best doctoral program in the country—the entire country," I said. "You can't say no to this. I don't care if you've never left your mother's broom closet. You can't say no." I looked at the letter again. "You applied to this program and they accepted you. Why wouldn't you go? You don't have any children. You don't have a husband. Why not? Who knows what's waiting for you there."

"A bunch of white folks and snow."

"Don't say that. You haven't even been there."

"But I have," Sharika said and I watched as the girl waiting at the counter looked at her watch and walked off. "I've been there a million times where some desperate folks let a black person in to fill some quota and then spend the rest of their time proving to the black person why she shouldn't be there. They make fun of how you dress. They make fun of how you talk. They make fun of how you think. I can't do that again."

"So you think them letting you in was desperate? A little equal opportunity?"

"Come on, Dawn. I got both of my degrees at a little rinky dink local college. I work in the poorest library in the county. Why would they pick that when I'm sure they have librarians from all around the country—the world—applying to their program? People with real experience. People with real know-how. And now I'm supposed to go up there and make a fool—"

"Please stop it," I cut her off. "I can't even listen to this nonsense anymore. You know none of those things are true about you. Those things might be true about them, but none of it is true about you. You're just as smart as anyone else who applied. Smarter. You got accepted."

"But I—"

"And I am not going to support you in this exercise of doubt. This is your dream. And no matter how afraid you are to leave this place, you will. You may have never been to Illinois, but you've read about Illinois. You've read *A Raisin in the Sun*. You've read *Native Son*. Hell, you've read . . . what was that book you read last month by Dy—?"

"Dybek. *The Coast of Chicago*."

"That's it! You read that, too! And I know that's not the same as being there. And those places are probably really different than"—I looked at the letterhead—"Champaign, Illinois, but the point is that you love reading and you know this library like no one else. All of that passion has got to amount to something big for you. You might need a little polish, but don't we all? You can't let that hold you back—not when an opportunity like this comes along. It's your time."

"You think so?" Sharika was tearing up and wiping her mascara everywhere.

"Crying?" I said. "Is crying a good thing?"

She smiled.

"Yes. I guess I'll have to talk to Mama about this," she said. "It'll break her heart if I go."

"I think it'll break her heart more if you *don't* go."

"Well, I guess it's time for me to fill out my response forms," she said, snatching the form and pulling her hands back to her hips.

"And I'm glad to hear that, because I was starting to sound like Sojourner Truth. *A Raisin in the Sun*? Where did that come from?"

We laughed and started walking back out to the help desk.

"Yeah, you were reaching."

"Well, you're worth it. I just have two things I need to say."

"What?"

"First, I want you to go to the bathroom and fix your eyeliner."

"It's messed up?" Sharika started wiping her eyes and making it worse, so I grabbed her hand.

"And next," I started again, "let's consider a new hair color before you go. Maybe something brown . . . or, I don't know . . . black."

"What's wrong with my hair? I like my hair blond. It's hot. And wasn't your little friend's hair blond?"

"Well, Sasha's like three shades lighter than you and she's on television."

"Please, we're the same color!"

"No, you're not—" I stopped myself, realizing I was getting nowhere on the hair. "Fine."

"Exactly. The hair stays. They'll just have to get used to the hotness in"—she looked at the paper in her hand—"Champaign, Illinois. And where is that anyway?"

"I don't know," I said. "Look, let me get out of here. I'll be back tomorrow. Can you hold down the fort?" I looked out over the floor to see that Mr. Lawrence and Mrs. Harris were gone.

"I got this. You know these are the slow days of the week," she replied. "And while I'm watching the books, you watch Ms. Thang."

"Why do you keep calling Sasha that?"

"I don't like her. There's something about her."

"Oh, she's just different. Hollywood type."

"If you say so," Sharika said as I walked to the door. "Just watch her," she added louder.

When I got to the exit, I look down the hallway and saw two hobbling old bodies heading toward the bathroom. "What is it with these two?" I said. I turned back toward Sharika. "Bathroom check!" I mouthed to her.

We investigated three nail salons before Sasha would approve of a technician. She'd done some feature about fungus in nail salons and scared the workers in the other salons after pointing out all of their violations. By the time we sat down in the plush massage seats to get pedicures at some posh spa downtown, I thought the only crime was that we were paying double what was charged at the first shop. While the first shop's version of a massage chair was a bucket and folding chair, there's nothing wrong with saving money.

I was slowly getting over Sasha's impromptu kiss, blaming it on the alcohol that had me acting funny, too. As I began looking her directly in the eyes again, I realized other people downtown were, too. Walking around with her was probably the closest I'd ever come to being a celebrity because people—and I mean old, rich, white people (which means Republicans in the South)—would stop and look at her kind of like they'd known her at some time in their lives and couldn't place her, and whisper to the person next to them. Some, I'm guessing the non-Republicans, even smiled. A few came over and asked for her autograph or a picture. Sasha was always beyond sweet and accommodating. And it was very interesting to see her in that way. She actually used her phone to take a picture of herself with a woman who didn't have one. She said she'd have her assistant mail it to the woman and I thought the woman was about to cry. "You eat this stuff up," I said to her as we walked.

"All in a day's work, baby," Sasha answered playfully.

"I don't know what it is about hometowns in the South," I said after telling Sasha about Sharika's letter and fear of leaving Augusta. We were sitting beside each other in the fancy massage pedicure chairs at the spa. "It's like, if you don't leave right out of high school, you'll never leave."

"That's not a Southern thing. It's a people thing. There are some folks in New York who have never left the city and people in Los Angeles act like they have their own country," Sasha said, laughing.

I bent down to help the technician roll my jeans up above my knees.

"So, what about you?" Sasha asked. She was enjoying the five extra minutes she'd requested to allow her feet to soak in the pedicure pool. "What's your dream? Are you going for your PhD?"

"I don't know. I never thought about it."

"Well, honestly, I didn't even know you were interested in library science in college. You never mentioned it. I was surprised when you said you were working at the library."

"It just came to me," I said. "I didn't work when I first got to Augusta. But I got bored when I got pregnant. I found an online program. That was it."

"Do you like it?"

"I like that the job gives me a little bit of money to help out around the house—and it's definitely not a lot of money. I get to be out of the house and meet interesting people. You saw them! It works for me. I enjoy it. I can't think of anything else I'd do. It's not like in Atlanta here. If you don't work for the medical district or the riverfront, there's not much else for someone with a general degree to do."

I eased back to meet the pulsating pressure from the chair.

"Sasha Bellamy?" A white woman I'd seen eyeing Sasha from the front of the salon now stood behind the technician doing Sasha's feet.

At first, I thought she was another fan, but looking in her face, I wasn't quite sure. She looked annoyed. Maybe angry. A little younger than both of us, she had a tight, college-girl body and the same diamond earrings Sasha wore the first day she came to my house.

"That's me," Sasha said happily, curling her lips up at the edges and poised to take a compliment.

"So you know my husband?"

"Excuse me?" Sasha said and she'd already pulled her fancy pen from her purse to sign an autograph.

"Phil Landon? You know him, right?"

"I know Phil," Sasha answered. "Are you a friend?"

"No, bitch. I'm his wife."

The nail tech stopped scrubbing Sasha's feet immediately, got up from her little stool, and walked farther back in the salon, saying something in what sounded like Mandarin.

"You're the black whore who's been fucking him," the woman said.

"Is there a problem?" I asked.

"No, Dawn, I have this," Sasha said coolly.

"Can you get the manager?" I said to the nail tech helping me.

"First," Sasha started, "I don't think my race has anything to do with this. And second, no, I haven't quite had the opportunity to sleep with your husband. Does he still have my number?"

"You think I believe that? I have all of the receipts from the hotel last week. When I get finished with you, you'll wish you never gave him your number."

People started getting up and walking toward the debacle.

"Oh please, honey," Sasha said. "The only wish I have is that you'd stop talking to me."

"Excuse me, miss." A woman I supposed was the manager tried coming between Sasha and the woman. "We can't have this here."

"Yes," Sasha said. "We can't have *this* here."

"Can you please leave?" the manager said to the woman. "We can't have problems with customers."

The woman angrily flicked her hand up at the manager but kept her deadly stare on Sasha.

"You're going to get what's coming to you."

"Miss, I need you to step outside," the manager tried again, getting a hold of the woman's arm.

"You get your hands off me," she said. "Do you know who my husband is?" The woman jerked away and hustled out of the door with all eyes following her.

"Pure foolery," Sasha said, dismissing the standoff by waving her hand at the woman's back. She leaned back in her seat.

"Foolery? What was that?" I asked, stunned.

The woman who'd been working on Sasha's feet was standing a few feet away, looking on nervously.

"You can come back," Sasha called to her. "Apparently, I'm not the violent one here. And this water is getting cold."

Sasha giggled and waved at a woman who was giving her a nasty eye from the massage chair beside her.

"What was she talking about?" I asked Sasha again.

"I want triple massage time," Sasha said to the newly returned nail tech. "And take off those plastic gloves. It feels like I'm being massaged by a garbage bag."

Sasha sounded haughty, superior in a way that I'd never witnessed. She was rolling her eyes at the nail tech and poking her feet out in the woman's face.

"Sasha, what's going on?"

"What is it?" Sasha asked. She rolled her resting head toward me.

"What do you mean, 'What is it?' Who was that woman?"

"That was Landon's wife. You didn't hear her say that?"

"I heard her, but what does she want with you? What was she talking about?" I leaned over to her chair to whisper. "Did you sleep with Landon?"

Sasha looked at me sharply.

"So what if I did?"

"*So what if you did?* He's a married man—that's so what," I whispered.

"So now it's my fault?" Sasha flashed a malicious smile that dissipated into a grin. "No, I didn't sleep with him. Calm down. I'm just annoyed at how ridiculous she's being. He's her husband. She needs to calm down and play her position."

"Confronting someone she thinks is sleeping with her husband isn't her position?" I asked.

"No, it's not," Sasha answered. "Look, if he's done with her, she needs to move on. Plain and simple. Marriage is little more than some ring and certificates. You can't expect people to stick around just for that. Be a good wife, and if he stays, he stays. If he finds a better wife in someone else, well, it is what it is."

4

Someone should've rang the fire alarm. Someone should've. But no one knew there was a fire. At least I didn't. And that's the funny thing about fires, you know? Most of us think when a fire breaks out, it just appears from nowhere. Stabbing, hot flames of red and orange flashing before our eyes like warning signs, giving us enough time to break a window and call for help. Run out of the door. Get the children out of their beds. But all fire isn't like that. Sometimes, it starts in the walls. In the attic. Beneath your bed. And can burn for a few minutes. An hour. A few hours. Sometimes days. Before you're willing to really see it and try to escape. But before that, there were signs. You smelled smoke. You heard cracking. You felt the heat. But you came up with a million excuses as to what else it could be instead of a fire. You opened a window. You turned your music up. You turned the heat down.

This was my fire brewing in front of me. And I was so busy trying to just kowtow and make good, have a friend in someone, that I was the one opening windows and turning up music and turning down heat. I wanted Sasha to be OK. Like, as my friend. And not smell the smoke, hear the cracking, or feel that heat. So I didn't. At least not those last days she spent in my house. I was busy making excuses for her.

Sasha was leaving in the morning. For real this time. She'd called the car and her bags were packed and by the door. The twins were buzzing around her at the dinner table. Cheyenne had made her a friendship bracelet at school and R. J. had a special surprise.

"We're going to miss you," Cheyenne said, her arm linked with Sasha's on the table. "No more pancakes in the morning. No more lasagna for dinner. . . . What are we going to do?"

"Eat what I fix you," I said.

"Or I suppose I could leave my lasagna recipe, too," Sasha said. She'd already given me the pancake recipe, but I'd stashed it away in Reginald's mother's old recipe box.

"Thank God for recipes," Reginald joked.

"So what's your special surprise?" Sasha asked R. J. And instead of looking away, he did something I'd come to expect when he was communicating with Sasha; he smiled.

He reached down under his seat, pulled up something flat that was wrapped in the red and orange wrapping paper I'd used last Christmas.

"What's that, sweetie?" I asked because I hadn't taken him anywhere to get something for Sasha.

R. J. proudly handed the gift to Sasha and said, "Thank you."

"Ohh." Sasha patted R. J. on the head. "Thank you for what?"

"For being my new friend." R. J. flung himself into Sasha's arms and hugged her so intimately I felt my blood stop.

"And thank you for being my friend," Sasha said before opening the gift.

"What's that?" Reginald asked as we saw what looked like a book appearing from beneath a snag in the wrapping.

"Is that a book?" I asked.

"*Goodnight Moon*," Sasha read the cover.

"What?" I leaned forward in my seat so I could see the cover. "Is that your book, R. J.?"

"Yes," he said.

"But that's your favorite book," I said. "Are you sure you want to give it away?"

"I could give it back," Sasha offered.

"Oh, nonsense," Reginald said loudly. "The boy gave it to you." He turned to me. "The boy gave it to her. He must want her to have it. Everyone stop pushing him." He pointed a fork that was half full of spaghetti at R. J. "Son, do you want her to have that?"

R. J. looked at Sasha and after a second, he smiled.

"Yes," he said. "I want her to have my book."

Sasha was standing at the bedroom window, staring out into a rainy night. She was talking about how she needed to become more active in her life, really make her dreams come true and stop standing on the sidelines. I was lying center in the guest bed, my arms and legs akimbo. My head spinning, struggling to keep up with the speech that was losing me fast. My eyelids were shutting down and the ceiling fan spinning above my head looked like it was about to swallow me up.

I didn't intend to go into Sasha's room that last night. I was actually in my bedroom sliding off my slippers when Sasha showed up at the door holding a bottle of wine, announcing that it was her last night in town and she wanted to spend some quality time with me—her best friend. She pouted loud enough that Reginald, who'd been in the bathroom shaving and was wearing only gym shorts, stepped into the bedroom and waved us away like little girls.

"I'll be back in just an hour, babe," I'd said, but lying in the bed with the ceiling fan spinning, I knew that hour had become two. I'd had three glasses of the red wine and felt that ocean of diamonds sinking into me. I felt like I could see through the ceiling. See into space. See myself as myself. Reading *Goodnight Moon* to R. J. Lying with Cheyenne in the purple bedroom. Kissing Reginald's spine until he turned to me. My eyes closed. I was floating.

"So, what do you think?" I heard this crash into my ocean.

I shook awake . . . only I wasn't sure I'd been asleep.

"What?" I said as the fan came back into focus and I turned to the window to see Sasha standing there holding a half full glass of wine.

"What should I do next?" She looked at me expectantly.

"Do? Do about what?"

"About what I'm talking about. About my dreams. About going after the things I want when I know I should have them," Sasha said. "God, Dawn, are you listening to me?" She sat down on the bed in her slinky ivory nightgown.

"I am . . . I am," I said, rubbing my eyes. "My head is spinning. A little too much wine." There were three Sashas. One at the window. One beside the bed. Another handing me a new glass of wine

"Well, that's every night," Sasha joked. "Here, bite the snake that bit you." She handed me the glass as I tried so hard to see her. Was she at the window, by the bed, or beside me?

"I can't," I said. "Too much . . . I've had too much."

"Take it," she insisted, lifting my hand and wrapping it around the little glass stem.

I took a sip.

"It tastes funny," I said. There was a gritty and almost chalky aftertaste. I smacked my tongue to clean it off.

"You're just buzzing," Sasha said. "It's the sediment. I told you before." She laughed.

"Oh, yeah," I said, looking from one Sasha to the next. "Red wine. The sediment . . ." I tried to hand the glass back.

"What?"

"I can't," I said. "I have work in the morning. I have to get up to read to R. J."

"You can take off again. I can read to R. J." She pushed the glass back closer to me.

"You know the rule: bite the snake that bit you. It'll make you feel better." She held the top of the glass as I held the bottom and raised it to my mouth. "Have some more."

She kept the glass there until it was empty. Not a drip rolled down my chin.

"Oh," I gasped, trying to catch my breath.

"That's it, Dawnie! I knew you had it in you! The old college try!" She hopped up in the bed and got on her knees.

"I'm sorry I bored you with all of my lame work talk."

"It's fine." I fell back to the pillow and looked at her face over mine. Her blond curls fell all around her head like a halo. The fan spun behind her.

"It's my last night. Let's just have fun. No serious stuff."

"But I have to go back to bed. I told Reginald I'd be back in an hour."

"Well, you missed that train, girlie." Sasha chuckled. "It's after 1:00 a.m."

"What?" I tried to scramble, but then I realized that Sasha was holding my hands down on the pillows. I tried to move, but the fan was spinning and spinning and spinning. And Sasha became three again. At the window. At the bed. On top of me.

"He'll probably be mad at you," she said. "Hey, I have an idea. I can come in with you and say sorry." She grinned and shook the blond curls. "We can have a slumber party. All three of us. Won't that be fun?"

"But, I—" My eyes were turning to slits and I saw darkness skipping in circles around my view. Sasha became smaller and then she was nothing.

I woke up in the guest bedroom alone. There was no candle burning on the dresser. No Sasha. The light was off and the fan had stopped.

Everything was fuzzy. More light and like a dream than it had been when I was awake. I reached out to see my hand.

"Sasha?" I called. "Sasha?"

I felt my way off of the bed and stumbled over each step to control my feet.

"Sasha?" I looked into the little bathroom Reginald had built off of the guest room when his parents died. "Sasha?"

I held the walls as I pulled my body through the house, walking and falling and calling Sasha. Everything. The couch. The refrigerator. The dining room table. Seemed brighter and nicer and more slow moving than I'd ever recalled. Or was it me?

I ran out of places and thought that I should go and ask Reginald if she'd left. Where was she?

"Reginald?" I called, nearing our bedroom. I pushed the door open and nearly fell down, but caught myself on the dresser beside the door.

I looked up. Only lights from the lamps on either side of the bed invaded the darkness.

Sasha was lying upside down at the top of the bed in her ivory nightgown, her legs up in the air, making a V over the headboard.

"Finally, you came to join us," she cheered. "I thought you were out for the night."

"What? Why are you—? Where's Reginald?"

The haze in my mind cloaked whatever anger or confusion or resentment I'd later feel.

"In the bathroom. Went to take a shower. Poor thing was fast asleep," she replied casually. "But now it's time to party!"

"Party? But—I—I?"

Reginald came out of the bathroom in a little towel he had to hold at his hip. He was still wet.

"Babe," he called, walking to me with one arm open. "You did *this*? I can't believe *you* did this for me."

He wrapped his arm around my waist and kissed me so softly on the forehead.

"At first, I, you know, I thought it was a joke, but then after Sasha explained everything to me, it made sense. I do deserve a little fun." He smiled and kissed me on the lips passionately. "Come on." He started pulling me to the bed.

"Wait." I pulled away the best I could. "Did you have sex? Did you two have sex?"

"No, crazy," Sasha proclaimed. "We were waiting for you."

Reginald sat me down on the corner of the bed and stood in front of me.

"Now," Sasha directed, "One of you has already kissed me . . . well . . . on the lips. And, so, it's only fair that the other has a chance." She pointed at Reginald seductively and turned her finger around to direct him to her.

"You kissed her?" Reginald asked and looked at me curiously for a little while, but I was too sluggish to reply.

"Come here, sexy," Sasha called.

Reginald climbed onto the bed and crawled right past me to Sasha's lips.

He kissed her upside down and I could see his tongue dangling in her mouth in the dimness.

She moaned and ran her fingernails up his chest.

He kicked back a bit and I had to move over to stay on the bed.

His head moved from her mouth to her breasts. He gently removed her nightgown with his teeth and Sasha squealed. Her head carefully contorted under his chest, she angled it to look at me at the edge of the bed.

"You're so fucking hot," she said, looking at me but clearly speaking to Reginald. She smiled this devious smile that let me know that no matter what I did, this couldn't stop. They wouldn't hear me. I wouldn't be louder than her. This had been happening for a long time. This night, this thing, had been building from the moment she'd walked into my house. And maybe before. And wouldn't stop.

Reginald's dangling tongue licked her nipples until they were full and Sasha's eyes left me to dance in space.

He ran his hands up the sides of her thighs, so carefully, so deliberately, so magically that I could feel them on me.

My hand began to move in circles at my thigh.

"No," I whispered into the dimness, but I could hardly even hear myself. I wanted to be touched. To be given love carefully and deliberately and magically. I needed it.

I looked at Sasha. Her beautiful blond curls spread out over my cheap cotton bedsheets.

Sasha moaned.

Reginald's tongue went from her breasts to her stomach to her navel. He made these playful circles there. And he laughed and she laughed.

"Kiss me," she said to him inching down from the headboard. "Kiss me."

He went deeper and his tongue and his face disappeared between her thighs. A lover I never knew wrestled her upside-down legs around his neck, dipped his back down lower, and instigated a full and heavy and mournful cry from Sasha's mouth.

But he didn't stop. He held her legs tighter.

She reached out to me. One slender arm, snaking down the white sheet to my hand.

I know I said "no," but my hand moved toward hers.

And the one that was at my thigh moved to the insides of my legs.

Sasha locked her eyes on mine and I whimpered. My body began to soften.

And then the ocean moved.

She pulled me to her with those eyes.

And this time my lips opened her mouth.

But she got loose. And turned around on the bed.

She pulled Reginald and I together.

He kissed me like I was golden. Ran his tongue up my neck and bit at my chin. He kissed me like I was her.

She pulled him back to her. He fell between her legs and with no question he entered her.

I didn't know where to take myself. Where to go with my ocean and my needs and screaming. My husband was having an affair in front of me and I wasn't saying anything.

They rocked and they moaned and Sasha held my hand so tight.

"Oh shit," Sasha yelled and her hand gripped mine tighter and her legs went rigid. Reginald wrapped his hand over her head and rocked faster.

She pulled me down to the bed beside her and he came over to me.

I wanted the same. I wanted everything the same. To have someone to laugh at my jokes and think I was marvelous and smart. To let me lead him into a meeting and cross my legs so he could see my ankles. To get him to do *this* to his wife.

I pulled him into me. I shook him like he shook her. I wrapped my legs around his waist and opened my insides so far back he moaned.

Sasha smiled like a teacher. I looked from her to Reginald and saw his eyes on my neck. On my throat. I imagined my hair was blond and my arms were slender. He went deeper inside and rocked me harder.

I yelled then. My legs went rigid and wild. I began to kick and kick as the ocean grew and the last kick when Reginald shook, too, was swift and direct. My heel stopped at something hard.

"Oww!"

There was a shout.

I looked over and Sasha was off of the bed and lying on the floor holding her foot.

"What happened?" Reginald asked, coming up off of me with his hands in the air confused.

"She kicked me off the bed!" Sasha cried. "She kicked me. My foot! My foot!"

I rushed to the edge of the bed to look at her.

Reginald turned on the light and went to her side.

"Are you OK?" He crouched down.

"It hurts!"

"Well, what is it? What happened?" he asked. He reached to touch her foot, but she moved away.

"I don't know," she said, now cradling the foot in her hand. "She did it!" She pointed at me. In my haze she looked like an image in a stained glass window, all colors coming together and then bursting apart.

"I didn't . . . I didn't mean it. I was just having fun," I explained. "I'm sorry."

Reginald went for the foot again, but Sasha was frantic now and wouldn't let him near her.

"I think my foot got caught on the side of the bed. I heard it snap. It's probably broken." She looked at me. "Did you do this on purpose? Was this supposed to be funny?"

"No . . ." I pleaded. "Not at all. I wasn't even . . ."

"It can't be broken. You'd be in way more pain," Reginald tried. "Probably just a sprain. Let me look at it." He reached again.

"Look, just get me out of here. Just get me to my room and away from her," Sasha said. "I told you she's jealous of me. She hates me. I tried, but she hates me."

"What did you say?" I asked.

Reginald helped Sasha off of the floor and she winced the whole while.

"You told Reginald I'm jealous of you?"

Sasha leaned on Reginald's shoulder and stuck out her limp foot that was already swelling.

"How am I going to work like this?" she said. "I can't go into work like this."

"Why would you say that to Reginald? I'm not jealous of you!"

I got up in the bed and began to inch over toward them. "You said I was your friend."

"You want to ruin my career," Sasha said.

"That's ridiculous," I said.

Reginald held out his hand to stop me from coming closer to Sasha.

"I'm gonna walk her to her room. Just stay in here."

"What?"

"I want to make sure she's OK. I'll be back."

"But what about me?" I asked.

"Dawn," Reginald said, "you've had a lot to drink. You need to lie down and get some rest."

"But I was just trying to . . ."

"Dawn," Reginald called louder. "Enough. You kicked her off of the bed. I need to make sure she's OK. Do you want me to leave her lying on our bedroom floor?"

"But—" I tried.

"Lie down," Reginald demanded, turning toward the door with Sasha hanging over his shoulder.

They began to walk out.

"But I—" I called to Reginald.

He turned his head to look at me.

"I'll be back soon," he said before walking over our threshold.

Sasha turned to looked at me over his shoulder. There was nothing in her eyes.

My mother was stuffing me into the empty closet under the staircase. I was still little. I know because her hands fit around my entire torso and there was nothing I could do to get her off of me.

"I don't want to go in here," I cried. "It's dark. It's scary."

"It'll just be a little while, Dawn," she said. "He won't find you in here. He won't think of it."

"But can't I go to my room? Be in my room by myself?" I was crying. My legs trembled in the cold draft.

"He's gonna come look for you there," she said. "Look, your daddy's been drinking; something bad got into him. Something real bad. The devil."

"Where ya'll at?" my father slurred and I heard his feet nearly caving into the steps above my head.

My mother pushed me hard, back into the wall. I hit my head and fell to the floor. I heard a click as my mother locked the closet door.

"Edith? Where are you? Where are you with that girl? Falling asleep in church? She knows better."

"Herbert, she ain't in the house," I heard my mother say. "She gone out to play now."

I crawled up to the door and peeked out of the bottom where a little slit of light shined in from the lamp in the living room. I could see my mother's black shoes right in front of me, hear my father's shoes shuffling toward her.

"Play? How the hell you let her out to play after what she done pulled in church this morning? Embarrassing me in front of everyone? She needs to learn how to act. Where's she at?"

His shoes were nearly on top of my mother's, but she didn't move from in front of the closet.

"She's gone. I told you. Told you everything. I'll talk to her about it later. I'll give her a whipping; don't you worry."

"Spare the rod and spoil the child!" My father stomped on the floor and turned away from her. "That's what the Book says."

"That Book says a lot of other stuff, too," she said.

"What do you mean, woman? You talking slick to me?" He unbuckled his belt. " 'Cause if I reckon, it does say a lot more, too. A lot about a woman obeying her husband."

"I ain't trying to fight with you. I'm just saying, maybe you need to wait until that whiskey wears off before you discipline our daughter."

My father walked away from the closet and into the dining room, off a bit to where I could see him. He was still in his church pants.

"What are you looking for?" My mother asked a question she knew the answer to.

He opened the bottom door of the cherrywood china cabinet I had to clean every Friday after school.

"I need a drink," he said. "Where's my whiskey?"

"You've had enough. It's all gone."

"Woman, it ain't your place to tell me when I've had enough. Now where is it?" He tossed some half-empty glass bottles out onto the floor. One rolled out over the wood and stopped near my mother's foot. Her hand, shaking and so pale from scrubbing other people's dining room floors, picked up the bottle.

"Thought you were gonna stop drinking," she said.

He kept rummaging through the cabinet and mumbling about a woman's place.

"Ain't want to have no girl anyway," he said.

"You get real mean when you drink."

"Told you I wanted a son. Girls is trouble. All of them."

"It's like you're somebody else."

"Open her legs to anyone who comes by. I bet you that's how she'll turn out! Like a whore. Like her mama."

"Like the devil gets into you."

"What you say, woman?"

My father sprang up off the floor and charged her so quickly it seemed like he was going to tear into the closet.

Her heels turned into the slit and her body banged into the door. The bottle hit the floor and glass scattered everywhere. The alcohol rolled beneath the door and wet my fingertips.

"What you say?" my father asked again.

"I ain't say nothing, Herbert," she cried. "I told you I don't want to fight with you."

He banged her against the wall and I watched as her heels raised high off of the ground over the slit and all I could see were the points of my father's shoes. I could hear the faint gurgling of her choking.

"I could kill you right now," he said. "You're lucky I'm with you. You're lucky you're alive."

I cried, but I knew to cover my mouth. I knew better than to let him hear me. She'd get it worse then.

Her struggle for air lessened to silence.

"Whore!" he yelled and all of her fell to the floor like a piece of rotten wood.

My mother's body covered the slit beneath the door. I sat muffling my cries in the darkness. I listened until my father found his whiskey and slammed the front door.

"Wake up, Mama," I cried, trying to slide my wet hand beneath the door to shake my mother. "Wake up!"

"Wake up, Dawn."

Reginald was shaking me.

I was still naked and alone in the bed, shivering in the early morning chill. My eyes were wet with tears from my dream.

"Wake up!" Reginald was holding my arm. He was fully clothed and wearing a jacket.

"What? Where'd you go?"

"I didn't go anywhere," he said. "I'm leaving now."

"Leaving?"

He let go of my arm and I sat up.

"Leaving for what? Where's Sasha?"

He went to the dresser and got his watch.

I got up and went to the bedroom door to see the door to the guest room on the other side of the end of the hallway wide open. "Did her driver come? What time is it?"

"A little after six," Reginald said. "Look, her foot is pretty swollen. Just a sprain, but she can't walk. I can't let her go home like that in a limousine. How's she going to get around and stuff?"

"She can call someone . . . I don't know." I put on my slippers and went to the bathroom for my robe.

"She's in the truck. Waiting for me."

I turned back to see him.

"Waiting for you for what?"

"To take her back to Atlanta."

"No. I'm going to talk to her."

"She doesn't want to see you."

Reginald stood on the other side of our bed, by the dresser, looking at me with cold eyes.

"She's pretty upset," he said. "And I told her maybe you two should just let things cool down a little before she—"

"Cool down?" I grabbed the bathrobe off of the back of the closet door. "I didn't do anything. She's the one who came in here and tricked me into having a threesome. I didn't want to do that."

"Now, she tricked you?" Reginald looked at me like I was crazy. "How did she trick you? Or was it the alcohol tricking you?"

"You don't believe me. Why would I try to hurt Sasha?"

"None of that matters," Reginald said. "I'm just going to take her home, make sure she's OK, and come right back."

"But what about the kids? What about work?"

"Just tell them I'll be home for dinner. And I canceled all of my appointments for today."

"You canceled work?"

Reginald hadn't canceled a job since his mother's funeral.

I tried to tie my robe with shaking hands and tears coming from my eyes, but I couldn't. I felt in me that something was wrong. And I couldn't say it. Because then I didn't know what it was. But I felt it. Something was wrong. Really wrong.

"I have to go, too," I cried.

Reginald grabbed my arms with both hands.

"How can you go with us with the kids here?" he asked slowly. "Look, Dawn, you need some rest. I didn't want to say anything, but you're drinking too much."

"I'm fine. Did she tell you to say this?" I asked. "She's the one with the—"

"She didn't tell me anything," he stopped me. "I know. I've seen it with my own eyes. You haven't been right in days. And I don't even think your mind is clear right now. Look at you."

He turned me to the mirror where my robe was wide open and I was still naked. My eyes were swollen. My hair was everywhere.

"Don't leave me," I whispered as tears began to roll at the image. "Please don't leave me."

He raked my hair down with his fingers and tucked it behind my ears.

"I'll be back," he said. "I'll be back before dinner."

5

Dinner got cold. Dinner was thrown away. Cheyenne had an attitude. R. J. wouldn't be settled down. I went to bed alone. And it was a sobering and restless night. Not a wink of sleep to be had.

I texted Reginald a few times. Called a few more times than that. There was nothing. I thought to call a friend or a relative to ask if anyone had seen or heard from him. But then I realized we had no friends. We kept in touch with no relatives. I thought to call the police or a hospital and report my husband missing. But I knew he wasn't missing. And that would be a lie. I knew where he was, but this silent and burning thing in my stomach wouldn't let me say it aloud. Instead, I was busy reviewing things in my mind. Do you know how that is? When you can't admit something to yourself, but you keep going over the facts anyway? You add it all up like a cashier at a register:

Sasha shows up.

My husband leaves.

I'm alone.

And there it is. In writing in your mind. You can't dispute it. But then, you tell yourself that you're crazy. That can't be true. He's just taking a long time. He's mad at me. Maybe I did kick her on purpose. How can I make this better?

I told myself I needed to relax.

And I might have. But I couldn't stop hearing myself begging Reginald not to leave me. And thinking of how crazy that was. I begged my husband not to walk out of the door with a woman who was supposed to be my friend. My last friend.

At four in the morning, my cell phone rattled the entire bedroom awake. I wasn't asleep, just lying in silence, and when I turned over after hearing the vibrating, I saw the light from the phone shining bright and blue, reflecting neon colors on the ceiling above the nightstand. I reached for it like it was water in a desert.

It was Reginald:

Got ur texts. Need time. Call u soon.

(That casual use of "u" would bother me for years.)

The light over the help desk at the library was out. One long, fluorescent lightbulb blew out and we were in near darkness all day.

"Light goes out downtown, the custodian in the building fixes it," Sharika said, using her computer screen as a lamp to see the bar code on one of the books on her cart. "Light goes out in the 'hood, we have to wait five days until someone will come fix it. Ain't that some racist shit?"

"I guess so," I said flatly, not caring to stop her cursing. "It's how things are here. How they've always been."

"Well, they need to decide what they're going to do. Either put the money into these libraries or shut them down. Poor people need books, but who wants to come to some beat-down, shabby library when you know they have better ones in the white folks' neighborhoods?"

"They have better everything in their neighborhoods. That's just how it is."

"Uhm . . . humm." Sharika shook her head disapprovingly and shot an evil eye across the floor at a boy who was folding back pages in a magazine. "Dante!" she called to him. "Stop folding those pages. I see you."

He looked up toward the dark help desk surprised and slid the half-folded magazine onto the table in front of him.

"Bad-ass kids up in here," Sharika said. "They'll break something that's already broken. Don't have a clue how to treat nice things. Can't give them anything."

She inched off of her stool and went to push the cart away to return the books.

"I'll do it," I said.

"What?"

"I'll return the books."

"You'll return the books? But that's my thing. That's what I do. You handle these crazy-ass customers and I do the floor work."

"I'll do it," I said firmly. I was getting tired of sitting there in the darkness and thinking of Reginald being gone. I kept looking at my phone. Waiting for a new text. Reading the old text. Trying to decipher it again. I'd responded, asking what he meant by "time" and reminding him that I needed him to come home to pick up the children so I didn't have to pay for after-school care again—he didn't answer.

Sharika's hand went to her hip. Her lips pursed together the way they do when she's about to read into something.

"What crawled up into your ass and died?" she asked.

"Excuse me?"

"Yesterday I thought something was wrong with you. I didn't say anything. I just knew and let it go. Didn't want to be all nosy, you know?" she pointed out. "But today, I know—"

"I'm fine," I said. "Let it go."

"If that isn't the weakest defense, I don't know what is." Sharika stepped away from the cart and stood right beside my seat. "You know you can talk to me, right? We aren't close, but I do consider you my friend. Hell, you listen to all of *my* problems."

"There's no problem." I got up and pressed past the little bit of space she'd left between us. "I figured I'd get used to pushing this cart around when you leave. And you need more experience with the customers." I began pushing the cart out to the floor.

"Dawn Johnson, you stop that cart right there and right now!" Sharika demanded.

And I stopped. Not because I had to, but because something in me wanted to. But I rolled my eyes anyway. Pretended Sharika was just wasting my time.

"You and I both know something is wrong. You came in here all scary-faced, looking like somebody stole your soul, and expect me to sit here and pretend nothing's wrong? That ain't me! That ain't where I'm from. Now, that might be how it is where you're from in the south side of Atlanta, but here, in these woods, we look the devil in the face and tell him he's a liar."

"Drama. Drama. Drama. What do you want from me, Sharika?"

"What's wrong?" She came over and pulled the cart from me. "I know it isn't the kids, because you'd be someplace else dealing with your babies. Is it Reginald?" She paused. "Is it that woman from TV who was here looking all funny?"

I grabbed the cart back.

"Hell no," she said. "Hell fucking no."

She put her hand on my shoulder. Tears came crawling up my back.

There was a slam from the front hallway where the bathrooms were.

Everyone looked up from their squares on the tables.

Sharika and I rushed to the hallway to see Mr. Lawrence stomping toward us in a rush.

"—tired of this," he said.

"What happened?" I asked. "Everything OK?"

He walked right past us and out of the library, slamming the door behind him.

I looked over at Sharika, but she was still looking down the hallway.

I turned to see Mrs. Harris heading toward us. Her head high. Her arm holding a book. She walked past our puzzled eyes and to the help desk.

"I'll be checking this out," she said with a forced air of sophistication.

Sharika and I went back to the desk, leaving the cart in the middle of the floor.

I took the book—*The Great Gatsby*—from her and held out my hand for her card without a word.

Mrs. Harris went looking in her purse, tossing things around and talking to herself.

Sharika, who was now right over my shoulder, looked at me.

A tear fell into Mrs. Harris's purse.

"Can't ever find anything in here," she said, her sophisticated voice broken. "Can't find nothing."

"No one's waiting in line," I pointed out. "You can have more time—"

"I don't need more time. I've had enough time!"

Sharika and I looked at each other again.

"I've given time and I've had time and I can't do this anymore."

She shut the purse suddenly, with no card in her hand and just looked up toward the ceiling.

"Everything OK?" I asked.

Sharika handed her a tissue from her desk.

She wiped her tears.

"I am not sleeping with that man," she said tightly.

"OK . . ." Sharika said. "Well, what are you doing with him?"

I nudged her in the ribs.

"What?" Sharika asked. "She brought it up."

"But it's not our place to—"

"I've been married fifty-three years," Mrs. Harris said as if we hadn't said anything and she wasn't speaking to anyone in particular. "Left my mother's house when I was twenty-two years old to be with Eldridge David Harris, a boy from my high school who was in Germany shooting guns and wanted to take me around the world. I was a new woman. Had nice shoes and long fingernails." She looked down at her wrinkled hands and I saw that her wedding ring was on her right hand. "And I was ready to see the whole world. And I knew he could show me." She paused. "The farthest we made it was Augusta. Right into his mother's house. I hated it. I started to hate him and that house. It wasn't what I wanted. Where was my world? Where were his promises? I felt like he'd tricked me with all of his big talk. Instead of the world, he gave me three babies and a broom. I wanted to leave so many nights. But I stayed. I made a life with him, because that's what I said I was going to do. I guess I'm too old to see the world now."

I slid the book down onto the counter.

"But that man"—she pointed to the closed doors Mr. Lawrence had just slammed—"he reminds me of that woman. How she smelled. How she walked. How she could tell a joke. Keep all eyes on her. With all of his faults, he does that for me. He brings me . . . joy." She looked into my eyes and shook her head. "But I can't put him through this anymore. I can't continue to lie to him or lie to myself. I'm too old to love again like that. Fifty-three years? I can't leave my husband. If I walk away, it's like I'm leaving my life"—she paused—"for him."

She slid the book back toward me.

"You girls are young—"

"Girls?" Sharika stopped her.

"Yes, girls," Mrs. Harris said again. "You're young. You still have a whole life to live. If there's something you want, you go out and get it. You see the world and don't wait for nobody to show it to you. You can do it. Don't let that be a mystery you discover when it's too late."

She picked up her purse and placed it gracefully on her forearm before pursing her lips to find some part of the composure she'd always had. She nodded to us and began walking to the door.

"But what about the book?" I held up *The Great Gatsby*.

"I've already read it," she said. "Keep it."

I told Sharika everything. From the blond curls on my white bedsheets, to *Goodnight Moon* and begging Reginald to stay. As I got sad, she grew mad. Mad like she was me. Mad like she'd been the one haunted in her nights and ignored in her mornings. I'd expected her to try to calm me down. Stop me from crying and say I was exaggerating. She'd tell me everything was probably fine. I'd go home and Reginald would be there waiting. But no. She just wagged her eyes from side to side as she considered the awful series of events.

"So this whore came up in your house and flaunted her bony ass in front of your family and now your husband hasn't come home?"

I nodded.

Sharika's eyes wagged some more. Her hand went to her hip again.

"Now why was this whore here again?"

I hated the way that word sounded. Like Sasha was a thief. Or a murderer. Someone no one in her right mind would allow in her home. But, you know, looking back now, I think maybe that speaks to the nature of a whore. Of a thief. Of a murderer. They're skilled. They don't show up in some T-shirt branding who and what they are. They just go to work and leave you to figure out the direction of the assault.

"She was at a conference. Some journalist's conference downtown. I don't know. I didn't ask," I replied.

"How'd she know how to get in contact with you? You said you hadn't spoken to her in years."

"I don't know, Sharika," I said. "Maybe she looked it up online. Maybe someone in the sorority—I don't know. I mean, why are you making it sound like I did something wrong?"

"I never said such a thing. I'm just trying to get my facts straight. You should, too. Look, if—and I'm not saying she did—but if this whore has somehow convinced your husband to up and have a rendezvous or whatever this is with her, then you need to know the truth of the matter, the beast you're up against. I knew that chick was trouble the moment I smelled her. Had that sugary-ass perfume on. Smelling like a stripper."

"You think she took Reginald from me?" I asked.

"I don't know for sure," Sharika said. She cocked her head to the side suspiciously and put both of her hands on her hips this time. "But I do know you need to figure out what your next move is."

"Excuse me, ma'am . . . ma'ams," a thin boy with thick glasses whispered. "Do you know where the most recent anthology of stories about the Star Trek series is located?"

"What?" Sharika shifted her weight from one hip to the next in her seat and shot her eyes at him. "Can't you see we're talking here?"

"But I—"

"It's out right now. It's usually in PN1997. It's due back next week." She turned back to me casually as if she hadn't identified a call number off the top of her head.

After a few confused stares, the boy gathered his things and went back to his seat.

"So?" she asked.

"I'm not going to do anything. I can't. I have to wait for him to call," I said. "What, you think I should call her?"

"Call her for what? So some whore can have the pleasure of telling *you* where *your* husband is? Hell no!"

"So, what?"

"So . . . I don't know . . . I don't know." Sharika shook her head worriedly. "You . . . you're always talking about love and what people do for love. You have to do something." She stopped and looked at the picture of Reginald and me floating on my computer screen and then looked back at me with wild eyes. "You have to get him."

"Get him?"

"Yeah. Go to her house and get him."

"I can't go to her house. I don't even know where she lives. Just the street name," I said, remembering Lover's Lane. "And even if I do find the house, what am I supposed to do? Drag him outside and make him come home?"

"No. You need to go there to stare this man you love in the eyes and demand that he tells you what's going on. Because something *is* going on."

"Yeah, that all sounds really good, but I'm not some teenager confronting her boyfriend. I'm a woman. A mother. And going to her house for any reason sounds irrational. It sounds crazy."

"No. That's love," Sharika said as delicately as a poet. "Doing nothing is crazy."

"Sharika, you don't understand. I let her in. I did that. I told him to like her. I wanted her to like him. I made this happen," I cried.

"Look, Dawn, I know you're older than me. And a little smarter than me. But I just can't believe you believe that. You didn't do anything wrong. If something was happening, your husband needed to stop it. But he didn't. Let's stop speculating and say what this is. Call a spade a fucking spade. He didn't stop it. Whatever it is. For whatever reason. And I know you want to be sad, but right now isn't the time for that." She took my hand and balled it up, placing it over my heart. "You take all of that blame you have in your heart and you get mad. You do something with that."

"Hi, Mrs. June," I said as pleasantly as I could, standing in the main office at R. J. and Cheyenne's school. "I'm here to get the twins."

"Oh, is something wrong?" she answered, getting up from her desk in a loud fuchsia dress that was nearly red and definitely too small. Her nails were the same color and as long as her pinkies. She'd been working in the office at the school since Reginald was a student and prided herself on looking young and staying in everyone's business.

"Yes. It's an emergency."

"Emergency?"

"Emergency," I replied tightly, so she wouldn't bother to ask me another question, and not only because I didn't want her in my business, but also because I didn't know the particular state of my business myself. Moments before, Sharika was stuffing me in my car and promising to back me up at the job by telling everyone at the main library that she was sure I had the flu and certain I'd infect the entire library if I didn't stay home for the rest of the week.

Mrs. June pulled a stack of papers from her desk and spit on her hand to thumb through to Johnson.

"Will you be needing any—?" she said, looking down at the pages.

Frustrated and frantic, I slammed my hand on the papers and she looked back up at me, afraid.

"I'll be needing my kids. R. J. is in Mrs. Nettle's class—room fifteen. Cheyenne is in Ms. Fern's class in room nine. Do you need me to go and get them myself?"

"Mama, where we going? To a basketball game?" R. J. asked, still giddy that he was leaving school early and, according to his teacher, missing an afternoon math quiz.

"No, R. J., and put your seat belt on," I said, watching him squirm around in his seat from the front of the car.

Cheyenne was sitting beside him, quiet and angry. I'd come before lunch and it was Natalie's birthday and she didn't get her cupcake and gift bag. She sucked her teeth and glared out of the window.

I had nothing to say to her. Altogether, she was enveloping all of my doubt. Had already asked all of the questions that made me look crazy and deflated every ounce of courage Sharika had pumped into me.

"Well, can we go to a basketball game?" R. J. asked excitedly.

"No basketball, sweetie," I answered. "Well, maybe."

"Then where are we going?" Cheyenne asked snidely.

"I told you when we first got into the car. We're going to get your father. To pick him up."

"But he has the truck. He can drive home." She rolled her eyes again and looked into my eyes in the rearview window.

Just then, I realized that I was lying to someone who knew the truth. She may have been young, but she wasn't dumb. Her anger alone made her better understand mine. Maybe she was happy I was sad. Maybe she was happy Sasha had come and taken her father away. I remembered how she'd laughed at Sasha's jokes, eaten her pancakes.

"When are we coming back?" she asked as we cleared Augusta and I could see the city with the highway slipping through it in the rearview mirror.

"I don't know," I said.

"Oh, a vacation!" R. J. exclaimed.

"But what about our clothes?" Cheyenne asked.

"I stopped at the house and packed some bags. They're in the trunk," I said to her reflection.

"Yeah, a vacation! We can go to a basketball game. We can go to the beach. Is there a beach in Atlanta?"

"No, baby."

"This is stupid. Next week is the last week of school. I want to be with my friends. Friday is Jayshanna's birthday," Cheyenne protested. "What about Daddy? What if he's on his way home? What are we going to eat? Where are we going to sleep?"

"I don't know. I don't know. I don't know!" I answered loudly and worn down. Her questions were like hot pokers, stabbing into my chest. "Look, we're just going to Atlanta to get your father, like I said."

"But Jayshanna's—"

"Cheyenne, you shut up and be quiet," I yelled at her in a way I don't believe I ever have before.

I looked at the mile marker on the side of the road. We'd be in Atlanta in two hours. Reginald hadn't answered my text asking where he was.

6

My eyes bounced from the odometer to the road to the trucks making afternoon deliveries and then back at the odometer again. I counted each mile, each long stretch of road I passed over like a red light flashing in my eye. First two, then ten, next twenty, and fifty. My chest tightened as if I was expecting something—a blow, a hit, a kick. I opened the window, all four and let the hot air come rolling around my neck. Back to the odometer, the road, the trucks, the odometer again.

"Go on in and say good-bye to your father," my mother had said after we alone managed to stuff my last box of clothes into the back-seat of the car. It was late summer and it seemed like every car in every driveway on our street was filled with the boxes of my class-mates leaving for college.

I closed the car door and looked at my mother standing on the other side. The heat had her bangs wet and stuck to her forehead.

"Go on," she pushed. "He's having his coffee. Just say good-bye and kiss him on the cheek. Tell him you love him."

"He ain't tell me he loves me. He ain't kiss me on the cheek and say good-bye," I said. I was taller than my mom already. Too big to be stuffed into a closet. And every day that I stayed in that house I

was becoming more loud and angry at all the closets she'd pushed me into, and all the reasons she'd had to do it. "Ain't even taking me to school. I went to the school he picked. What more does he want from me?"

My mother walked around to the side of the car where I was standing, limping carefully on a bad leg she'd worn down with work. She was still young. Still beautiful. But time was hard on her body. It creaked in places it shouldn't and slowed far faster than my father's.

"He's just scared," she said. "You can't tell when he's scared yet?"

"I can tell when he's angry."

"You're his only child. You're leaving. He's scared something might happen to you. That you'll leave this house and forget your Bible. Lose your way."

"Mama, don't say that to me," I said. "He might be scared, but it ain't about me losing nothing. He just wants to control me—the same way he controls you."

"Girl, I suppose it is time for you to leave this house. Your mouth is getting bigger than your fist." She came in close to me. "Now, you're getting older and you are getting smart. But I'm still your mother and there're some things I know about this world and how it works that you don't yet understand. You may be moving out of my house, but you're still going to live by my rules. And if I tell you to do something, I expect it to get done—and quickly. Now, you carry your narrow tail in that house and you tell him—"

"But he ain't even care enough to take me to school. He hates me. And I hate—"

"You stop that talk and go in that house," she whispered harshly, pointing at the house.

"Mama, I'm not—"

"You want to get out of here?" she asked. "You want to go to that school? Who you think gonna pay for it? Who? Me? On my knees? Scrubbing walls and begging for weekend work? I can't do it. I can't. You need him. You need him!"

He prayed, one hand pressed against my forehead, the other holding his Bible with the curled edges, until my feet were swelling over the edges of my shoes and Mama slid a chair up behind me in the middle of the living room floor.

But he wouldn't let me sit down.

Told her to move the chair and turned to some other curled page to pray for some other thing I hadn't yet done, but he was sure I'd do.

A word against greed. Lust. Against dishonoring my family. Lying. Stealing. Cities burning. God coming with a wrath so horrid I'd be burned alive. And, for this, I should be grateful. Should love this God in curled pages who'd sent a man with liquor on his breath to warn me not to grow up.

His hand got more heavy on my head. I pushed up on my heels and told myself not to cry. I couldn't, not now. This was almost over. I was leaving. I was never coming back. Not to this God.

His voice got louder and turned to rain clouds in my ears. I rolled my fingers into balls and felt that I wanted to hurt him. To slap him to the floor and kick him into the kitchen sink. Make him pray not to be a whore.

I felt Mama holding me then. She held my fists to my sides.

"She don't need no mercy, Edith," Daddy said. "She got demons in her. Going to that school to be a whore. To leave my house and turn her back on the Lord."

He slapped my head with his hand and pushed me back into my mother.

"I see you, devil. Come in my house and ruin my family," he said. "Get out of this child. I see you, devil. I see you. I see you!"

He whipped the Bible up over my head and began beating me with it.

"I see you, devil! I see you!"

He pushed me and Mama down to the floor and began beating both of us, first with his book and then with his belt. Heavy and hard and angry.

"No, Herbert," Mama cried. "She ain't done nothing wrong!"

"What you know about what she done wrong? She following you! She's a whore like her mother. A whore!"

The belt came down on my head so many times I stopped feeling and started thinking. This was it. This was enough. The last moment had come.

The belt came down on my face.

And I grabbed it.

"I'm hungry, Mama!" R. J. groaned with his hand pressing into my shoulder.

Pulled from the burning memory of my father's belt wrapping around my bare arm, I saw the sun lowered over the front of the car. We were just thirty minutes east of Atlanta and cars in a desperate race through traffic were piling up on either side of us.

I peeked back at R. J.

"Get back in your seat," I said wistfully.

"Can we get something to eat?" he whined. "I need something to eat. I don't feel good."

"We'll stop in a minute," I answered, watching him in the rearview mirror as he buckled himself back up. I looked over at Cheyenne. Her eyes were closed, but she was only playing sleep. I could tell because her head was straight up and pointed toward the sunlight coming in through the window.

Slowly, she crept her hand off of her lap and slid it over to R. J. She clasped his hand and squeezed it tightly like she used to do when they were very small and just walking and she, through some knowing intelligence, could feel that her brother was about to cry.

And this is where I actually have to stop telling this tale for just a second. Because it wasn't until that moment when I saw my babies sitting in the backseat, clutching hands like they were still toddlers, that I realized what was really going on. I'd been hurt by Reginald's odd behavior, angered by Sasha's clear betrayal, and even silently mad at myself for being so blind and ignorant for so long. And I'm not slow or stupid. I know that about myself. I know I have faults, but I'm smarter than some simple woman who's dumb enough to let another woman come in and drag her husband off into space. That's not me. I'm a lot of things, but that's not me.

There was something else. Something that was keeping me from seeing things as they were. Seeing things the way I saw them at that moment in the car. Clear as day. It was like I was waking up. I was starting to feel like, up until that moment, each and everything that was happening to me seemed like it was just an echo of my life. I don't even know if that makes any sense. But it was like, after that first night that Sasha came into the house, everything was fuzzy, not real, and kind of like a dream, even that night in the backyard, even that night in my bedroom, even that morning when Reginald left. It was like I'd been railroaded or run over or robbed in my own house, while I was awake.

And that, well, just the idea of that, infuriated me. Put a loud fire in my heart. Do you know what that's like? When you can feel anger rumbling inside of you. And not some sense or emotion. A real fire. Fury. My life, my completely imperfect, clichéd, and tedious life, was under some kind of siege. And I was furious at the idea of that. Because it was mine.

Even looking back on it now that I'm on the other side and can see things as they were, I don't know if I can actually put into words the kind of sudden panic I flipped into at that moment. It wasn't about me getting into a car to go and get Reginald. That was just a part of a drama that failed to have meaning just yet. It was about me losing myself. About me being tossed into a situation where my children could now lose themselves, or what they thought they were. And that was unacceptable. Sharika was right. I couldn't let this just be. I had to do something.

Something got into my head and that old and shaky car managed to skate over three lanes and snake off of the highway where I sat and watched the kids eat chicken nuggets and French fries as

I made a plan. I couldn't just show up at Sasha's house with R. J. and Cheyenne. I couldn't put them through that. I had no idea what Reginald would say or if he was even still there. I needed to protect them.

"Are we in Atlanta?" R. J. asked, licking ketchup off of a French fry.

I nodded and smiled at another woman across the restaurant, who was sitting with two small babies.

"Isn't this where you're from?" he added.

I nodded again.

"You're lucky I'm home." There was no smile. No hugs or kisses. This was just the sound of my mother's voice as she opened her front door and disappeared into the house before we got to see her.

R. J. and Cheyenne looked up at me.

"Go inside," I offered as pleasantly as I could and smiled. I reached for the screen door.

The three of us filed into the foyer and I could hear my mother still talking to us, though she'd walked into the kitchen.

"Been meaning to get dinner started," she said distantly. "But no sense rushing to cook when it's just me. Didn't know I was expecting company."

"Oh, we won't be needing anything to eat, Mama," I said loudly and my voice just echoed through the silent staleness of the house.

We walked into the living room and I sat in the middle of the twins on my mother's clumpy, floral-print couch that was so old it had sunk so close to the floor my backside nearly touched the heels of my shoes.

"That's Grandma?" R. J. asked and Cheyenne nodded to him.

An old Girl Scouts picture of me with braces and tight pin curls sat on a wooden table beside the couch. There were pictures of the twins when they were just six months old on the mantel above the fireplace. No pictures of my father.

"Of course you can eat," she said, her voice getting closer. "Long drive from Augusta."

"We already stopped for lunch."

"What? Fast food?"

She appeared in the hallway leading into the living room and stood right in front of the old closet door. Her eyes were saggy and stale. Her hair was all gray, all gray.

I told myself I wouldn't do it—that I wouldn't reach out for her unless she reached for me. But looking at her, seeing her standing in that old house, in that old place, I saw less of why I wanted to keep my distance and thought of how long it had actually been since I'd seen her. It had been a long time.

"Hey, Mama," I called, getting up from the couch and walking toward her.

If this was some family reunion movie where the estranged daughter returns home to a loving family waiting with open arms, I would've been smiling and holding my arms up and out toward someone who was doing the same. But there was no family reunion here and all I had to act on was what I knew.

She stood frozen in front of the hallway closet as I kissed her on the cheek, held her hand like we were old classmates.

"Dawn," she said, smiling a little. "You're looking thin."

I turned to the twins, who'd nervously moved in toward one another to fill my empty space on the couch.

"What ya'll waiting for?" I asked. "Come say hello to your grandmother."

R. J. looked to Cheyenne and she looked at me.

"It's OK," I mouthed to her.

She got up and walked slowly toward us as if she were approaching a stranger and really that was what my mother was to her, and probably more so to R. J. I tried quickly to remember the last time they'd seen her. I hadn't taken them to my father's funeral. That was the last time I'd seen her. It had been three years ago.

Cheyenne poked out her hand toward my mother.

"Hi, I'm—"

"Child, I know who you are," my mother said so sweetly it sounded as if I was ten years old again. "You're my grandbaby!"

Cheyenne's face warmed so quickly. She smiled and R. J. came running up behind her.

"And I'm your grandbaby, too," he said.

"You ain't no baby," my mother said. "You're a big boy, a little man."

She outstretched her arms and pulled both of the twins into her chest as I watched.

"Ya'll so big," she said and her eyes turned glassy and sad. "Grown up so fast. I don't think your mama was this big when she was ten."

The twins looked at me slyly.

"She wasn't?" R. J. asked.

"No," my mother answered. "She was a tiny thing. Bigger than a dime, but smaller than a penny."

They all laughed and R. J. said the oddest thing I think I ever heard him say.

"I don't know you, Grandma. But I miss you."

My mother found something in the kitchen and even though I'd refused a need to eat five or six times, food was in the pots and she was standing by the stove.

She'd given R. J. and Cheyenne a bag of green beans she'd picked out of her garden in the backyard and they were sitting at the kitchen table snapping and laughing like two kids who'd had this as a responsibility all of their lives.

My mother and I made small talk by the stove. I asked about people on the street. She mentioned people from the church. We said everything that we weren't thinking and the worst part was that we both knew what we were doing. We didn't look into each other's eyes. We didn't ask anything about one another. What was there to say? To ask. After I'd left for college, scarred in welts from the bottoms of my ears to my ankles, the little relationship we'd had dwindled to nothing. Campus was just a jog of miles away, but we hardly saw each other and spoke even less. She was stuck in my father's shadow, and soon, to me, she became him.

There was nothing I could say about that. And what I've learned is that when you can't talk about the past, talking about the present is almost impossible.

My mother should've been asking why and how the daughter she hadn't seen in three years had shown up on her doorstep in the middle of the day with her grandchildren and no husband. Why my eyes were so puffy and it seemed like something was on my mind. She should've been asking where Reginald was.

But she couldn't.

"I only got four pork chops," she said after an awkwardly long break in our conversation.

"Four's fine," I said. "I told you we're not too hungry. Maybe they'll eat a little later."

"Four's fine? That's just enough for us and the twins. That's all the company I'm expecting?" she asked, and in that question was a heap of expectation.

"Yes."

"You all will be staying the night?" She turned to the dish of pork chops she'd been turning in raw eggs and milk.

"I think so," I said with my voice cracking.

She looked up at me for the first time. She dropped the pork chop she was turning into the dish and wiped her hands on her apron slowly, keeping her eyes on me.

"Hey, ya'll," I called to the table. "You two go out to the car and get our bags."

"We're staying here?" R. J. asked.

"For tonight," I said. "Now, get the key from my purse and bring the bags inside."

"You can take them up to the room next to your mama's old room," my mother said. "The one with her name on the door."

"That's Daddy's old study," I said to my mother after R. J. and Cheyenne left the room.

"Turned it into a guest room. Don't have a lot of guests, but don't have a lot of need for a study either. Gave the books to Goodwill. You sure we don't need an extra pork chop for your husband?" she listed quickly and it was clear the only statement she really meant to make was the last.

"Mama, I know what you're thinking. You probably want to know where Reginald is, and it's cool, everything is—" I swear I was about to say "OK," but I couldn't. It seemed a silver dollar was caught in my throat and any lie I wanted to force out got stuck. I felt my body sigh.

"Don't you even try to finish that sentence, honey," my mother said, pulling her apron off. "Insult my intelligence. Even a maid knows something's wrong when the daughter she hasn't seen since they buried her father in the earth shows up at her front door with two kids and no husband. Even a maid."

I laughed uneasily.

"What is it?" she asked. "Where's Reginald?"

My mother's face stayed solid as I told her only half of what I knew about where Reginald was. I couldn't take hearing the truth again. And I couldn't handle thinking what she might think of me if she heard what the truth really was. All that was necessary was that he was somewhere on Lover's Lane and I needed to get to him. I'd brought the twins there because I couldn't think of anywhere else to go.

"You told them? You told them kids their daddy's gone?"

"Not directly, no. They know something's up. But I just . . . I don't know if he's gone, really." I tried to sound convincing. "And I don't want them to feel bad. Like they did anything. And what happens when he comes back?"

"You still banking on that?"

"Banking on it? Mama, you make it sound like we're talking about a sale at the mall. This is my husband. My marriage. My family."

"Yeah, I know what that is," she said. "I had one, too. But then my child ran off and—"

"Mama, I don't have time to go through all this. I shouldn't have come here. I knew you'd—"

"Knew I'd what? Bring up the past? Bring up how you just run up out of here like it was the worst place in the world and then marry the first man who ties your shoe? Didn't ask your daddy for permission or nothing?"

"Oh, no, this was a mistake," I said, hearing the kids trampling up the stairs with our bags.

"Don't you dare walk out of here," she said to my back as I turned to walk out, "like you got someplace else to go. Ain't no other reason you'd be here anyway. So what you need me for? You could've gone to a hotel. Need me to look after them? Is that it? Do you even know where he's at?"

"Just the street," I said, turning around.

"Ohh," she heaved.

"Lover's Lane," I said, hearing Reginald say it to me in my memory.

"Lover's Lane? Where's that?"

"Buckhead, up north somewhere."

"Buckhead? So, you going up to see them white folks to find your husband in some house you ain't never seen? Is she white?"

"No, Mama," I said. "I told you she went to school with me. You met her before—"

"Who cares if I met her before?"

"Look, I don't want to get into all of that. I just need you to watch the kids for a little bit."

"Yeah, I'll watch them. But who's gonna watch you?" she asked.

"What do you mean?"

"You going up there all upset and what you gonna do? Fight somebody? Get hauled off to jail? That's what you gonna do?"

"I just need to talk to him."

"And what if he don't want to talk? You think you going to be able to just leave? No. Your heart ain't gonna let you do that. I've seen women burn down houses. Kill. Kill themselves. Thinking they were just gonna go and talk to someone. You ain't heard from him, and that's because he don't want to be heard. What make you think he wants to talk?"

"Well, that's fine, Mama, but what am I supposed to do then?"

"Pray."

I just stood there and looked at her.

Even in my anger, there were so many things I'd wanted to say to my mother over the years. To pick up the phone and laugh and tell her what it was like being married. Having children. Learning to deal with life as it came to me. Things that made me a woman. So many things she'd missed. So many things she needed to know. How clean my house was. How I never let my children go to bed hungry or dirty or cold. How everything she'd taught me about making beds and cleaning staircases, washing dishes and warming bread had somehow snuck into my life. But there was something I'd left out of the things I'd wanted to tell her. One thing I'd given up over all those years. And on purpose. One thing I never wanted to say to anyone, especially not her. I didn't pray anymore.

My father always said that your desire for light keeps the devil busy. And just as surely as you'll see the sun, he'll make sure darkness comes right behind it.

I always thought it was rather sad to look at life like that. Like saying a glass is half empty rather than half full, and fully expecting it to be empty soon. His way of thinking made happiness seem so temporary, so flimsy and inconsistent. He expected sadness. He expected darkness. He waited for darkness to take the light. And if it didn't, he took it himself.

The sun went down and my mother sat at the dining room table playing some card game with the twins. They were betting with pennies and nickels she'd found around the house and R. J. and Cheyenne were laughing.

They seemed so natural with her. And I had to keep reminding myself that I shouldn't have expected less. They'd asked about her so many times when they were very little, and when Reginald's mother died, Cheyenne buried her face into my lap and cried that she only had one grandmother left.

I'd guessed that over the years their hearts had become as hardened as mine, but I was wrong. Maybe they needed to see her. To snap beans and play cards with her. Maybe I'd been wrong to keep them away because *I* wanted to stay away. But after one year, the second year got easier, and then I didn't have to explain anything anymore.

I sat on the couch watching TV in the living room, listening to them argue over nickels like I had with my mother when I was ten. Only then, when we heard my father's key in the door, we'd flush the cards and coins into my mother's purse and pretend we were praying. He'd warn my mother that playing cards was a sin and go for his bottle in the china cabinet.

I felt like I was in limbo. Struggling through my past and worrying about my future. Like I was standing on a tightrope and going in any direction meant I would fall all the way down.

I clicked through the channels feeling like something was coming to me, but I have to tell you I had no idea what it was, as obvious as it was.

"Hey, that's Aunt Sasha," R. J. said, peeking over at the television from the dining room. "Right, Mama?"

I think my heart saw her before I did, because it was pounding and ringing so loud in my ears I hardly heard Cheyenne answer for me or what he said next.

"Did you say your daddy's with her?" my mother asked, adding meaning to the mumbling I'd heard.

I was fixated, stuck and frozen on Sasha's face on the screen. That same blond hair. Those eyes. She was smiling. Laughing. She held up her hand to say something to a man sitting in the interview seat beside her and I saw her freshly manicured hands.

We were all silent. And right then I knew what my kids knew. I knew I was hiding nothing. They knew everything.

"I have to go," I said, getting up from the couch.

"Go? Where are you going? It's dark outside," my mother said, her eyes digging into me to say so much she couldn't in front of R. J. and Cheyenne.

"Just a little errand," I said loudly and smiled. "I'll be back. Can you watch the kids?"

I went to get my purse from the table and my mother was right behind me.

"What are you doing?" she whispered sternly. "I told you not to go out there and do anything stupid. You need to wait here and pray for direction. Not run out in the street and get yourself arrested."

"I did pray," I lied. "And I got a response. I know exactly what I need to do." I looked at the television. Sasha's show was going off in thirty minutes. I could be downtown to CNN in fifteen.

"Mama, is everything OK?" R. J. asked.

"Everything is fine," I said, stepping back from my mother. "You just stay here with your grandmother. I'll be right back."

Apparently, CNN is a big building with lots of big security guards. But I've been a woman long enough to know how to get around big buildings and big guards. Let me rephrase that. I've never had to sneak around a building that size or lie to security guards whose hands were as big as my head, but it's amazing what you can do when you're full of fury and know that in the South, you can get just about anything if you say the right things to the right people. I smiled and told those guards they must be tired from working all day. I didn't want to be any trouble. I was Sasha's sorority sister visiting from Augusta. I wanted to surprise her. I even showed pictures of her that R. J. had taken with my digital camera.

They all seemed a little suspicious. But I pointed out that the pictures had been taken just days before. Clearly, we were friends if she was serving my son pancakes. Everything was fine. They loosened up a little and one copied my driver's license after I begged him not to call Sasha and ruin my surprise. Another walked me to her dressing room and said he could get fired if I was anything but legit. I assured him everything was fine in my most pleasant voice and kept him distracted with a tale about Sasha's fondness for big, black, bald men.

"You sure?" he said, rubbing his bald head as he let me into the locked room.

"Sure? *I know.* That's all she used to date."

"So, I stand a chance?"

"Why wouldn't you?"

He laughed and grinned as if he was imagining Sasha on his arm.

"OK, well you just stay in here, little lady, and wait for her!" he said.

"And that's what I plan to do," I said. "Thank you."

I closed the door behind him and exhaled heavily, not realizing I'd been holding my breath since I'd walked into the building.

I took a few deep breaths and steadied myself as I tried to remember why I was there and what I wanted to say to Sasha. My mother was right. The flames of my anger were fanning so high, I knew I might lose control if I wasn't clear about what I was supposed to do. I didn't have any questions, because I didn't expect any answers. I was coming to the conclusion that everything Sasha had ever said to me was a lie. And I was wondering what lies she'd told that I hadn't discovered yet. I just wanted her to know how trifling she was. Laying up in my house and lying to me. Taking my children's father away from them in the middle of the night like a thief. I wanted to look her in the face and let her know I wasn't a fast loser. I could fight. I would fight.

There were candles and flowers and lipsticks and makeup brushes scattered everywhere in the room. An open closet full of new suits and a huge box of designer shoes. A monitor over a little couch beside her makeup table showed Sasha was still on the screen.

I stood up beside the door for a few minutes watching her. Then I sat down. But then my legs were growing so jumpy with my nerves that I had to get back up. I paced the floor. I jumped at each voice I heard from someone walking down the hall, worried that it was her assistant or a makeup artist or just someone other than Sasha coming to discover me in the dressing room.

I looked at myself in the mirror. My brown face. No makeup. No lipstick. Just my tired eyes, still puffy from this morning. I leaned over the vanity, closer to the mirror. My eyes were starting to look like my mother's. Losing the bit of shine they had left. I wondered who this woman was staring at me in the mirror. Dawn? Sneaking into the CNN building and posting up in the dressing room of the woman who was obviously having an affair with her husband? Was that me? It couldn't be. Nothing in my plan ever suggested this. I wasn't some angry black woman going out into the world to fight. I had children. I had a home. I had to be better than this.

A tear rolled down my cheek and I let it sit on my chin until it dove into the vanity.

"I need to go home—" I tried, turning around to walk out.

But the dressing room door opened and I jumped back, scared.

"Oh, oh no, I'm sorry," an exceptionally—and I do mean *so* exceptionally—handsome man said, holding the door open. "Did I scare you?"

"Yeah, I . . . I . . . was leaving."

"I'm sorry. I was looking for Sasha."

We both looked at the screen to see the credits rolling on her show.

"Guess she's on her way up soon. I'll catch her in the hallway."

He stepped back to let the door close and I noticed that he looked familiar. He had light brown skin, slanted, secretive eyes, and strong cheekbones.

"Wait, are you . . . are you A. J.? A. J. Holmes?" I called.

The door was about to close, but he came back inside.

"Yeah, that's me," he said and his voice was friendly but humble. He put his hand out to shake mine.

"Dawn," I said. "Dawn Johnson."

"And you're. . . ."

"I went to college with Sasha. We were roommates."

"Really?" He chuckled. "I couldn't even imagine what that must've been like."

"It was memorable."

"So you guys are hanging out tonight? You know Sasha can get you into almost anywhere. Hawks game tonight?"

"Oh, I don't think we'll be going to see the Hawks."

"Well, all right," he said, smiling, and his jaw eased back like he was someone in charge, perfectly confident. "Well, let me know if you all need anything." He lowered his voice a little. "I've been here a little longer than Sasha. I can have better connections."

"Thank you," I said, not realizing I was laughing and grinning at this man. I was melting. I couldn't help myself. "And, that was a great special you did last year about black women and natural hair. I never thought I'd see anything like that on CNN."

"You caught that?"

"Yeah, it was good. I've been meaning to go natural, and it was cool to hear so many black men say they like it."

"Yeah, I'm an au natural brother. I've been trying to tell your friend to kick the weave tracks to the curb, but you know."

"Yeah," I said.

"Yeah," he said.

And we stood there grinning and nodding until there was a clatter and loud voices in the hallway.

"I don't give a shit, Suzy," I heard Sasha say. "There was no reason for me not to have that information. I've been gone for two weeks. You'd think that was long enough for you to do a little bit of research. I was up there looking like a damn fool."

"Well, here she is," A. J. said, pushing the door open.

I straightened my back and spread my feet apart like I was about to fight.

"Here who is? Who are you talking to?" Sasha asked before coming into the room. "Was my door open?"

"Your friend is in here," A. J. said, slipping out of the room as Sasha came in with a short, Asian woman following close behind her. "I'm sure I'll see you again." He nodded at me and signaled for Sasha to call him.

"Ohhh, I didn't know I was having company," Sasha said as if she wasn't even surprised to see me.

"I'm sorry. I don't know how she got in here," the Asian woman said apologetically. "I locked the door but, I guess—"

"Please, Suzy, just . . . just go somewhere," Sasha scolded her, "and figure out why you work here."

The woman stood there confused for a second and then hustled out of the room.

Sasha slammed the door behind her.

"What?" She looked at me. "You came here to fight?"

"Fight? Why would I want to fight you? You're my college roommate. We pledged together. You just came all the way to Augusta to visit my family. Made my children pancakes. Why would I want to fight you?" I smiled wickedly in a show of strength, but I guarantee it took everything in me not to tackle her into the back of the dressing room door. The way she moved, spoke, and even smelled just scolded me. Here I was on the edge of everything and here she was having a day at the job and looking at me like I was some spectacle. "And, oh, I almost forgot, you fucked my husband. . . . But why would I want to fight?"

Sasha walked to the closet and kicked off her shoes into the box.

"Oh, save the drama, Dawn. You know you don't even know how to curse. Here's your first lesson: be careful who you say did the fucking."

"What is that supposed to mean?"

"It means I didn't make Reggie do anything he didn't already want to do."

"Whatever. You stop calling him that."

"Whatever, then," she said, stepping closer to me, almost daring me to hit her. "Look, I know you didn't come all the way down here and sneak up to my dressing room, which I never would've thought you'd have the nerve to do, so go, soror, for that"—she pumped her fist in the air like a cheerleader—"but I know you didn't do all of that to come here to tell me what I can and can't say. And you're also not terribly slow, so I know you're not here hoping to pick a fight with me, so what do you want?"

"I want you to know that you're a trifling . . . tramp. And I know exactly what you're trying to do."

"Oh, really, do tell." Sasha stepped around me and went to the vanity to pretend she wasn't really interested in what I was saying. She began wiping off her makeup as I spoke.

"All that talk about how you want a man, and how the next one you meet is going to be a father," I said as she pulled off her earrings and aped my speaking in the mirror. "Yeah, I remember that, Sasha. And I know you couldn't care less about Reginald. You just want a sperm donor. Someone to take pictures with. But it's not going to work. It won't last. He'll figure out he's just a pawn in your little scheme and leave you just like all of the other men—the one who slept with your neighbor, the one who slept with your assistant, the one who gave you syphilis in college."

Sasha became visibly angered and slung her metal bracelet into the mirror making little hairline cracks spring from a pinhole break.

"Fuck you," she said, looking like she was about to spit at my image in the mirror. "And you know what"—she turned around to me—"I did fuck Reggie—"

"I said don't call him that," I warned, balling my fists.

"And it was good and he's not going anywhere, so you can pack up yourself and carry your ass back to Augusta where you belong." She rushed and pushed me into the wall beside the closet, pinning me by holding both of my arms. "You think you can compete with me? You think he wants to be with someone who's just a nobody? A no-fucking-body? I can make him something. I can make Reggie a real man. Not some lawn-cutting country fool."

"I said"—I pushed back against her, slamming her into the opposite wall and pinning her arms—"don't call him that!" I wrapped my hand around Sasha's neck and wanted badly to squeeze, but instead I just threatened her, staring into her eyes as the seconds ticked.

The short, Asian woman came into the office with her head down, looking at a stack of papers.

I stopped and looked at her and Sasha regained control, pushing me back into the other wall.

"What is going on?" the woman said, looking up. "Security!" she yelled. "Security!"

"That's right," Sasha said slyly. "Call security to get this bitch out of my dressing room. I think she's on drugs or something."

"Ma'am, you're lucky she didn't press charges," a plump black woman with childlike spiral curls in her hair and a name tag spelling "Sperry" said to me over a desk in the CNN security center. She'd been typing all of my information into the computer in front of her and promised I'd never be let back into the building. "We have a strict security policy here. And we'll prosecute to the fullest extent of the law." She slid my driver's license across the desk to me. "We have good people who work here. And we protect them at all costs."

"Sasha doesn't need any protecting. In fact, you all should probably work harder to protect the rest of us from her."

"That's none of my business," the woman said flatly. "What *is* my business is why you thought you were just going to sneak past my officers and go into a dressing room to attack one of my clients. That was stupid. What if she'd pressed charges? If you went to jail? Ms. Bellamy said you have children. Did you think about them when you broke that mirror?"

"I didn't break the mirror," I said, but this little fact was a small defense for how I was feeling. Something had been broken. I'd been dragged by my collar down a hallway and held in a little square room like a criminal. And to all those who watched—the little Asian woman with her papers, A. J. and his confused stare, others with open mouths and pointed fingers, Sasha and her smile as she brushed her shoulders off—I was a criminal.

"She said you did—"

"She said? She said?" I snatched my driver's license off of the desk and looked at the woman's bare finger, where a slight tan of once-hidden skin revealed a missing ring. "Have you ever been married?"

"That's none of your concern, Ma'am."

"None of my concern? Really?" I said. "Let me guess, he cheated on you?"

She looked off and said, "Yes, he did, but that's still none of your—"

"And what about the woman he cheated with?" I asked. "What would you do if you knew exactly who she was and where you could find her?"

She looked back at me and I saw in her face the image of myself I'd seen in Sasha's mirror.

"I would and did kick that whore's ass," she said coldly.

"Exactly—"

"But couldn't you have gone to her house or some other place? Please, coming up in here ain't doing nothing but bringing me more trouble. I have to suspend two officers. And explain to my boss how in the hell they let you upstairs."

"Well, I'm sorry about that."

"Look." She looked into my eyes. "You just needed a better plan. One that didn't include my job."

"I don't know where she lives."

"Ahhh . . . phewww . . ." She sat back in her seat and looked at me crossly. "It's almost time for my break." She looked at the clock. "I have to go call my ex-husband to make sure he doesn't have my kids around that slut he had the nerve to marry." Her voice changed and she looked at the computer. "I still need you to fill out this statement though—saying you didn't break the mirror, and you didn't come here to fight Sasha Bellamy. Right?" She winked at me.

"No, I didn't come here for that."

"OK. So, I'm going to step out of the room and make my phone call. You can sit here and finish your statement." She pushed away from the desk and I noticed that her voice had shifted from discipline to polite deception. "Now, don't you come around here and try to sneak a peek at my computer. There's lots of private and sensitive information on here." She eyeballed me closely. "Addresses and information about employees. You just look up the last name and there they are."

"Yeah, that sounds like sensitive information," I agreed.

"But don't you come over here looking for stuff. Could cost me my job. Especially if you ever tell someone how you got that kind of information."

"I wouldn't do that, because I wouldn't look at the computer."

"Well, I'm glad you wouldn't do that. Because then I'd have to hurt you myself." She stood up and the plump woman became tall and plump. She grabbed her keys and walked toward the door. "The call I need to make usually takes about five minutes. You can leave your statement on the desk."

"I'll do that," I said.

"And don't you dare look at that computer."

7

My mother's house was dark and quiet. While no one inside knew what had happened at CNN and they were all probably asleep and dreaming, my embarrassment made me creep into the house like a teenager who'd snuck out and was trying to avoid her parents. My cell phone had died, so I plugged it into the wall in the living room and went to the dining room table to just sit and think. I'd written Sasha's address down in the palm of my hand. Just the numbers, in big, looping, red ink. 593. That's where she was. That's where Reginald was.

I looked at the dusty chandelier over the dining room table. It was a pear-shaped bulb covered with chipped, leaf-shaped pieces of glass falling down all around it. When I was little, maybe five, my mother had gathered all of the leaves off of the chandelier and put them into a pot with water and vinegar to soak. I saw the pot on the table and looked into it to see the little glass pieces sunken into the water, sitting in the bottom, sparkling and shining like diamonds. My mother was in the kitchen, so I put my hand inside to touch the diamonds. I fingered them in the water, turned them around, and then took one out to hold it to my finger like a diamond ring. I held it up and smiled. One day I'd have a ring like that. When I was big and a woman. I held it up farther, so it could catch the light shining in from outside of the living room window and I must've lost my balance in the chair because I fell over and both me and the pot of diamonds fell to the floor.

I screamed, but the sound of all of that glass and the pot crashing into the wood was what made my mother come rushing in from the kitchen, my father from upstairs.

I wasn't hurt, so I jumped back up and tried to pretend nothing had happened, but the evidence, those chipped glass leaves, were scattered everywhere.

"What is this?" my father asked.

"Oh no, Dawn, what did you do?" my mother asked, getting down on her knees to inspect the broken pieces.

"I was just playing," I said. "They're diamonds."

"I told you to leave it alone," she said.

"Leave it alone? You should be watching her!" My father's voice boomed around the room like a siren.

"I can't watch her every minute of every day," my mother complained as we stood around her.

"You can't watch her?" He bent down and slid his hand around her neck from the back, squeezing it so I could see his knuckles stick out. "You can't do anything I ask you to do." He pushed her down into the wet floor like a dog. "Get this cleaned up and watch her!" he said, finally letting her go and walking upstairs without even looking at me.

It was the first time I'd ever seen them like that—seen my father try to hurt my mother—or maybe just the first time I recall.

I rushed to her side as she gasped for air and continued picking up the leaves.

"You OK, Mama?" I asked.

"Just help me get this up," she said. "I need to get this up before he comes back downstairs."

Remembering the look in her eyes, the detached, silenced look in her eyes, I turned from the red 593 on my hand and saw my father's old liquor hiding place at the bottom of the china cabinet staring at me.

I got up from the table and went to open the door, hoping and then not hoping I'd find something in there. He never stopped drinking until everything was gone and I was sure my mother hadn't put anything else in there after he died. But with my memories and my realities, I wanted what my father always needed: a drink.

There was a full bottle of Scotch inside. I always hated that rubbery taste that took over every sense as you struggled to get it down. But as they say, after a man has his first glass, the second is like water. And my third didn't even require ice.

Soon the bottle was half empty. And I had my legs spread up on the other chairs beneath the table. I stopped pretending to sit up and just slouched down in the seat, cursing the night for my life. If Reginald left me, if he really left me, I wouldn't even have anywhere to go. I had no savings; hell, the library hardly paid me enough to buy groceries, and with R. J.'s medical bills, if he got sick or if any of us got sick, I'd have to . . . I'd probably have to come back home.

I looked around the room—the scene of the place I'd hated so much my only plan in life was to leave and never ever come back—and thought there was no way I'd make my children live my nightmare.

And what about Reginald? In his house on Lover's Lane. In the bed with Sasha. Their meetings. Their big plans. Their future. All of this, and the past with me was so much of a nightmare that he had to leave without saying anything?

I poured another glass and sipped until I couldn't feel my tongue anymore. Sipped until my memories and thoughts were just clouds over the chandelier.

And then my cell phone rang. It kicked into the dark house like a fire alarm and the vibrating made it coast all over the living room table. And I knew who it was. And why he was calling. I sat for the first ring, but then ran for the second.

I didn't say anything.

"What the hell is wrong with you? I've been calling you all

night. Why in the hell would you go to Sasha's job?" Reginald's voice was so loud I had to move the phone from my ear.

"Hello," I said.

"What is wrong with you, Dawn? Why would you go to her job?"

"You said you would call. You never called. What's going on? Why haven't you come home?" I knew what was going on. We both knew what was going on. But I wanted him to say it to me. To say to me directly that he was having an affair with Sasha.

"I told you I'd call."

"But you didn't," I charged. "And you didn't answer my question—what the hell is going on?"

"Nothing . . . I mean . . ." he stuttered. "I just need some time. Like I told you."

"Told me? You didn't tell me anything. You just crept out of our house like some little boy. Ran off and sent me a damn text to solve the case of my missing husband."

"I just need some space."

"Space for what, Reginald?" I asked and I could hear myself screaming then. "Space for what?"

There was silence, but I waited. I waited and waited, because I swear I wasn't going to allow him to just get off the hook with some half-baked lie about needing space.

"Why did you have to go to her job? If you would've just waited until I called you," he said weakly.

"Well, I couldn't wait. I couldn't wait. And your children couldn't wait. And have you even considered what your little disappearing act is doing to them? They wake up in the morning and their father is just gone? What am I supposed to say to them?" I snatched the phone from the charger.

"Where are they?"

"Where are you?"

"Dawn, don't play games. Where are my children?" he asked, but it sounded more like an order.

"They're with me."

"Where?"

"OK, I'll tell you," I said. "I'll tell you where we're at if you tell me where you're at."

There was loud banging on the phone and I could tell Reginald was hitting it against something hard.

"You tell me where they're at. They're my kids and they have nothing to do with what's going on between me and you."

"See, that's the thing, Reginald," I said. "I still don't know what's going on between you and me. Until Sasha showed up at our house, you seemed fine. And now, suddenly, you need space and you're taking off and not calling to check on the children you now so quickly care about."

"Now you didn't know I wasn't happy?" he spat. "Please, you know I haven't been happy in a long time. You just don't do it for me. But now I know what I need."

"And what's that? What do you need, you fucking bastard?" I cried. "You sound like a tape recorder. Is she sitting there, is she sitting there telling you what to say?"

I saw my mother rushing down the steps in her nightgown. R. J. and Cheyenne were behind her rubbing their eyes.

"Never mind her," he said. "This has nothing to do with her."

"How doesn't it?"

"I'm not going to talk about that with you right now," he said and I'll say that was the farthest his voice, his thought, his concern had ever been from me. It was like I was speaking to another person. "Now, you claim I've abandoned my kids, so I want to see them."

"Oh, you want to see them now?"

"Is that my daddy?" Cheyenne asked, coming over to me.

"Come here, Cheyenne. Your mother's on the phone," my mother tried, but Cheyenne wouldn't budge.

"Yes, I want to see my children this weekend. I'm coming to get them," Reginald said.

"Get them? Get them and take them where?"

"Where is no matter to you. Now stop making this hard!"

"Making it hard? *I'm* making it hard?"

"I want to speak to my daddy," R. J. cried sleepily, stepping up behind his sister.

"You know what," I started, "I'm going to make this really easy for you. If you want your children, you'll see them. You'll see them right now!"

"What are you saying?" he asked, but I hung up the phone.

"What are you doing?" My mother pushed the twins out of the way and grabbed the phone.

"Nothing. He said he wants to see the kids, so he'll see the kids," I answered coolly, but the alcohol added a sway to my voice. "Ya'll go on upstairs and hurry up and put your shoes on," I said to R. J. and Cheyenne.

"For what, Mama? We're going to see Daddy?" R. J. asked as the phone started ringing again.

Cheyenne stepped to get it.

"Don't you dare touch that phone," I forbade her and she stopped fast. "You two go upstairs and put your shoes on."

"But it's twelve o'clock at night. You can't have them out there so late," my mother said and the twins looked from her to me.

"Go," I ordered and they scrambled up the stairs.

"What's this?" my mother said over the ringing phone. "What's going on with you?"

She got closer to me and frowned.

"You've been drinking," she said. She looked over at the nearly empty bottle of Scotch. "Got that devil in you?"

"Oh, Mama, please stop that."

"Don't you know that ain't no good? Didn't your father show you what that stuff does to you?"

"My father showed me a lot of things," I said.

"You can't take those kids out of this house. It ain't right."

"It ain't right? No, what's not right is what's being done to me," I cried. "And I want them to know what their father is doing and who he's doing it with. I won't keep his secret so he can save face."

R. J. and Cheyenne came back down the steps in their shoes and nightclothes.

"This isn't about you or him; it's about them," my mother said. "And I won't let you do this."

"Oh, Mama. Save the speech." I grabbed the phone from the couch.

"Don't do this," she said. "It's the devil in you." She looked into my eyes. "I see it. I see your daddy. You've got to stop it. I know you wouldn't do this if you weren't drinking. And now you want to drive. At least let me come with you."

"Come with me?" I laughed. "You want to come? For what? To protect me? Please, you couldn't protect me from him all those years ago, and you can't protect me now."

Cheyenne and R. J. sat so close together, their little bodies fit into one seat in the back of the car. R. J. was crying and had his arms wrapped around Cheyenne's neck.

I watched them from the front, blinking in seconds to keep the alcohol from fading my vision.

And I knew I was wrong. Knew I shouldn't be listening to my cell phone tell me how to get to Sasha's house in the middle of the night, drunk and taking my children along for the ride. But right and wrong had just left me. I was aching. Aching in every part of me. And nothing in me could control it. I was there, but then I wasn't. The lanes raced beneath the car. I was screaming, angry. Hot. I couldn't hear anything knocking in me. It was like I was hollowed out and desperate. And I knew it wasn't just Reginald. Couldn't be. There was more riding me in that car. No man could pull me from protecting my children. Risking my life and theirs. But I wasn't me. I was someone who was angry at me.

I got off of the highway exit and the pleasant little voice on the GPS on my phone told me to make a right. There was a long road ahead, winding and dipping down. I went so fast the car flopped on a bump. Our bodies hopped out of our seats and fell down hard.

"I shouldn't have let her into my home," I said to Cheyenne's wet eyes looking at me in the mirror.

Cheyenne pointed up ahead to the windshield in front of me.

"What's that?" she asked.

I flicked my sight from the mirror to circling blue lights flashing ahead on the narrow road. There were two lanes with police cars set up on either side. A row of cars sat in the dark behind the police cars. Another, right down the middle, was streaming through.

"What is it?" Cheyenne pressed.

"I think it's the police," I said delicately. I slowed the car and came up gently behind the car in front of me that was edging into the streaming cars. Police officers came up on either side of that car and flashed their lights inside. The driver held his wallet out of the window.

"What do they want?" R. J. cried.

"It's nothing, baby, just a roadblock." I tried to calm him, but my whole heart was beating so fast I felt it was about to knock me over. I heard it in my head, my ears, and through my mouth. How could I pass them? I was drunk. I could smell myself. My face was wet with tears. The children were still crying. I tried to wipe my eyes and pushed on the gas when the car in front was released. I told myself to smile. Sit up straight. Say it was a long night. I was just trying to get my children home to bed. I sucked in my stomach. I don't know why.

"Ma'am," a voice behind a white light shining in my window called, "can I see your driver's license and proof of insurance?"

I could feel my forehead getting hot and wet beneath the light.

I smiled and went into my purse. Through the corners of my eyes, I could see the light bounce over my shoulder and into the backseat where another light was shining.

I started saying something about how dark it was and that I was surprised to see the roadblock up so late, but then the light came bouncing back to me and retracted back behind a round, lemon-colored face.

"Ma'am, are you aware that your children are crying in the backseat?"

I don't remember if I said "yes" or if I was just thinking it, but next, I was out of the car and standing against the bumper with four police officers around me.

"I didn't drink anything," I said, answering one of the officer's questions for the third time.

"Mrs. Johnson, you couldn't tell us where you were going or why you're in the area. And your children are nearly hysterical," he said. "Don't you think it's time you started telling us what's going on?"

"I can," I said. "I will."

"Now," the lemon head jumped in, "how much have you had to drink?"

"Not a lot," I answered quickly.

"So, is it 'not a lot' or 'none'?" the officer with all of the questions asked.

"I just had a little," I tried. "I'm having a really bad day . . . and my husband," I started crying, sobbing so heavily my nostrils were filled with salty tears. I could hear Cheyenne screaming for one of the officers not to remove R. J. from the car.

"Mrs. Johnson, this isn't about your day. This is about you drunk driving," the lemon head said.

"I'm not a drunk driver," I said. "It's not me. It's just a bad day. I'm trying to get my children to my husband."

"Get off of him," I heard Cheyenne scream and I turned immediately from the officers to see someone pulling R. J. from the backseat. His arms were flailing and he was crying silently in anger.

"No, that's my son," I said, reaching toward him, but it felt like a million hands came down on my body and held me to the trunk.

"255 Means Drive!" R. J. yelled harshly at the female officer trying to hold him still. "255!"

I saw the park. The playground. R. J. waiting for me in the sandbox. Him smiling into the sand. It felt like, looked like, and smelled like home. All around me. I wanted to be there, too. Back before all of this. When we were together.

"He just wants to get to the park," I cried, trying to squirm away from the hands on my back. I kicked and kicked, hitting legs and arms and chests. "Let him go," I screamed. "Let my baby go!"

I was being lifted high and passed along a torrent of blue suits, pink hands, and round faces.

I saw Cheyenne reach for me and I fought to get to her, but I couldn't.

I saw R. J. reach for me and I reached back for him, but I couldn't reach him.

Soon I couldn't see my hands or feel them. They were tied to my back like I was an animal and I felt the hard and cold leather seat in the back of the police car slap against my cheek.

"I'm not a drunk driver," I hollered out to the hands stuffing me into the car. "I'm not a drunk driver!" I shouted and then I saw dark clouds rolling into my eyes in spirals. They gathered all in together and then everything went black.

There was something wet on my forehead. Something cold and soft and wet. I opened my eyes and a strong light came shining in. I blinked and tried to look up at the soft thing above my eyes.

"Ohhhh," I murmured. Something pounded in my head as I tried to move.

"Stay still, Dawn."

I blinked again and squinted under the pain in my head and saw my mother standing over me.

"Mama?"

I tried to move my legs and realized I was lying in a bed. I saw a television hanging on the wall behind my mother.

"You can't move. The doctor said you shouldn't move," she said, leaning into me over the bed rail. "You hit your head pretty hard."

"My head?" I went to touch the sharp pain in my head, but I couldn't move my hand. I looked down to see my hand chained to the bed rail. "What?" I pulled at the chain. "What is this?"

"Calm down," my mother whispered. "*They're* outside."

"Who?"

"Is there anything you want to tell me? They're going to come in here."

"Who's coming in here? What's going on? Where . . . Where are R. J. and Cheyenne?" I rattled the chain.

"Oh, stop it, now, please calm yourself." She looked over her shoulder outside of the room, but I couldn't see what she was looking at.

I heard a door open and my mother stood up, crossing her arms over her chest.

"Calm down, sweetie," she said pleasantly. "I think everything is going to be OK."

She moved from the bed and I saw a thin black woman with short blond hair walking in. She was wearing a pantsuit with heels. A golden badge was hanging from the waist of her slacks.

My mother reached over the bed railing and grabbed my hand.

"Who is this?" I asked. "Did something happen to my children? Where are my children?"

"Your children are fine, Mrs. Johnson," the woman said. "I'm Officer Russell." She kept her hands at her side. "I'm with the Atlanta Police Department, Children's Services."

"Children's Services?" I looked at my mother. "What's going on?"

The woman traded stares with my mother and my mother nodded to me.

"I'll wait outside," she said, gripping my hand. "I'll be right outside that door if you need me."

I tried to push up in the bed, so I could sit and see around the room, but my head was throbbing and the chain kept sliding down to the bottom of the rail.

"Be careful, Mrs. Johnson," Officer Russell said. "You've really hurt your head. That's why we had to bring you to the hospital."

"What's going on? Can someone please tell me what's going on and where are my children?"

"Well, let's start with last night. Do you remember anything?"

I saw blue lights flashing. Cheyenne's finger pointing to the front window. An empty glass on the dining room table.

"The police officers. The roadblock," I tried.

"Yes."

"Something was wrong with R. J. I had to get to him."

"Mrs. Johnson," the woman started, sitting down on a small corner of the bed where my feet couldn't reach. "You were driving drunk."

"Nooo," I cried faintly. I could remember the lemon face poking into my window. The smell of the back of the police car. I was kicking. I kicked the window. Glass went everywhere.

"Your blood alcohol level was four times the limit in the state of Georgia. There are some things I need you to know."

"Where are my children?"

"Your children are fine. They're with their father," she said calmly.

"With Reginald? No!" I pulled at the chain again and pulled the wet rag my mother had laid across my forehead off and threw it to the floor.

"Mrs. Johnson, I need you to calm down," Officer Russell said.

"I know this is your first offense, so I need to explain some things."

"I don't care about what happens to me. Get my children. Please," I begged her. I cried and kicked in the bed. "I need to see them."

"You'll see them soon enough." She put her hand on my leg to stop me from moving. "I know you're upset and confused, but you have to listen to me right now. Do you understand?

"We have a mandatory minimum sentence for drunk driving in the state of Georgia. And you were driving with your children in the car, so they were automatically to be put in protective custody. Luckily, your husband called your cell phone while police were detaining you and he was able to come pick up the children. So they're safe. But we are pressing charges. And he's been given temporary custody."

I felt embarrassed and ashamed. Felt like I was lying in that bed naked. Alone. Cold. I looked away and at a bare white wall as the officer went on. I heard half of what she said. Maybe less. I kept thinking of Cheyenne and R. J. and what they'd seen. How they'd cried and begged me to turn the car around. Their two bodies stuffed into one seat. They must've been so scared.

"When you passed out," I heard her say after a while, "the officers weren't sure what was wrong with you. They knew you'd been drinking, but when they spoke to your friend—"

"My friend?" I turned back to Officer Russell.

"Yes, a Mrs. Bellamy? Sasha Bellamy. She was with your husband when he called. She told the officers you might be using drugs."

"What? That's crazy. She's crazy," I explained. "I don't use drugs. She's just trying to steal my husband. That's what this is about. That's why I was out there." I looked at Officer Russell. "I know I shouldn't have been drinking, but I was upset. It was just one time. I'd had a fight with my husband and it was wrong for me to do that to my children, but I don't use drugs."

She patted my leg like I was a psychiatric patient or wounded soldier.

"I hear what you're saying, but you need to know that when the officers brought you to the hospital after you passed out and they told doctors they weren't sure if you'd been drinking or using drugs or what kinds, they had to test you."

I shrugged my shoulders expecting a clear denial of anything Sasha had said. I'd never used drugs. Not once in my life. Not even a pill beyond what I'd taken for pain after having the twins.

"You tested positive for methylenedioxymethamphetamine or MDMA."

"What's that?"

"Ecstasy."

In all my anger, in all my fear and embarrassment, I actually laughed at this. Not loudly, but just like I was sure she was joking. Ecstasy? It was a joke. And if that was a joke, maybe all of this was. Maybe everything was fine. Some big joke the world was playing on me. I felt like the chain on my wrist had loosened.

"I don't use drugs. Something must be wrong."

She pursed her lips and reached for a clipboard hanging on the foot of the bed. She slid out a sheet and handed it to me.

"This isn't from me," I said, reading exactly what she'd told me, and my fear returned immediately. "I don't use drugs. There must be a mix-up. There has to be."

"Mrs. Johnson, we see this all of the time. Suburban mother working hard, needs some relief. The pills are easy to come by. They give you relief. You hid it with alcohol."

"But I didn't—" I tried.

"But there's only a matter of time before you can't hide it anymore. Before you hit a wall," she said. "And I think you hit your wall last night."

"I'm not hiding anything. I didn't hit a wall. I admitted I was drinking and I said I was wrong. If there's a fine or something I need to pay, I can do that, but I'm not a drug user."

"Why aren't your children in school?"

"They are. It's the end of the school year," I said, trying to let her hear how rational it all sounded, but even listening to myself, it just didn't. "Just one more week. I took them out, so we could come here . . ."

"Come here for what?"

"My husband." I paused and looked back at the white wall. "He's having an affair with Sasha."

"And what about your job? You haven't been there in days. Had someone been covering for you?" she asked.

"Oh, Sharika said she'd help me out while I came to see about my husband."

"So you took your children out of school and left your job to find your husband when you knew exactly where he was?" she asked matter-of-factly.

"I didn't know where he was. I knew, but I didn't know." I covered my mouth with my hand. I heard it now. I heard my own confusion. What was going on? I didn't know. I knew I hadn't used drugs, but right then I didn't know anything.

"I've been working in this area for fifteen years and I've seen a lot of things."

I looked back at her.

"And in my opinion, and I'll be honest with you, you don't really seem like the type of mother who'd use ecstasy, and judging by your response, you hardly know what it is. But that doesn't exclude both science and investigation," she said and I could tell by her voice that she was a mother to someone or many. "The test was positive and your coworker, the people at the library, your husband, your best friend, your mother, your children, everyone says they've noticed a change in you. So something is going on. Maybe in time we'll find out what it is, but right now, you need to prepare yourself for the fact that your husband has temporary custody of your children and you're going to jail. I would suggest that you get a lawyer."

8

I had to spend a day in jail. And when it was time for me to go before the judge, he was less than understanding. I sat in a row of women with our legs chained and when the judge called my name, the only lawyer my mother's limited savings could afford came shuffling up to the front of the courtroom searching for my name in a stack of wrinkled papers.

I wanted to hate him, but inside I was cheering for him. I needed to get home, wherever that was, just to remember who I was. They'd taken my clothes and shoes, felt through my hair, humiliated me so many times I'd stopped eating and going to the bathroom.

I could see my mother sitting in the back of the courtroom in one of the wooden rows that looked like pews. She was quiet, kept her eyes on the judge and her hands on what I was sure was a Bible in her lap.

"Reginald had to bail you out," she said in the car as she drove us home. "After I used my savings for the attorney, I had nothing left, so I had to call him. Couldn't put up the house. That's all I got in the world."

"I'm sorry, Mama. Sorry about all of this."

We rode in silence the rest of the way. I looked out the window and she looked at the road. We were together, but I don't ever remember feeling so alone. In fact, counting cars flashing by, I thought of how I don't recall ever having a real intimate moment with my mother. She'd try to slow down, to touch me, or hold me, but if it wasn't the church or my father, it was the Bible or God coming between us. My first breakup, my period, when I lost my virginity, when I pledged my sorority, she missed all of it. Even my wedding. Reginald and I decided to have it in a park in downtown Atlanta that was just a romantic stroll to the reception hall, and she and the Good Reverend decided that it was against God's orders not to have the service in his house. I called and begged her to come, cried into the phone that I couldn't find it anywhere in the Bible where it said I had to get married in a church and I needed her to be there. She said she'd think about it and then I heard my father's voice. The phone went dead.

That's how things went all my life with my mother. And after a while, I put her and all of the other people in the same category—do not disturb. If my trouble was too much, I'd keep it to myself. I was safer that way.

Like glasses of Scotch, after the first day in bed, the second is just easier, and the third feels like home.

I remained rolled up in the old sheets in my old twin-sized bed upstairs at my mother's house for four days. I took calls from the lawyer about when I'd be able to see the twins and organizing my mandatory community service activities to complete the judge's sentence. I still had months of community service and a fine. He also suggested that I get a clinical evaluation for alcohol and drug dependency and a therapist. I refused. I knew what was wrong with me. And it wasn't drugs or alcohol. I didn't know how to explain to anyone that I was telling the truth. All they saw were the results, and after the attorney had me tested, they came back positive for MDMA three times. It didn't make any sense. I was lying in that bed, not sleeping and not dreaming, trying to figure it out.

"You have a phone call," my mother said, popping her head into the bedroom.

"The lawyer?" I asked, not bothering to lift my head from the pillow or look directly at her.

"No, it's a woman." She came toward me and I looked up to see her holding the phone's receiver cupped in her hand. "I think she's from your job," she whispered. "Her name, it's something African or French. Not American."

"Sharika?"

She nodded and I reached out for the phone.

"I'll take it," I said.

"You eating dinner tonight?" my mother asked, handing me the phone. "I'll just warm up what you didn't eat last night."

She walked back to the door and turned to look at me like I was an insect.

"Sure, Mama. That'll be great," I said, lifting the phone to my ear and waiting for her to leave.

"Yoooooooooooooooo," Sharika howled into the phone. "Dawn! I've been calling you! Tried your cell phone like a million times. What's going on over there?"

I don't know if it was because I'd hardly heard another human's voice in days—aside from my mother's and the attorney's—or how quickly Sharika's sound flipped me back into my past, but I started crying nearly immediately after she said my name. Big, sloppy tears welled in my eyes and when she asked a question and went silent I couldn't speak for the knot doubling in my throat.

"You there?" she asked. "Are you crying? What's wrong?"

"Nothing," I murmured. "It's just, just so nice to hear your voice."

"Ohhh," she purred. "Well, I've been trying to call you, but the line went straight to voice mail."

"That was probably when I was in jail—"

"What was that like?"

"Awful and then worse than awful," I said. "The worst part was that I didn't expect to go there. I thought there was something I could do, but as soon as the doctor pulled the bandage off of my head, I was carted downtown in the back of a van."

"I'm sorry to hear about that," Sharika said. "You know some detective called here. Everyone at central knows you've been out. I couldn't lie. It would've been my ass then."

"Please, you don't have to apologize, Sharika," I said. "I understand. I don't think either of us saw this coming."

"Yeah, that's exactly how I felt. It just seemed so unreal, you know? How everything happened. I actually went and did some research."

"Research about what?" I asked.

"About Ms. Stinky Bellamy and that conference you said she was in town for. I don't know what it was, but when you told me she was here in Augusta for some conference, it didn't sit right with me. I mean, conferences come here all of the time, but we know about them—especially if someone from the news or something is going to be there. We hear about them. And I didn't hear anything about a journalism conference."

"So what did you do?" I sat up in the bed and looked at the knot on my forehead in the mirror on my old dresser.

"Just asked around. Spoke to some people downtown. And you know what? There was no conference. Nothing anyone could recall."

"What?" I stood up.

"No conference. You heard me right. There was no conference."

"But she said she was in town for a conference," I explained as if this would negate what Sharika was telling me.

"Well, she was certainly in town, but it wasn't for a conference," Sharika said. "Any idea what else could've brought her to Augusta?"

I sat back down on the bed and tried to remember Sasha's message on my machine. Reginald saying she was coming over. The car in the driveway. Her suitcase. The red candles on the dresser in the guest room. Phil Landon's nervous eyes on her legs at the car dealership. Then there was his wife at the nail salon. Her angry face. Her cold eyes. She'd pointed at Sasha. *"I guess you're the black whore who's been fucking him,"* she'd said. *"I have all of the receipts from the hotel last week. When I get finished with your ass, you'll wish you never gave him your number."*

"What, Dawn? What do you think?"

"I don't know. There was something. Something with Phil Landon."

"Phil Landon? From the car dealership? The jungle fever skirt chaser?"

"Skirt chaser?"

"Yeah," Sharika said. "You never heard about him? Oh, I forgot you're not from here. Both he and his daddy have chased every black tail in Georgia." She laughed. "We have like four caramel-colored families in Augusta that can trace their roots back to the Landons. And you know what that means. The only problem with those guys is they love black women, but they won't marry one to save their lives."

"What? But he was so nice," I said. "And Sasha said he was her—"

"Friend?"

We sat and listened to each other's thoughts. Sharika was sure she could get more information on Landon. He'd dated and dumped some girl she'd gone to high school with. His wife showed up at the house one afternoon, threatening to take her to court, saying she had receipts. I couldn't believe what I was hearing. I couldn't make sense of it. If Sasha was having an affair with Landon, why would she come after Reginald? And if Landon had dumped Sasha like Sharika was implying, why would she take us to his office? Why would he agree to a deal?

"I'm going to put my ear to the street," Sharika said, like we were in some old blaxploitation movie. "See what I can find out."

"Thank you," I said, feeling a little bit of soft rain over my fury.

"Well, if you ask me, that's what friends are for."

"Thank you for being my friend."

My mother had chucked a spoonful of lima beans and ham chunks into two bowls on the kitchen table. There was no salt, no pepper, just beans and ham clumped together.

I moved the food around. Ate a little. Picked the pork from the bone and used it to suffer through the beans.

I couldn't stop seeing Landon's wife standing there alone in the nail salon. How Sasha responded to her. How Sasha responded to me when I asked if she was actually sleeping with that woman's husband. She smiled. She grinned.

If she was capable of acting like that, behaving that way toward a woman she didn't know and then toward someone she'd slept across the room from for two years, what else was she capable of? What else had she done?

"Mr. Morgan gave me information about a doctor," my mother said, talking about the lawyer. "I can call if you want."

"I don't need a doctor, Mama. I told you and I told him, I don't need to see a psychologist or psychiatrist or whatever."

"Now, I know our people don't commonly go to these doctors, but Mr. Morgan said it'll be good for you, and considering everything that's going on—"

"Everything that's going on? What exactly is going on, Mama?" I asked. "You and Mr. Morgan seem to want me to see this doctor about what's going on, so what's going on? You tell me, because I don't know. Maybe you know. Maybe he knows."

"I don't kn—"

"And there it is. You don't know. And neither does he, so how can you tell me to get help for something neither of you understand? Not one of you! I don't have my children. My husband is . . . Who's supposed to fix that? How can they?" I hollered. "They can't. No one can fix this but me."

"I still think that maybe you could at least try it. Who knows. With prayer and a little help, you might be able to—"

"Mama, please stop it!" I rattled. "What is it with you? What? Do you believe those test results? Do you believe I'm using drugs?"

"There were three tests," she answered. "They all said the same thing."

"But what do I say?"

"I don't know what you say. You show up at my house. You scream. You run off. Drink up that old liquor," she said. "I don't know what you say."

"I'm your daughter! The least you could do is believe me when I tell you I didn't use drugs."

"Then how did they get into your system?"

"I don't know. I've been thinking about that. I just don't get it," I said. "But until I do, I need you to back off. And trust me."

"It's not just about me trusting you. For this weekend—" she said uneasily, bringing up a topic I'd forced into silence.

"Forget about it," I cut her off, pushing the bowl away from me. "I'm not going to see my kids in that house. Not with her."

"Well, then, how else will you see them? The judge gave Reginald temporary custody and he ordered supervised visits until they can clear your drug test and psychological evaluation."

"I don't need to be supervised with my own children," I said. "I'm a good mother. I'm a damn good mother and Reginald knows that. He's just listening to Sasha and letting her fill his head with all of these lies."

My mother looked off and I could see in her face that she thought I was tumbling through excuses.

"Here we go again," I said. "First you think I'm crazy and need a therapist, then you think I'm using drugs, and now you don't believe me when I say Sasha is the person behind all of this. God, Mama, who do you think I am?"

"I don't know who you are. I really don't," she said. "You left this house in a rush and you never turned back. You acted like me and your daddy was monsters."

"One monster's just as scary as two," I said.

"He wasn't that bad."

"Wasn't that bad? Were you there? Do you remember?"

"He was hard on me, but he wasn't ever really hard on you. I protected you. I protected you as much as I could."

"Well, it wasn't enough."

"You're OK now. You turned out fine," she said, getting up from the table and carrying the nearly full bowls with her. She flung them into the sink and there was a crash of glass. "I did what I was supposed to do. I put a roof over your head. Got you in school. Took you to church. Fed you. Gave you an extra blanket at night. I couldn't do none of that without your father and you know that." She stepped toward the sink and looked out the window into the dark night. "I wasn't nothing but a baby when I came to Atlanta. No education. No skills. Had to get on my knees and scrub floors. You know what that's like?" She looked at me over her shoulder and then looked back outside. "No you don't know what that's like. Because you ain't never had to do it. I made sure of that. I made sure you had a daddy who'd stay. A home in a nice neighborhood. That you were smart. That you'd never be like me."

I began to cry and took my eyes off of my mother. I couldn't look at her. She'd had her hands holding onto the sink like she was about to fall down. She was weeping and shaking with her back to me.

"I made sure you went to college. Fought like hell to get you out of this house. Begged your father to pay for it. I begged! Begged! On my knees! Raw. On this floor. Right here." She stomped on the floor. "And I knew, I just knew that it'd come back to me. That you'd go out in the world and be something and come home and show your mama. Show her that even if everything wasn't right, she did something right. But you left me. You found that man and you left me."

"I couldn't come back here," I said. "I promised myself I'd go anywhere, but I couldn't come back here. That's the only thing I wanted. That was all I thought of when I left. That I couldn't come back."

My mother turned around to me.

"When I met Reginald, that was his promise," I said. "He was going to take me away. Take me away from here."

The day we met, Reginald said my dress reminded him of a flower bed. I was just nineteen, as skinny as a stick man and still stuffing my bra. I didn't know how to take his compliment. Flowers were pretty. They were all over my dress and even springing up on the sleeves of my sweater. But did I want to look like a flower bed? A whole flower bed?

I was standing in front of my old dorm, an ancient sweat box with tiny bedrooms and prison-like windows.

He was wearing a huge sand-colored hat with sweat permeating the brim. Standing in a bed of flowers near the steps.

"You like flowers?" I asked, hoping he'd say yes at least and maybe I wouldn't feel so bad about looking like a whole flower bed. I was on my way to class, and while Spelman is an all-girls school, I had a few guys from Morehouse in my classes and I didn't want them snickering at my fashion choice when I walked in the door.

Reginald looked up from the flower bed and smiled. He was young. A little older than me. Had nice teeth and dark brown skin.

"I wouldn't have told you if it was all that bad. Now would I?" he said. He plucked a purple flower from the soil and handed it to me.

I kept our first date a secret. I'd just pledged my sorority and I was learning fast that there were rules to being a sorority woman. More rules than there were to being a Spelman woman—and that was certainly enough. I had to watch whom I dated and where we went. Watch what I wore and what we said. I had to watch everything. And if I wasn't watching, they were.

"How could someone as sweet as you end up pledging a sorority?" Reginald asked on our third date at a dinky hero shop in the West End. He'd gotten a huge sandwich with onions and ketchup gushing out of the sides. I thought it was gross, but he pointed to the sign out front: "Gutbusters!"

By then, I already knew how much Reginald hated the sorority, and anything to do with it. He found all of us pretentious and shady. Said we were actually the "Negro problem"—a bunch of black folks who thought they were white and measured success by money and names.

While I didn't necessarily see these things or have a problem with my Spelman or sorority sisters, he was saying all of the right things to me at the right time. See, I wasn't exactly Spelman or Alpha pledge material. Who someone was, what her family name meant when we lined up to become women of the school, meant that she could be shot right to the front. The daughter of a dignitary, a family of graduates, contributors, the list went on. They all had their own sections in the sun, clubs and traditions. The next set was the second generations and daughters of faculty or staff members; their parents had a little money or status. Maybe a feature in *Ebony* magazine. And last were the sisters there on scholarship. The ones who were first generation to the school. Who knew better than to say who their parents were or what they weren't doing.

I fit somewhere between the second and third lists of sisters. I was never mysteriously shut out of activities or told "no" to my face like some other girls I knew. My father was a pastor and many people had heard of our church, so my matriculation into the circle wasn't so difficult. I was kind. I was smart. But I knew not to ever tell anyone that my mother scrubbed floors. And then she started working for one of my Spelman sisters.

"They're not so bad," I told Reginald. "We do community service. We try to make the world better."

"If you believe that nonsense, you've already sipped the punch," he joked. "Do I need to save you from the cult of the Alpha sisters?"

"No," I laughed. "It's not a cult."

But it was. Or maybe it just felt like one once they all figured out that I was dating Reginald. My big sisters just stopped talking to me. My line sisters, the women I pledged with, said I couldn't date him. "He didn't go to college," someone said. "You can do better. He's beneath you."

This only made me love Reginald more. I snuck out. I lied. I had late-night kisses and tight hugs. We were rebels. We were in love. When I was about to graduate, he asked me to marry him. He said he wanted to take me home and build a life with me. That was everything I wanted. To leave Atlanta.

I knew I couldn't have both him and my sisters. I chose him.

The judge suspended my driver's license. I couldn't drive a car on my own for a year, unless I took a driving course.

My mother had to drive me to Sasha's house on Saturday to see the children.

I fought it. I called the lawyer. I called the courthouse. I cried and tried to make threats, but in the end it was clear that for a long while, the only way I could see my children was on Reginald's terms. And after over a week of being away from two people I hadn't gone so much as ten hours without in ten years, I had to break.

My mother prayed through the entire ride. Begged me not to say anything to Sasha. Not to break anything. Said she understood my anger, but that if I wanted the twins back, I had to prove I wasn't losing my mind.

"I'll be fine," I assured her, but I wasn't sure about that. Riding in the little car down the wide streets with freshly manicured lawns and white people staring at us from every front step, I felt myself unraveling and I held onto my gut to stop from vomiting.

On Lover's Lane, the grass was so green, it looked like it had been spray-painted. Perfectly pruned flowers seemed to sneak up on towering home fronts that somehow were both intimidating and friendly with their matching mahogany French doors and latticed windows. The houses were so big, they looked like offices or community centers. I wondered what kinds of people lived in those houses. What they did. How they'd gotten so wealthy. How they saw my children. How they saw my husband. And how he, a man who claimed for so long to hate these people, saw them.

My mother pointed to a house tucked so far back behind bushes and rows of tulips you could hardly see it.

"This is it," she said, stopping the car in the middle of the street.

"You sure?" I asked. I looked down at the address that had once been written on my hand.

"Yes." She backed up and tried to park the car close to the curb, but we looked around and saw that not one car, not one, was parked in the street.

"You think we should park here?" she asked.

"Where else?"

We looked around again as if we'd find some sign or person telling us it was OK to leave my mother's little Toyota on the street.

"But it's such a long walk to the house," my mother pointed out. "A mile!"

"That's not a mile, Mama," I said, but I wasn't sure. It was a long way.

We looked at the house. The car was still idling.

"Maybe you could call them," she said.

"I'm not calling them. I'm not pulling into that driveway. Let's just park," I insisted, reaching over to the ignition.

"Is that Reginald?" She nodded to the house and I looked to see Reginald skipping down the driveway, waving his hands. He was wearing khaki shorts and loafers. A thin white T-shirt.

"Pull into the driveway," he said, holding his hands around his mouth like a megaphone.

"See, he said to—" my mother tried, but I snatched the keys from the ignition.

"No!"

I got out of the car without my purse or my thoughts. Seeing Reginald for the first time since he'd left me in our bed, I was past any edge. I wanted to fight. I was beyond asking why or being pleasant for the judge. This man walked out on me.

"Where are they?" I asked, but it was more like a command.

"You should park in the driveway," he said after a weak wave to my mother, who was standing by my side.

"What driveway?" I asked sternly. "You don't own a driveway here, so you can't say where I can park."

"Oh, Jesus, are you going to be like this? Don't come inside if you're going to act like this."

"WHERE ARE MY CHILDREN?"

My mother grabbed my arm.

"Calm down, Dawn," she begged.

"Yes, listen to your mother," Reginald agreed. "That'll be best. I never knew you'd act like this."

"Act? I'm acting the way you made me act," I said. "Just take me to my children."

We trudged up the driveway and through a little path of bushes to the front door. I was behind Reginald. My mother was behind me. I could hear her praying.

Reginald opened one side of a set of French doors and R. J. and Cheyenne were standing in front of a winding marble staircase I'd only seen on television. The newel posts were taller than the twins.

I ran to them and sank to my knees like they were still two feet tall. I gathered them into my arms and rocked and rocked, kissing their cheeks and asking if they were OK.

"Let me see you," I said to R. J., pushing him back and looking at his face.

I did the same to Cheyenne.

They smiled at me pleasantly, but the look in their eyes was more distant.

Then I realized that their arms were to their sides and not around my neck. Cheyenne had one hand in her pocket. She was wearing jeans I hadn't bought her. I hadn't bought any of the things they were wearing.

"I've missed you guys," I said. "Missed you a lot. Didn't you miss me?"

"All right, everyone, let's go into the sunroom to get some lunch," Reginald said loudly, trying to usher us with swinging arms.

"No!" I argued. I looked back at the twins. "Didn't you miss me? Didn't you miss your mama?"

"Dawn, just come and eat." My mother put her hand on my shoulder. "They're probably just hungry."

R. J. looked down at his feet.

I sat there on the floor before them for a minute, but then I got up.

I felt so defeated. I wasn't expecting a whole lot. But hugs. Kisses. I miss you—those weren't expectations. Those were just standard. These were my children. They had to miss me. They had to want to touch me.

Reginald explained that Sasha had gone shopping. Elka, the cook, had made lunch. A year later in therapy, I'd describe his voice, his body language, even his scent as pedestrian. He was flat.

Detached. Like a tour guide showing us around a funeral home or a host who didn't exactly want to have the party.

He was saying something as we walked. Pointing to things.

My mother smiled and held onto her purse.

And just when I was about to lose myself and scream that this was all my nightmare, R. J. came walking up beside me and took my hand.

I looked down at him and he smiled. A tear rolled from my eye. I squeezed his hand and looked forward at Cheyenne following so closely behind her father's footsteps, he nearly tripped. She looked nervous. Very far from me.

A moon-shaped pool provided the center for the sunroom. It was pink with S. B. painted into the floor in black.

"That's not a pool for children," R. J. explained cautiously. "It's for adults. Daddy and Sasha use it at night and—"

"Come on, son, let's sit down," Reginald stopped him. "I know your mother wants to talk to you guys. Not hear about that little pool."

R. J. stopped talking about the pool, but after we took seats around a glass table that was nice enough to be in someone's living room, Cheyenne made sure we heard about everything else in the house. There was "her" room. She was painting it "lavender." There was the game room. She couldn't wait to show her friends. And Sasha had already told her she could have a slumber party in the movie room.

"I don't think your friends can come this far," I said. "Maybe we can have a slumber party at our house. Don't you miss our house?"

"Sometimes," she mumbled.

"We don't have a movie room, but we have our living room with the big pillows on the floor. The purple beanbag from your room. Don't you think they'd like that, too?" I asked.

"Maybe."

Elka, whom I identified by a name stitched in red into the

white dress she was wearing, set a platter of sandwiches on the table.

"Salad for you?" she asked me.

"No, I won't be eating," I said.

"Salad for—" She'd turned to my mother.

"She won't be eating either," I said.

Reginald was the only one who reached for one of the sandwiches. He insisted that the twins eat and when they didn't fill their plates, he did it for them.

"Don't be shy because your mama's here," he said before biting into his sandwich. He looked at my mother. "They've been eating up a storm since I got them," he explained with his food in his mouth.

"Oh, I'm happy they're healthy," she responded awkwardly.

His cell phone started ringing on the table. Still chewing his food like a horse, he picked up the phone and looked like he was reading a text message.

"It's Sasha," he said anxiously and I'm certain I was looking at him like he was crazy. "She's just pulling up and wants my help with bags." He jumped up from his seat like it was on fire. "I'll be right back."

Reginald hurried out, leaving his cell phone and half-eaten sandwich behind.

"So," my mother opened, trying to fill the hush at the table, "you two having fun in this place?" She smiled at R. J. adoringly, but I did sense a little agitation in her voice and it surprised me.

"Well, we can't play on the couches in the living room," R. J. admitted. "Auntie Sasha let us do it on the first day, but then she told us not to go in there."

"Don't call her your aunt," I ordered. "She's not your aunt."

"She's Daddy's girlfriend," Cheyenne said, cutting me in half.

I was about to correct her, but my mother slid her hand onto my knee beneath the table.

"Your father is married to your mother," she said, "so he can't have a girlfriend. In God's eyes, that's a sin."

"So?" Cheyenne muttered. She rolled her eyes and looked away from the table.

"You don't believe sin is wrong, baby?" my mother went on.

"What's a sin?" R. J. asked me.

"You don't know what a sin is?" My mother stared at me, but my eyes were hung on Cheyenne and her coldness. She went on to describe the Ten Commandments and tell the story of Moses and Sinai.

"I wasn't trying to hurt you," I said to Cheyenne beneath my mother's telling. "I would never try to hurt you. You know that? You and R. J. are the most important people in the world to me. I love you."

I reached across the table to touch her, but she moved away.

"I promise nothing like that will ever happen again," I added. "I promise that to you and R. J." I looked at R. J. "Mommy made a bad mistake. And I swear it will never happen again. Can you forgive me?"

"Yes—" R. J. answered.

Cheyenne got up from her seat and started running out of the room.

"I'll never forgive you," she hollered. "I wish you would die!"

I got up to follow her, but she was stopped by Reginald and Sasha walking into the room laughing and talking. She ran right into Reginald.

"What's wrong, Chey?" Reginald asked, leaning low to her.

"I want to go to my room," Cheyenne cried, wiping tears.

"But your mama is here to see you, sweetie," my mother said.

"I want to go to my room," Cheyenne cried frantically.

"Let her go," I said, feeling bad that she was hurting so much. Cheyenne was born distant from me. But even in her cutting words and swipes at my head, I never wanted to see her upset. I never wanted to be the person who made her upset.

Reginald released Cheyenne and she ran from the room.

"Can I go, too?" R. J. asked his father and then looked at me confused.

"Sure you can," I said as sweetly as I could. "Can you give me a kiss first?"

"Yes!"

R. J. kissed me on the cheek and I kissed him on the forehead, holding him close to my chest for as long as I could. I wouldn't look right at Sasha, but I could tell from the dark lens of her sunglasses that her eyes were on me.

"See you again next time," I said to R. J.

"When, Mama? When can we go home?"

"Sooner than you think," I said to him. "Sooner than you can blink your eyes." I kissed him on the forehead again and he scattered out of the room.

"Mrs. George," Sasha called to my mother, "it's so nice to see you."

She and Reginald walked over to the table where my mother and I were both now standing. She was wearing shorts the same color as Reginald's and a tight cream tube top that pushed her breasts up to her neck. Her huge sunglasses were tucked beneath a tan floppy hat that seemed more appropriate for June than early May.

"Oh," was all my mother could spare.

"Well, for sure the circumstances leave much to be desired, but it's a pleasure."

"Oh, thank you."

"Dawn, how have you been?" Sasha's voice was slow and pandering. She spoke like I was a mental patient.

"How do you think?" I asked.

"Well, I haven't seen you since the incident at my job, and I wanted to make sure you were doing OK. You seemed a little off." She took off her shades and grinned this grin at me. It was psychotic. Crazy. Nearly diabolical. Just the way she'd spoken to

Landon's wife at the nail salon. Suddenly, I heard everything she'd said in a new way.

"Cut the bullshit," I said. "I know you lied to the cops and told them I was using drugs."

"I didn't say that," she said with marked fake concern. She slapped her hand over her chest with surprise and looked at my mother. "I just said that she'd been acting strangely. And that maybe something was going on. Maybe it could be drugs. I was just acting in your best interest. Being a friend." Her voice cracked and she leaned over to Reginald. "See, I told you she can't ever say anything good."

"Oh, I have some good things to say," I said. "Some good things to say to both of you and maybe it's time for me to get started right now."

"Oh no, let's just go," my mother came in. "We've seen the children. Let's just go."

"No, I'm not leaving," I shouted.

"Don't make a scene," Reginald said. "You'll only make yourself look bad."

"I'll look bad? No, *you* look bad! Running up behind this phony like you don't have half a bit of sense to see that she's just using you."

"I'm not using him," Sasha said.

"Oh, you save your act for Reginald. He's just as weak and simple as you."

"Now, hold on, Dawn," Reginald said. "Let's not do this name-calling. I haven't said anything about you."

"Well, try!" I demanded. "Try. Say something wrong about how I was your wife for ten years. How I cared for your parents and your children and kept your house clean. Loved you. Even when it wasn't convenient! Even when you made me turn away from every person in this world who loved me! Tell me!"

My mother was pulling me out of the room.

"And this is how you do me? This is how you repay me?" I asked. "This is what you do to your family?"

"Let's go," my mother said to me as we neared the door.

Sasha sauntered behind Reginald and his stupid-looking face. Elka walked out of the kitchen holding a tray of drinks, but then turned back around.

"You're not a man. You're not even half of a man. And I'm going to prove it to you. I swear if there's nothing I do before I leave this earth," I said, pulling away from my mother, "I'll prove that to your weak ass!"

I tried to charge Reginald, but my mother caught me at my stomach and swung me out of the door.

"Nice visit," I heard Sasha call from the other side and I tried to get through the door, but I was still in my mother's arms.

"Stop it," Reginald said to Sasha. "Just let her go."

When we got back into the car I must've called Sasha every foul word I ever learned. I was sitting beside my mother, but I didn't apologize. I was just that angry. Just that pissed off.

"When did you lose your faith?" my mother said after I ran out of nasty things to say.

"What?" I thought I heard her incorrectly.

"Your faith . . . when did you lose it? Because how you were acting in there, it was clear you didn't have any."

"Oh, come on," I said. "There's nothing wrong with me or how I acted. Did you see her? Did you see how she was acting?"

"How *she* was acting has nothing to do with you. She's obviously not walking with the Lord, but you, you weren't raised like that. You know the Word."

"Now we get to it. I guess the Good Reverend still has his power. But you know what?" I looked at her. "I haven't exactly seen you running off to church. When was the last time you went and sat in a pew? Or did that get too old when God called Herbert George home?"

"You keep pushing this off on everyone else. It's Sasha. It's me.

It's your father. How I worship God has nothing to do with you. And the relationship your father had with his maker is none of your business."

"Relationship? Please. He used God. And as far as I'm concerned, if there was a God, he would've struck Dad dead the day he choked you in the dining room," I said. "Maybe you forgot that I was there. Maybe you forgot that I was in the closet. But I'll never forget that. And I'll never forgive him or God." I turned to the street. "I don't need to have faith. I have myself."

"One day, you ain't gonna be enough," she said solemnly. "And when that day comes, I hope you lay these burdens down and do what I taught you to do. Prayer changes things. Faith is the most powerful thing in the world. Not you."

9

It is a fact that I slept on the floor that night. I sat on the bed for a little while. I listened to my mother walking through the house praying and scrubbing every surface she could find. We were tired. Just tired. And if I tried to explain that to you, I'd say you'd have to have experienced something so excruciatingly painful that all you want to do is feel something more deep and dark than that. What I learned that night with my face to the floor, like it had been in the closet when I was too young to imagine my life becoming such a tragedy, is that some people try to fight that feeling of exhaustion with drugs. Some with alcohol. Some even with sex. Some with things and pleasure. Some death. I wanted to feel more pain. I wanted to feel my bones splitting and aching on the wood as I held my eyes closed and pretended to sleep. I wanted for my back to sink into the floor and hurt so bad so I could let this pain go and move on.

When we'd gotten home, my mother had told me about her parents. The grandparents she always said were dead and buried in Mississippi. Now she admitted she didn't know if they were dead or alive. She said her father was a bad drunk. And one night he was so liquored up, he tried to drown her mother in a lake. All three of them almost went under as my mother tried to save her.

My mother slit the wrist on her father's left hand that night as he slept. He woke up and chased her off of the farm. She ran and never went back, but she said she had two younger sisters in the house and they said he never hit her mother again—he never really slept again either. She got a bus ticket to Atlanta. Didn't know a soul. Hardly knew how to read. But she could clean.

"I only wanted three things when I got married: to have someone who could give me and my children a life," she said, holding her arms straight out toward the steering wheel, "and that he would not beat on me, and never drink. That was it. When I met your daddy, I knew I was safe. He was a preacher. He never drank and he said he'd never hurt me. If I worked, he'd work. But then I saw he was drinking some days and then every night. See, back then working men didn't use drugs . . . they drank. That's what they did. He'd say one thing on the pulpit, but come home and be just like one of them souls he tried to save. I insisted he stop. But it had a hold on him. Just like it did my father. I was going to leave. I wanted to leave. But then I had you and I thought I could save him. I'd fought that demon before and I'd risen to the top. I could do it again this time. I could fix him. I could survive him. You could survive him. When you left I was angry and I was mad that I never saw you. Mad that you never came around. But I understood. And a little part of me was kind of glad. I thought maybe you'd survive. Maybe you were off living a good life and having everything I didn't have. You hated your father. Hated me. But you had love. And that meant someone floated to the top that time. When you showed up at the house, I knew we were both still drowning."

When I woke up, my mother was sitting on the bed. The sun was up. I could tell she'd left the house by the shoes she was wearing.

"I went to see Mrs. Jackson," she said.

"What? Why would you go see Mrs. Jackson?" I asked, referring to the woman she worked for. While she was full time until my father died, her aches and pains were too much to continue full time, so she only worked once a week now and mostly went to keep Mrs. Thirjane Jackson, a black woman who thought being a Southern belle was all a woman should do with her life, company.

"I thought she could help. Maybe give us some tips. She knows everyone. Has connections."

"Why would you do that? No. We don't need her help," I said annoyed. Not only was Mrs. Jackson a chatty, judgmental royal, but she was also the mother of Kerry Jackson, someone I went to school with who knew many of my sorority sisters. "She's going to tell Kerry and I know Kerry will tell Marcy."

"So?"

"So I don't want all of Atlanta to know my business," I said. "They gossip about stuff like that."

"I don't think that will happen. Kerry's a nice girl. She wouldn't gossip about you."

"Oh, no! You told Kerry?"

"She was there when I was talking to Mrs. Jackson."

I slapped the floor in disgust.

"No," she went on. "She's not like that. She's been through a divorce. She's been through this. Her husband—"

"So now I'm getting a divorce?"

"I hope so."

"I don't even know Kerry," I got up from the floor and heard both of my knees crack.

"That's not true. She remembers you from Spelman. She wants to have lunch with you," I heard this after I'd already turned to look at my swollen face in the mirror.

"She what? No! No, you didn't—" I turned back to her.

"No, I didn't ask. She asked. She said she wants to talk to you. Catch up." My mother sounded like I was five years old and she was convincing me to make friends on my first bus ride to school.

"I can't believe you," I said. "And I'm not doing it. I am not going to lunch with Kerry because she feels sorry for me."

"I can't cancel. I already set it up."

"You set it up? For when?"

"Today."

I walked out of the room.

Kerry Jackson was Spelman's Black Barbie. She was the kind of girl who, when other girls were around her, they couldn't help but look. She was beautiful. Dark and had long black hair. And she came from a good family. Had money. Got good grades. Had a great reputation. Her mother went to Spelman and pledged our chapter. But Kerry didn't join. Some people said it was because she didn't like that the chapter wasn't "taking in" girls her color and it was clear that they'd only take her because she was a legacy since her mother was a member, too. That made a lot of people hate her. I remember the day after Sasha and I crossed into the sorority, we were with our sisters in the cafeteria, wearing our jackets and singing and Kerry walked in. She was alone, dressed in all black with a single strand of thick aqua pearls around her neck and right wrist. We kept singing and dancing, but when she came in, eyes left us and went to her. They couldn't stop looking at her. And I was with them. What she did—that she wasn't trying to be a part of the crowd—made her stand out to me. And add the fact that my mother worked for her mother. I watched her from behind for the next two years and prayed she'd never turn around. And when she did, I'd wave and smile. Never speak. That would acknowledge something we both knew and didn't want to talk about.

When I reluctantly walked into the restaurant later that afternoon after talking to my mother, I was looking for the beautiful girl I saw in the black dress and aqua pearls. My mother drove me across town to Murphy's where I was supposed to meet Kerry at 1:00 p.m.

I looked around the restaurant after telling the maître d' I was meeting a friend. She mentioned a woman sitting toward the back at a table and I peeked, but I was sure the woman with the short afro reading a book wasn't her. I said I'd wait. I stood around for ten minutes watching a couple share pictures on their phones at the bar.

I looked at my watch and saw that it was getting late. Maybe she'd gotten stuck in traffic, I thought: we were in Atlanta. Maybe she'd canceled though, I thought, after realizing that she was about to meet a woman for lunch whom she hardly knew. I scanned the room and somehow I kept going back to the woman with the short afro.

This time, she looked up from her book and toward the front of the room. She took off these black spectacles and there was Kerry.

I looked for a second to make sure it was her and then I made my way to the table.

"Kerry?" I said, ambling through the maze. "It's me, Dawn. I was waiting up front."

"Oh, I'm sorry!" Kerry got up and hugged me. She was wearing a loose pea green yoga set and when she moved, her top seemed to flow over her skin.

"You look so different," I announced almost involuntarily.

"Oh, everyone says that." Kerry laughed as the waiter pulled out my seat. "I can't be that different. Really? Come on."

"No, you've changed. Changed a lot," I said. "You look beautiful."

"Thank you," she said. "So what's up with you, Ms. Lady? How have you been?"

"Alive. I'm sure my mother gave you an earful. She told me she spoke to you and your mother."

"Oh, thank God you know." Kerry exhaled. "I was thinking I'd have to sit through this lunch and get you to tell me what's going on yourself. You know she swore me to secrecy."

"Yeah, after she told all of my business," I said.

"Well, join the club!" She picked up her glass of water and clinked mine. "Look, you don't have to feel any pressure. If you don't want to talk about what's going on, we don't have to. I was just hoping to get you out of the house. I remember when I was where you are at. I'd go days in the dark."

"Thanks," I said. "So what were you reading?" I pointed to the book she'd stashed in the chair beside her. "I'm just being nosy. I'm a librarian."

"Oh, that's wonderful." She reached for the book and put it back on the table. "It's just a textbook. I'm finishing my Master's in Public Health."

"That's . . . wonderful," I said, laughing at repeating her word.

"One more class and I'm done! This one is killing me."

"What are you going to do with it—the degree?"

"I'm going to open a clinic for handicapped mothers," Kerry explained. "A place where they can come and get special services and see doctors who are experienced with their needs. I've already got a location, start-up money, and interested physicians."

Kerry and I had a long conversation over lunch. We didn't talk about Reginald or Sasha. I told her about the library and Sharika going back to school. Mr. Lawrence and Mrs. Harris. The teenagers. The twins. Cheyenne's attitude. How it felt when I learned about R. J.'s autism.

She listened and cheered me on. And while I still felt like I was half dead, she gave me hope without offering it.

She told me a little about her divorce. How her husband had cheated on her, and twice with the same woman. She said she'd slept on a floor, too. Had to be dragged out of bed. But she was OK. And knowing she'd been where I was at made it seem like some kind of change was possible.

She was so together. She wore her victory over her divorce like a piece of armor. I didn't know if I'd ever get there, but it was nice to be reminded that maybe I could.

"I cut my hair," Kerry said, digging into the bowl of warm peaches with cobbler crust and vanilla bean ice cream we'd agreed to share for dessert. "That's when I knew I was ready to move on. I got up and went into the bathroom and just cut it all off."

"Why?"

"I still don't really know. I think I was tired. Tired of all of those years of my life I'd wasted trying to be someone's wife, and someone's mother, and someone's daughter—it was all too much."

"But what did your hair have to do with that?"

"It was just what I thought made me beautiful. What I thought made people like me. It was everything they'd talk about: 'Kerry's hair is so long . . . Kerry's so dark, but she has that pretty, long hair!' But when Jamison was gone and I was left sitting in that big house with just myself and my son, I was like, 'Fuck it! I'm tired of doing this hair!' So I cut it off and I haven't let it grow back since. I've cut a lot of things." She spooned the last scoop of ice cream onto my saucer. "What are you going to cut?"

"Cut?"

"Yeah, cut from your life? You can't get a whole new life unless you let some of the old things go."

"I don't know if I need to go cutting things just yet," I said. "Seems like right now people are busy cutting things for me." I stopped and let the waiter place our bill on the table and waited until he'd walked away and I was sure he couldn't hear me. "That woman took him. She came into my house. She took my husband. And every time I think about that, I have to think that maybe I'm wrong. Maybe she didn't take anything. Maybe I never had it."

"So what are you going to do?"

"I want my kids back. I want my house. My mother thinks I need a divorce."

"And you?"

"I'd be a liar if I said yes," I said. "I feel yes. Of course. I'm furious. But it's been a long time. And I keep thinking maybe Reginald's confused. Maybe he'll wake up and see Sasha for what she is. Maybe . . ." I stopped. "I'm too embarrassed."

Kerry insisted that she pay for lunch. She said I needed to be treated—formally.

"How'd you do it?" I asked as we walked out of the restaurant. Kerry had agreed to drive me home, so my mother didn't have to drive all the way back downtown to get me. "How'd you get through all of that stuff and come out like this?"

Kerry was quiet. She reached into her pocket and pulled out a card that was so yellow it was almost neon. She handed it to me.

"What's this?" I asked.

"It's what healed me."

HHNFH was spelled out in sparkling diamonds that were perfectly placed in the center of the card above a phone number.

"Hell Hath No Fury House," she said.

I laughed at the name.

"Are you serious? What's that?"

"I wasn't going to tell you about it unless you asked," Kerry answered. "It's a special treatment and counseling center for women thinking about, going through, and those who have been through divorce. It's where I went after I cut off all of my hair and people thought I was crazy. They help."

"Hell Hath No Fury House," I repeated, still laughing. "You can't be serious." I looked at Kerry. "You're joking. A counseling program for divorcing women? No offense, but I don't need that. I'm OK. Is this why my mother put you up to meeting me? I told her I don't want a counselor."

"She doesn't know anything about it," Kerry said.

"Well, I'm sorry. Just meeting with you was cool. I already feel better than I did this morning. Got some air. I'm just not feeling like being around a bunch of angry women all day." I tried to hand the card back to Kerry, but she stepped back.

"You're not angry?" Kerry asked flatly.

"I'm depressed," I said. "I'm . . . angry. But I don't need this kind of help. I can get through this myself." I held the card out, but Kerry folded it back up in my hand.

"Just keep it," she said. "Just keep it."

When Kerry and I got to my mother's house, there was a compact car with one of those magnetic signs over the top that said PIZZA sitting right out front.

"Looks like someone's having pizza for dinner tonight," Kerry joked as I got out of her car.

"Yeah, I guess so," I said, noticing that there was a man, a black man, sitting in the front seat. I thought it was odd for my mother to be ordering pizza; I didn't remember her being a pizza eater and I was confident she was going to try to serve those lima beans again, but there were no other cars out in the street and the car was parked right in front of her house. Her car wasn't in the driveway. "Hey, thanks for lunch. It was a great idea." I closed the door and bent down to talk to Kerry through the open window.

"I enjoyed it, too. Maybe we can do it again."

"That sounds great."

"And don't forget about HHNFH."

"Got it right here in my back pocket," I pointed out, tapping my pocket.

I waved at Kerry driving off and turned to see the man getting out of the pizza delivery car.

He had a pizza box in one hand and an envelope in the other.

"Can I help you?" I asked.

"Hope so," he answered, smiling kindly. "Are you Dawn Johnson?"

"Yes," I said, surprised that he knew my name. "But I didn't order pizza."

The man tossed the pizza box onto the hood of his car and it slid over a little bit like it was just an empty cardboard box.

He handed me the envelope.

"You've been served."

"I what?" I asked with the envelope in my hand. "Served? But I . . ." I read for the first time a name that would stay with me for a very long time: Terri D. Loomis Law. "What's this?" I looked back up to talk to the pizza delivery man, but he was already pulling off, leaving me in the street holding the envelope.

I went into the house and sat down at the dining room table to read the letter inside of the envelope. I didn't even close the front door. My purse was still on my shoulder. I read.

It was a petition for divorce. Reginald was citing "irreconcilable differences." Somewhere in the pages it said there was a "conflict of personality" and "constant bickering." He wanted to split our possessions, excluding the house, which was in his name, down the middle and full custody of the children—Cheyenne Loren and Reginald Brian. He cited that I was losing my job and had recently been arrested for a DUI and failed a drug test.

I dropped the paper. My head was spinning. My neck felt clammy.

These words, these ideas had been floating around for days, but everyone made it seem like a "divorce" would be my idea. I wasn't prepared for it to be Reginald's. His estrangement was obvious. I didn't think he'd want a paper to prove it. And not so fast. This was happening too fast. How could he be sure? Not sure that he wanted to be with Sasha, but that he wanted to leave me? And take my children? I couldn't let him take my children. If he left, it had to be alone. He couldn't have them.

I looked at the papers. Let my arms fall to my sides and just sat there and looked at them. The silence in the empty house became deafening. My ears rang. I felt the pain, the burning, empty, tiring pain rushing back to me. I looked at the china cabinet.

"Nothing? Nothing in here?" I cried, shuffling around my mother's old carafes in the bottom cabinet. There were no bottles left. My mother must've thrown them out. One of the carafes rolled out to the floor and then another as I rummaged through. "Nothing. Nothing!"

I saw sunlight rolling in across the living room floor. The front door was open.

A carafe rolled and hit my mother's foot.

"What's this?" She walked quickly into the dining room. "What are you doing?"

"I can't find it!" I explained, but I don't know what I was talking about. Right then it was the liquor, but there was something else.

"No, not a drink. You don't need that," she said. "I threw it all out. No more. I should've done it before when your father died. It's gone now. It's all gone now."

"But I need it," I cried.

"No, you don't." She came over to the table. "What's this letter? Who's it—" She started reading.

I kept looking around in the cabinet for something I couldn't find.

"He wants a divorce?" my mother read.

I got up and looked through the drawers, but I couldn't find it there either. I ran into the living room. It wasn't in any of the drawers in the end tables.

I looked at the staircase and thought maybe it was upstairs. Maybe it was upstairs.

"What are you looking for?" my mother asked, coming up behind me.

"Something to stop this. Something to stop everything. The pain. And Reginald. Sasha. Me. I need something to stop this," something in me said. I ran up the stairs and went straight to my parents' room.

"What? What's in here?" my mother asked. She was crying then. Puddles of tears were gathering in the sides of her eyes.

I went to the closet and started pulling stacks of hat boxes from the top shelf.

"What are you looking for? What is it, baby? Tell me!"

At the back of the closet was a rusty green lockbox. I snatched it.

"Your father's old gun? What are you doing with that? No . . . no . . . you don't need that!"

I opened the box. He never once locked it. I pulled out the gun and dropped the box.

"Dawn, please stop! Please! In the name of Jesus, please stop this right now!"

"Give me the keys," I said.

"I can't. You're not supposed to drive."

"Give me the keys!"

"No, I can't."

I grabbed my mother's purse and tried to find the keys, but I was shaking so badly I could hardly see anything.

"Give me the keys, Mama! I need them. I need to stop this!" I tried to sound reasonable. But I was screaming at her and she shook.

"I can't," she cried. "I can't."

I pushed past her and started walking toward my room.

"What are you going to do with that gun?" she asked, following behind me. "You'll hurt yourself. Give it to me. Please!"

I didn't say anything. I just kept walking. I was seeing fire. Seeing flames. Literally in my eyes.

"You want me to call the police? You want me to call the police and have them lock you up? I'll do it. I'll do it to protect you. I can't have you out here like this. You'll kill yourself!"

My mother reached for the gun, but I pulled away. She got on my back and tried to get her arms around me, but I shook her off and ran down the hallway into the bathroom.

I went inside and turned to see her coming down the hall to me.

"What are you doing?" she asked. "What are you doing?"

I slammed the door closed before she could reach me. I held it closed and locked it.

She pounded so hard on the wood it sounded like it would split.

"Lord Jesus, please help my child!" she cried again and again.

I put the gun on the floor and sat on the toilet. I looked at it and thought of how it could make everything stop. I could get away. I could be free. I was so angry at myself. I felt like I'd done this. I'd done everything wrong and now here I was. Me and a gun in the bathroom.

My mother's screaming got louder. She was wailing. Past weeping. Wailing.

I finally began to cry.

I hadn't noticed it before, but the whole time, after I read that letter and saw that Reginald was petitioning for child support, I hadn't cried.

I looked up at the ceiling at something I couldn't see, but needed to know was there.

"My God!" I cried, and the heat in me boiled out of my mouth so fast that I lurched forward to my knees, falling to the floor beside the gun.

"My God!" I cried. "God, help me!"

10

I'm a grown woman now and I was a grown woman then, but I have to say, thank God for mamas. I thought I knew something about being a mother from having my own children. From staying up late at night cleaning up vomit from stomach viruses and rubbing lotion on chicken pox. I thought I understood the power of a mother and how the strength in that role alone can make miracles happen even when I thought God himself couldn't care less. But when I heard that bathroom door come crashing down and I thought my mother had called the police, but really it was just her with a chair in her hands, I realized that the strength of a mother is God. It has no limits. It has no apologies. It has no order. It's a bail of water coming to put the fire out.

When I cried out for God, my mother came kicking in. She pulled me off the floor and held me in her arms and promised she'd never let me go again. She wasn't going to let me kill or be killed. She was going to fight with me and we were going to win.

And then it was like a little bit of the sun was in the room with us. Lying in my mother's arms, I saw a glowing in the corner of my eyes on the floor beside the gun. We looked at it at the same time. It was the little yellow card from my pocket.

* * *

"You call me when you're done. I'll be right out here waiting in the parking lot," my mother said the very next Monday outside of the Hell Hath No Fury House. "I won't leave you."

"I know, Mama," I said. She'd stayed with me in my bedroom the night before and we'd called HHNFH in the morning to see what I needed to do to get more information. This came after a long talk where we agreed that I needed help if I was going to get the twins back and feel any sense of normalcy in my life. The woman on the phone said I was lucky because there was an orientation that night. All I needed was a pen and a pad. Be there at 7:00 p.m. It was free.

The House was really a house. A little red and white craftsman in the middle of a swarm of gray buildings. There was a mailbox. A white picket fence. A porch with a row of rocking chairs.

"I'm proud of you for doing this."

"You've said that a hundred times," I said.

"Well, you said you weren't going to get counseling and now you agreed. I think that's a lot to be proud of."

"Hold on," I started. "I agreed to get help. We don't know if this is all counseling or what." The woman had been very vague on the phone. "I'm just going to see what it is. If it helped Kerry, maybe it can help me."

"Good words," my mother said.

The house was furnished in a mix of dainty Victorian antiques and country whimsy. There were pictures of women from aged black and white photos to color all over the walls in different kinds of antique frames. Some I recognized—Princess Diana and Juanita Jordan—but others looked like women who were just from around the area.

There was a woman sitting at a desk in the foyer. She smiled at me. Introduced herself as Sarah Ferguson and asked if I could sign in. There was a spiral notebook with REGISTRY written on the cover.

"I wanted more information," I said.

"Don't worry. They'll cover everything in the meeting," she

replied. "Just relax." She bent over and picked up a dramatic champagne bucket with little cards in it. "And take a name tag."

I picked out a card and then another.

"But these already have names on them," I said.

"Yeah, we don't go by real names in the meeting. Some members are very private. Just pick whichever name you like. It won't matter. We're all going through the same thing." She held the bucket out to me. "Go on."

I pulled out another card. Jennifer Aniston.

"Great choice," Sarah Ferguson said. "I love her hair."

I pinned the card to the pink sweatshirt I'd found in my mother's closet.

"Now, go on into the room and have a seat," she said, pointing to a set of sliding wooden doors. "We'll get started in just a few minutes."

At first there were just four women, including myself, in the meeting room. It was a huge space where it was clear they'd gutted out a wall dividing once-formal dining and living rooms. Fifteen or so chairs were arranged in a circle and a table with juice and cheap cookies was set up in the corner.

We were just sprinkled around the room. It was obvious we were the new people, quiet and focusing mostly on the buzz of the ceiling fan.

"It's getting hot out there," one woman said. "Much too hot for May in Atlanta."

We all nodded, but went back to watching the fan.

Soon the room got noisy. Women with badges reading Elin Nordegren, Sandra Bullock, and LisaRaye laughed aloud at the punch bowl like old friends and one said, "Wait until we get started! I am so telling on you, Ms. Kathy Ambush!"

Madonna, who was seated next to me, asked who that was and I said I didn't know, but later the "ringleader," whose name tag said she was Carol McCain, would explain that Kathy Ambush was Clarence Thomas's first wife.

"OK, you furious women, settle down," Carol McCain said, walking into the room in a black yoga outfit similar to the one Kerry had been wearing at lunch. I saw a sign out front that said there was a weekly yoga session in the backyard. "We need to get started and I hear we have some new women today, so there's no time for your angry chitter-chatter."

The women growled at her playfully and started taking their seats.

"For those of you who are new, I'm your ringleader, which simply means I'm the group leader for this week. I'm one of three psychologists who run this Hell Hath No Fury House and we're a nonprofit counseling support group for women who are considering or going through divorce. We provide these free group sessions three nights a week to about seventy-five women in the metropolitan area and we also do private meetings daily upon request—those will cost you." She stopped and everyone laughed. "We like to think of HHNFH as a gathering place for stunned souls. For women who thought their marriages would last forever but were shocked and scorned and made furious by the reality that they didn't." People were clapping and nodding along. "Our goal is to help our furious sisters admit to their pain, accept it, and get on with the work of healing their lives. Our approach is different than most. We don't want you to pretend what's happening isn't affecting you. We say, get angry. Break something. Tell people how you feel. We believe that accepting those actions is the only way you can move on. In meetings, we commonly have three rules: no names, no lies, no fake recovery. If you don't want to tell the truth, be quiet. If you haven't moved on, admit it."

Sarah Ferguson handed out an agenda. There was a review of old topics from the week before. One woman who'd slashed her husband's tires had to go to court and she gave her update. Another woman finally agreed to let her ex-husband see their children after two years and she shared what it was like seeing him again.

"No, Ivana, you shouldn't have scratched his eyes out. I'm glad you didn't," said Vivica Fox, who was white with red hair.

"But I want to so badly. Is there something wrong with that?" Ivana Trump looked at the ringleader.

"No, I can't say there's anything wrong with *thinking* about it. My question concerns why you think you want to do it and what it would've solved had you done it," she said.

"It's been two years since the divorce, but I still feel it like it was yesterday," Ivana Trump admitted. "He took me for a ride. A real ride. Stole my money. Froze my bank account. I couldn't feed my children and then he told the judge I wasn't a fit mother. Thank God she could see through that. The day the divorce was final, he was laughing. And said he was happy to get rid of me and my baggage. I wanted to hurt him. I wanted to wipe that smile off his face and make him hurt like I was hurting."

I found myself leaning in and nodding with the other women. Ivana's story wasn't mine, but it sounded like mine. She sounded like me.

"The only thing I could do to get over that was to keep the kids from seeing him. I know it was wrong. He was a shitty husband, but he was good to my girls. But I just, I wanted him to hurt."

"But you moved on," someone said.

"Took me two years of being with you guys and a lot of wine, but I did, and I felt like the bigger person this weekend when we went to meet him. I was OK. But when I saw him, I still wanted him to know where I was at and how I was feeling. I didn't really want to hurt him. I know it wouldn't solve anything, but it was a good image. He just has such beady little eyes."

"Mine, too," said Juanita Jordan.

"Mine, too!" someone else called.

"Well, what about the new furies?" the ringleader asked. She had all of us new women in the room introduce ourselves by saying why we were furious and how we knew we were.

"My husband, Reginald, he wants a divorce," I said, expecting to go on, but I didn't know what else to say. I didn't know what I wanted to say to these strangers.

"And how do you feel about that?" the ringleader asked.

"Angry. I feel very angry. The situation, it's . . ." I paused and looked around the room, stopping at the woman who'd said her ex-husband stole her money. "I thought I knew him better than this. But I guess I didn't."

We kept going around the room and then a few older members answered a question the ringleader had posed the week before: what are the good things you remember about yourself before you got married?

The women opened the writing pads they had on their laps and began to read aloud, taking turns.

"I had great hair," Madonna said.

"I was a dreamer," Sarah said.

"I could give a great massage!" Juanita said.

"I was a good hiker. I hiked the Appalachian trail," Vivica said.

"The whole thing?" someone asked.

"The whole blasted thing!"

"What about you, Jennifer?" Madonna asked me. "Do you remember anything good about yourself?"

I couldn't remember doing anything that was good. I'd gone to school and said my prayers. But those were things that were expected. I didn't have any talents or hobbies. I hadn't hiked a two thousand-mile trail. I was just living.

"I was open to life," I said after a while. "Open to where my life was going."

There was a collective sigh and I felt Madonna's hand on my back.

The ringleader shared the assignment for the next week. We had to define our power. I followed everyone else and wrote this short question on the writing pad I'd brought. While I thought it was vague and kind of odd, I looked at the words and thought I'd at least try to answer.

The women skipped out of the meeting like kids heading to recess. They laughed so loud I thought maybe the punch had been spiked. It was interesting though; I was wanting to laugh with them.

"Good first day, Jennifer," a short black woman who'd been wearing a name tag with Kelis on it said to me as I stood outside searching for my mother's car. She pointed to the name tag I'd accidentally left on my shirt.

"Oh, I forgot to take this off," I said, unpinning the card.

"Oh, keep it. I'm sure you'll be back."

"Why did you say I had a good first day?" I asked.

"You just seem furious enough to make it. It's the ones hiding their pain that I worry about. The quiet ones."

"I can't be quiet. I tried that and I almost hurt myself."

"Didn't we all," she said, stepping off the curb to get into a car that had pulled up. "Didn't we all."

I waved at Kelis as she rode away and noticed a camera crew standing in front of the building on the opposite side of the street. It was already dark outside, but I could see a camera with lights focused on a man holding a microphone.

"Is that A. J. Holmes down there with his fine self?" a woman asked Juanita as they walked out of the picket fence behind me.

"I think it is," Juanita answered, stretching her neck forward so she could get a better look. "Give me back ten years and he might be my second husband!"

"You'd have to get past me first!"

They laughed and walked down the street arm in arm like teen girls.

I watched A. J. for so long I didn't notice that my mother had pulled up right in front of me. He was like something from a movie. Past good-looking. He didn't even look real. I thought to wave a few times, but then I figured he must have women waving at him all day and he looked really busy. And there was no way he'd remember me. Not in my mother's pink sweatshirt. And I was sure my unibrow was back. I think I was blushing before I reminded myself that I was supposed to be angry. Or furious. And working through that. Not looking at A. J. Holmes. That's when my mother honked the horn.

The camera crew, A. J., me, and everyone left in the house jumped at the sound of the horn.

"You see me right here?" my mother yelled to me, lowering her head to look at me through the passenger side window.

"Yes, Mama," I said, opening the door, completely embarrassed and wanting to get off of that street as quickly and quietly as possible.

"Dawn? Is that you, Dawn?"

It was too late.

A. J. was walking across the street with his microphone in his hand.

"Who's that?" my mother asked.

I closed the car door and turned to A. J. as he came up on the sidewalk where I was standing. I saw the faces of the women in the house pressed against the window. Some had come out to the porch.

"Yeah. Hi. Hey. What's going on?" I held my hand over my forehead.

"Working," he said, holding out his microphone.

"Yeah, I saw that. I was going to say hello, but I figured, you know, that you wouldn't remember me."

"Please. Men don't forget beautiful women."

"Thank you?" I said like it was a question.

"So what brings you down here?" He looked at the house. "Some kind of sorority house?"

"No, it's just a support group for women," I said. "And what about you? Why are you working down here?" I tried to change the subject.

"A story I'm working on about international attorneys operating without licenses in the state . . . very interesting stuff."

"Sounds like it," I chuckled.

"Yeah, I didn't feel like coming out here so late, but it was the only time we could catch this particular attorney on camera," he said. "But now I'm happy I did. I got to see you again."

Just like in the office, his kindness was effortless. Almost unbelievable. Men like him didn't say things like that to women like me. I was a librarian. I had gray hairs. I was covering my unibrow. I could hear my mother asking who he was from inside of the car.

"It's nice seeing you again, too," I said.

"Hey, I was wondering, are you free . . . like ever? Maybe we could hang out."

"Hang out?" I asked, hearing my mother's calls for attention getting louder. I bent down and looked at her in the car and said, "Mama, wait!" very harshly and stood back up to face A. J. I forgot to cover my unibrow. "I don't hang out."

"You don't?"

"I'm married." I couldn't believe I was saying that, but it was the only way I knew to respond to that kind of attention from a man. And it was the truth. I was still married. Even if my husband was sleeping with A. J.'s coworker.

He looked at my ring finger. "Guess I should've noticed that sooner."

"It's fine. And I'm very humbled, but I'm not dating."

"Whoa, I asked you to hang out! Not out for a date," he pointed out.

"So you're saying you didn't mean a date?" I was so embarrassed.

"I did, but since you're saying no, I'll change that motion," he said and we laughed.

"Look, you seem like a nice guy, but right now I'm going through some things," I said. "And I can't believe I'm saying this to you of all people, but maybe another time."

"So, get back to you?"

"Yes," I laughed.

"The pretty ones are always the hardest," he said. "Well, you know where to find me."

"I sure do."

Sharika nearly sounded like she was having an orgasm on the phone as I told her about my run-in with A. J. She moaned and groaned about how fine he was and asked if I'd taken a picture.

"No, why would I do that? I was looking tacky enough in my mother's sweatshirt," I said. "And even if I wasn't, I was so shocked that he was talking to me that I wouldn't remember how to take the picture." I laughed and rolled over on the couch. My mother was sitting in her chair watching the news. We had one agreement: no CNN.

"Why are you laughing? He's hot for you!" Sharika said.

"Nah. He's one of those guys."

"What kind of guy?"

"Those kinds who prey on different kinds of women for attention. They only like you so you like them. So you'll sleep with them," I explained. "I went to college with a bunch of dudes like that."

"What makes you think he's one of them?" Sharika asked.

"He's so attractive and successful and smart," I said. "Come on! Why would he really try to seriously date me? He has like a million or a billion women chasing him. Special women. Exotic women. Not 'plain Janes' like me."

"Some men like that. Not any I date, but some." Sharika laughed. "I say, just be nice to him. You never know."

"And what kind of man tries to talk to a married woman? He claims he didn't see my ring, but come on!"

"Oh no, men can always tell when a married woman is mentally available," Sharika said. "It's like in *Madame Bovary* when Rodolphe corners Emma. He knew she was married, but she wanted to give up those panties, too!"

"I doubt he's ever read that."

"He read you, though!"

"Fine. It doesn't matter anyway. I'll probably never see him again. And while my marriage is a disaster area, it still exists. I couldn't consider something new until I know for sure what's going. Just the idea of something new terrifies me. I think A. J. might just be a good thing to look at and think about."

"Suit yourself," Sharika said. "But don't call me when you need your potato salad stirred. I don't go that way!"

"Oh, you are so gross! Why do I talk to you?"

"Because you don't have any other friends," Sharika quipped. "And the last one—"

"Please don't continue that statement," I said, cutting her off.

"Fine. I guess I'll go into why I actually called you," Sharika said. "I've been doing a little investigating over here. I stopped by Landon's dealership today."

"For what?" I sat up on the couch.

"A little car searching . . . and flirting. I wore my yellow stretch pants."

"No, you didn't." I covered my eyes.

"Sure did. Walked right past Landon's office and, whoops, I dropped my keys," Sharika said dramatically.

"What happened?"

"He came out—after I dropped them the second time—and asked if I needed help. I asked if he needed help and he invited me into his office. Did you see that office, girl?"

"Yes," I said. "What happened next? I can't believe you did this."

"He sat me down. I complained that my feet had been hurting all day from looking at cars. I pulled out my baby oil and massaged my ankles."

"That's gross."

"Don't knock it until you try it," Sharika said, laughing like she was imagining that she was a character in one of the books she'd read. "Landon wasn't grossed out. He was panting. He asked if I was free for dinner. And after I readjusted my breasts and my bra and talked about how much I loved rich white boys, I told him I'd never go out with him, because word on the street was that he was dating the sister on CNN. 'Who told you that?' he asked. I said it was a little birdie."

"Did he ever admit to having dated Sasha? Sleeping with her?" I asked.

"Oh, that's the small fries. My yellow stretch pants get big fries. He said he did have a little friendship with her—that's nasty-speak for an affair—but he broke it off when she refused to let him wear a condom and said she wanted a baby."

I nearly fell to the floor. "He said that?" I shouted. "A baby?"

"What baby?" My mother woke up from having the television watching her sleep.

"Nothing, Mama," I said. "Go back to sleep."

"He said she has fibroids and she has to have her uterus removed within a year. She's hot for a baby daddy."

"She did say something about getting pregnant!"

"Well, that's all I got," Sharika went on. "After I let him massage my ankles, he said the day he broke it off with her, she refused to leave the hotel and completely spazzed out. She stayed there for days, ran up a bunch of bills, and the next time he saw her, she showed up in his office with some black couple begging for work. He was sure she was just doing it to flaunt her next victim in front of him."

"That must've been us," I said. "That must've been Reginald and me."

"Yeah, and there's the bad news. Landon has no intentions of giving Reginald that contract. He said he was just trying to get Sasha out of his office. Sorry."

"I knew something was wrong. That whole setup seemed too good to be true. And the look on Landon's face . . . Reginald's going to be so disappointed when he realizes it was a scam," I said. "But why would she have done that if she knew he'd only fake the contract to get us out of there?"

"So she could seem like Jesus walking on water and turning water into wine. She was just trying to upstage you and scare the crap out of Landon. The rest is none of your business. I know you probably feel bad about Reginald not getting the contract, but he was the mouse who ate that cheese. He'll have to realize who Ms. Thang is on his own."

"I can't believe this."

"Believe it. Old girl is scandalous. A real-life black widow—well, she hasn't killed yet, but it's only a matter of time," Sharika said dramatically. "There's no telling what she might do. Landon said she's one of those people who wants to get her way no matter what. And she's desperate right now. You better watch your back."

"Watch *my* back? What more could she do to me?" I scoffed.

"Trust me. There's plenty she can do. She'll hurt you if she thinks you're in her way. I'm surprised she didn't try to hurt you already."

Something in me clicked. I heard Sasha's voice telling me to drink the last of the wine, holding the cup to my mouth even when I said I'd had enough. I told her I was dizzy. She said I needed to loosen up.

"I need to call you right back, Sharika," I said as this sudden suspicion washed over me.

"But I wasn't done," she protested.

"It'll only take a minute. I swear."

"Fine."

I hung up and looked over at my mother sleeping.

It couldn't be true. There was no way. I got up. I needed to think. To remember.

I remembered the white chalk in the bottom of my glass every night. *"It's red wine, silly,"* Sasha had said. *"That's just sediment from when they made it. It happens with expensive bottles."*

I paced around the room. My thoughts sounded ridiculous, but nothing else made sense. There was no other way for ecstasy to get into my body.

My mother didn't have a computer so I had to look up what I was thinking on the Internet on my cell phone. I couldn't believe I hadn't thought of it before. I searched: the effects of MDMA—emotional warmth, decreased anxiety, enhanced sensory perception, recklessness. I moved from link to link. They all said the same thing. One noted that when taken with alcohol the effects were even more pronounced. Users experienced chills, sweating, blurred vision, faintness, a loss of consciousness.

I remembered the night in the backyard. How the whole ocean seemed to be coming into me. I'd put my tongue into Sasha's mouth.

I nearly dropped the phone.

"I knew she was crazy! I knew she was chicken-coop crazy!" Sharika screamed into the phone after I called her back.

I went into the kitchen so my mother couldn't hear the conversation.

"So you believe that? You really think she'd try to drug me?"

"You said yourself you felt like you were sleeping that weekend. Right? And we both know you don't use ex. I wouldn't put this past her at all."

"But it just sounds so crazy. I keep remembering everything and it sounds so crazy. People don't really drug people," I said.

"Ask all those chicks who get raped in clubs. It's real. Happens all the time."

"That's different. Those are rapists. Have you ever heard of a woman drugging another woman? Why would she do that?" I asked.

"I don't know, Dawn. If you wanted to steal someone's husband, what do you think the best course of action would be? We're not talking about the most sane person."

I believe my mouth hung open for two days straight. My mother kept asking me what was wrong. But I couldn't say it. For so long, I'd felt like I was out of control physically and bodily in my own home. I was losing control in my life. And what was most deceiving about this reality was thinking that it was all somehow my fault. That I should've known better. Now I knew that most of the decisions I'd made that weekend and the days following weren't my fault. That wasn't how I normally behaved. Yelling at R. J., randomly taking off from work, staying up all night, sleeping all day. That wasn't me. That was what Sasha did to me.

I was stunned. I felt violated. Cheated. I wanted to scratch her eyes out. I wanted to call the police. But for what? Sharika and I thought that anything I said would be unfounded. I had no evidence. My husband had left me for her. Everyone would say I was just a jealous, angry woman. And I was. And knowing that, admitting that, was the most powerful thing I could do.

I heard someone say one time that "when you know better, you do better."

Now that I knew Sasha's game, I had to do better.

I woke up one morning and decided that it was time for me to get back in control. I just had to figure out how.

That next Monday, I got to the meeting at the HHNFH early and ready with my pen and pad. I was ready for old business. I had some questions that needed answering.

"Last week, our ringleader asked us to define our power," I said. "When we left, I admit that not only did I not want to answer this, but I also think I didn't know *how* to answer. Maybe that's why she asked the question."

We all laughed.

"Preach, Jennifer," Madonna said.

"I don't think I've known for a long time if or why I'm powerful. I add up everything I do to just needing to do it. If my husband needs something, I just do it. If my children need something, I just do it. The house. The car. My husband's business. The people at my job. I step up and I dig in. I never thought for a second that meant I was powerful." I slid my pad under my seat and stood up like some of the older members had last week when they spoke. "My son has mild autism. I don't talk about it with many people. It's hard. Very hard. Most people don't understand it. They think he's just bad or spoiled. One woman even asked if he was retarded—whatever that means. I thought my husband didn't want to be bothered with him. That he was embarrassed by him. But I was embarrassed, too. I wanted so much to fix him. I wanted him to be OK. To be just like the other kids. So he could enjoy life. I pushed him. I pushed myself. I pushed our family. I ignored my other child. I said I was doing it all for him, so he could be better. I thought that was what made me powerful. What made me a good mother. But now I think it was all for me. He's fine with who he is. And he's fine with sometimes not having me hanging over his shoulder. I think his sister needs me more than he does. I *know* his sister needs me more than he does. And I'm going to try to be better. I have faith that things can get better. And that's what makes me powerful. My faith that things will get better."

I got a standing ovation and a lot of hugs from famous women.

When my mother came to pick me up, I got into the car and said, "Thank you."

"Thank you for what?" she asked.

"For reminding me about faith."

A secret sister from the HHNFH gave me what they called a "Divorce Grant" and I was able to upgrade from the flimsy lawyer my mother had found in the phone book to one who handled most of the cases of the members at the house. I was pretty certain the "secret" sister was Kerry. She'd called me days before to see how I was doing and to tell me that Reginald had contacted her ex-husband's company to set up a meeting. She said she'd gotten 50 percent of the company in the divorce settlement and there was no way she was letting her ex do business with Reginald. I told her I had a custody hearing coming up and I was worried about my attorney. The next thing I knew, there was a call from thc HHNFH talking about giving me a grant I hadn't applied for. I was shy at first, but then with everything on the line, I had to take it. I promised myself I'd give Kerry back every dime once I got myself back together. The ringleader said most women just paid back into the grant. In the justice system, a woman without good representation wasn't likely to see any justice.

After two weekends of me meeting with the twins at the local McDonald's, my new lawyer filed a petition saying me seeing the children in Sasha's house could be psychologically damaging for them. I waited in court to hear the judge's ruling on returning the children to me. My attorney made a special case, noting that I'd passed two drugs tests and was in counseling. I'd had no further contact with the police since that night at the roadblock.

"I can't promise you anything," my lawyer said as the judge walked into the courtroom after taking a break to read over his notes. "But let's keep our fingers crossed."

Cheyenne and R. J. were sitting out in the hallway with Sasha. I growled at her like I'd learned to do from the other women at my HHNFH meetings, but I quickly found my poise when I went to hug the twins. I kept reminding myself that this wasn't about her.

R. J. wouldn't stop kissing me and talking about the pink pool, but Cheyenne hardly looked at me. I knew I had to get her back quickly or I'd lose her forever.

In the courtroom, the judge brought down his gavel and proceeded with his ruling after we sat down. Reginald was seated on the opposite side of the room with his attorney. He had on a tailored suit with cuff links and a pinky ring. No wedding ring.

I turned to my mother and she pointed to the ceiling.

"Pray," she mouthed.

"God help me," I said, turning back around.

"Now, this ruling was difficult," the judge said. "Here in family court, we try to keep the best interests of the children at the center of what we do—even when the parents don't." He looked over at me and I was sure I'd be back at McDonald's the next weekend. "But," he went on, "any parent knows that no parent is perfect. We make mistakes. We fail. We try to do better. Even when we should've known better. Mrs. Johnson, I've looked over all of the interviews from your children's teachers and their pediatricians, even some parents of their friends. And they all say you're an outstanding mother. Now, your actions say otherwise, but your reaction to this situation is very impressive. Counselor, what information do we have to solidify your client's claims that she's able to support her children?"

Right then, Reginald stood up and shouted, "She can't. She has nowhere to live and she doesn't have a job!"

His attorney pulled him to his seat as the judge warned that he'd lock Reginald up if he had one more outburst in his courtroom.

"Judge Bruner, my client is currently living with her mother in a four-bedroom house in Atlanta," my lawyer explained. "She's been placed on a leave of absence from her job with the Augusta Public Library System until she resolves this matter of guardianship and is able to return home to find suitable housing. In the meantime, her mother has pledged to support her daughter and grandchildren. She has part time work."

"Is this true, ma'am?" the judge asked, looking at my mother.

"Yes, sir, your honor."

"Well, with all of this information, I believe it's in the best interests of the children that they be returned to their mother until a final custody hearing following the divorce petition."

"Wait!" Reginald jumped up again. "She's on drugs. I know it!"

"Mr. Johnson, please have a seat," the judge said unamused. "Please don't make me lock you up today."

Reginald's attorney grabbed him quickly. They argued and Reginald stared over at me with a pointed finger.

I felt like sunshine. I hadn't won the war, but this battle was coming to a close.

"Thank you," I said, hugging my lawyer. "Thank you so much."

I ran out of the courtroom and gathered the twins together like they were two hours old and still able to fit together in my arms.

"We're going home?" R. J. asked, but I could tell by his voice he meant the house in Augusta. Reginald had already changed the locks and had a letter sent to the attorney saying I couldn't enter the residence. I was surprised by this action, but I guessed what the women at HHNFH said about people in divorce was true: it brought out the best and worst in people (but mostly the worst).

"We're going to Grandma's house," I explained to R. J. "You remember her house? With the garden out back?"

"I want to go back to my park," he said. "I miss my park."

"I know, baby," I said. "We'll go back there soon."

"What is going on?" Sasha demanded, trying to snatch R. J. from my arms. "You can't have these kids. They're mine."

"Hardly," said one of the court officers, pulling Sasha back. "I need you to back away from these people and let them leave."

"What? What are you talking about?" Sasha pulled away from the officer.

Reginald walked out of the courtroom with his attorney and said good-bye to R. J. and Cheyenne before the officer escorted them into a waiting room with my mother.

"What happened, Reggie?" Sasha asked dramatically.

"I don't know . . . The judge had all of these lies Dawn filled—"

"No, no!" I jumped in. "The judge had the truth and that's why I got my kids back."

"So! Do you think this is going to change anything between Reggie and me?" Sasha said spitefully after quickly getting over the fact that I was taking the children. "We're still going to be together." She jumped in my face and whispered in my ear, "You can have those bad-ass kids anyway. They were tearing up my damn house. Cheyenne and that attitude. R. J. and those freaking outbursts. I'd never have kids like that. I just want the man."

I pulled back my arm to punch Sasha, but my attorney caught me and started pulling me away.

"You know, I hated the idea of that, but the more I think about it, the more I don't care," I said. "I guess we'll just talk about that in court." I pulled away from the attorney and stepped closer to Reginald. "You do know what they call that in court? Adultery? Sound familiar? And there's no need to talk about what happens to adulterers in divorce settlements. . . . Guess I'll be moving back to Augusta faster than you think."

"You'll have to prove it first," Sasha shouted as Reginald stood there looking stunned by my threat.

"Yeah, you're right. I'll need to prove it in court—" I stepped up to Sasha and whispered in her ear, "But even if I can't prove it there, there's a new public courtroom today: it's called the Internet. And I plan to start a full-on campaign to air every piece of your dirty laundry to every person who will listen. You don't need proof for that. Just an e-mail account."

Sasha looked like she was about to faint.

"You wouldn't dare," she said as my attorney got ahold of me again. "You wouldn't dare!"

"I guess you'll have to wait and see."

My mother had prepared what can only be described as Thanksgiving dinner. There was a turkey. A ham. Sweet potatoes from her garden. Macaroni and cheese. Stuffing. Gravy. Everything. There was so much food on the dining room table, we had no place to put our plates.

"Is it Thanksgiving?" R. J. asked, looking around the table as we took our seats.

"No, just a special dinner," my mother said. "I wanted you two to know how happy your mama and I are that you're home."

"Home? This is our home?" R. J. looked around. I was so afraid he'd shut down with all of the changes, but he was more talkative than ever. He'd talked all the way from the courthouse.

Cheyenne was the one who was quiet. More than usual. She was still keeping her distance, but I let her know that I was fine. I was her mother and her place was with me. I wouldn't want it any other way. A psychologist who had met with the twins before we left the courthouse said she'd take some time to come around. I shouldn't push. I just needed to be consistent.

"Every head bowed, every eye closed," my mother said proudly.

We gathered hands around the table.

I didn't bow my head and I didn't close my eyes. I just watched everyone. I looked at my family, looking like a family.

11

I was a part of the crowd laughing at the punch bowl at the HHNFH meeting now. I'd been Madonna and Vivaca, LisaRaye and even Ivana (three times for Ivana—I really liked how that name looked on my chest). I was making fast friends with these women as we openly shared our greatest fears and anger about this hand love was dealing us. Or was it life? Because our lives were what was being dismantled by the loss of our love. It was interesting to see how we all dealt with it. Some women, even the ones who'd left their husbands or were the ones who got caught cheating, were in a rage. They wore their anger in silence. Just sat there in the meetings. Or wouldn't stop talking about how much they hated their husbands even when the ringleader was trying to move us on to talking about ourselves. The ringleader said anger was fine. Expressing it was OK. Being furious was to be expected. But when we denied those emotions or just stayed in them, we risked becoming scorned. And scorned was something far more permanent than fury. It was something that stayed with us and sat inside of us. I knew what she was talking about. I knew if I'd stayed in that bathroom or taken that gun and done anything with it, I would never have recovered. And I was still a long way from anything that resembled a nonfurious woman, but I refused to be scorned.

One time at a meeting I traded name tags with Star Jones. I was Whitney Houston and everyone kept making me sing. And I sounded awful, but she didn't move. She sat there sending texts on her phone. Just quiet. She reminded me of Cheyenne. "You want to be Whitney?" I asked. "No." She looked at her phone. "She has bad hair." I nodded. "You could be right. But she's also not built to break." I pulled off the tag and handed it to her. "And neither are you."

It was then that I finally realized why we didn't go by our real names at HHNFH. It wasn't because of the visibility of some of the women who came in the front door covering bulging eyes with Chanel glasses. It was because we were all in the same situation. We were all sharing the same pain. And who we were wasn't what mattered. It was what we were going through that connected us.

"So, ladies, today is career day," the ringleader said at the start of my eighth meeting at HHNFH. "You were all supposed to bring in personal résumés that were updated with your projected career moves. If you want to be the next Oprah Winfrey, I should see President/CEO of Harpo Entertainment as your current employment status. Let's see what we have."

I was noticing something. When the weekly work assignments at the meetings were focused on something driven by anger or pain, the ringleader had to work hard to get folks settled down. They wouldn't stop volunteering to present their assignments. Some outtalked her and insisted that we continue talking about the top three reasons we shouldn't hire a hit man to take out our former spouses (which was a comical assignment, yet beneficial and probably in line with what at least three women had secretly considered at one point).

In contrast, when the ringleader gave us an optimistic or positive assignment, requiring lots of personal reflection—write a love poem, draw a heart on your sleeve, even saying what was once good about your spouse—she had to force us to the floor. The assignments were done, but sharing what she'd requested was like a vocal reclamation of our former selves. It was an outward declaration that we knew we had to move on. And so many people weren't ready for that. I know I wasn't. I hadn't looked at my divorce papers since the twins came to live in the house with me and my mother.

"Ms. Shaunie O'Neal, I see you have a folded-up sheet of résumé paper in your pad," the ringleader said, speaking to one of the newer women who'd been coming every other week.

"I don't have anything new," she answered, shaking her head nervously. "I'll pass."

Everyone was quiet. Passing was, of course, allowed and even promoted if you thought you would be put in a position to lie to the group, but it was rare.

The woman next to Shaunie O'Neal put her arm around her shoulders.

"OK, what about the rest of you? Where's my next Jackie Collins?"

Some people laughed.

"Come on; don't be shy. Remember, the only way that you can fully visualize your life moving forward is if you plan for it. You have to know where you're going or you'll be stuck in the past." She went and stood in front of the fireplace. Above the mantel one of Maya Angelou's poems, "Phenomenal Woman," was painted on the wall in script. I hadn't noticed the poem at first, but then, at my third meeting, I went and stood by the fireplace and read it. I'd memorized that poem when I was just a little girl. I'd said it at a talent show at my school. "All of you have the potential to be amazing. To be the best. To be exceptional. This is not the end of that opportunity. It's the beginning." The ringleader went on, "I know projecting for your future is scary for many of you, because in your eyes that might mean being alone. And that's frightening. But you can't think that's all there is. Being married, being with someone doesn't and shouldn't define you. You can't let your daughters think that's all there is. You can't let the little girl inside of you think that's all there is. Speak up."

I raised my hand.

"Great, Ivana," she said. "Why don't you come up to the mantel and share since you're so courageous."

I stood up and unfolded my résumé. It was a cream-colored sheet of paper with my name on top. I had to straighten my sagging pants once I got to the mantel—another thing I was learning about divorce was that because of the stress, you either gained or lost a lot of weight (I was falling on the weight loss side and none of my clothes fit).

"Can I say something first?" I asked the ringleader.

"Sure. Be our guest."

I looked around the room slowly and didn't stop my stare until I was looking at the poem above the mantel.

"Everyone said I was going to be something special when I was little—my mother, my friends, the people at my church. And when I got accepted into college, they kept saying it. Everyone was so excited about me going to Spelman. So excited about me getting a college education. They told me—*told me*—I was going to be a doctor or a lawyer. They said that to me. They said I was so smart that I had to be one of those things," I said. "Looking back, I had no clue what they were talking about. I didn't feel special. I didn't feel smart. I had no desire to chase any of those opportunities they said were for me. And that was because I was just trying to get away from my past. I didn't have the energy to care to know how special or smart I was. I had to just use those things to figure a way out of my circumstance. I only used Spelman to get out of the house. And then, once that happened, I signed up for the next step. The only thing that would ensure that I wouldn't have to look back. I hate to think of my marriage that way. I loved my husband for the independent man he was. But I also know that independence was only used to make me more dependent. And, as a result, I don't think I ever really sat and thought of anything beyond him. I went to grad school. I got a job at the library. But it's just a job. It's not a career. It's not something I care to do. The worst part is that I can stand here and say it's not what I want to do with the rest of my life, but I still don't know." I held up my résumé. "This sheet of paper has my name, my current job, and 'mother' on it. I wanted to fill it all in. Make it two pages and add a staple. But you told us not to lie." I looked at the ringleader. "And I couldn't. I don't know what more I want out of life and I don't know how long it's going to take me being on my own to figure that out. It's scary to think I can be so old and not really know myself enough to see my future . . . how I can contribute to the world . . . change it. All I have right now is my basic instinct, and that's to take care of my children. Give them a home. And let them know that Mommy is not going to be beat. And I know that's not as cool as saying I want to be the next Oprah, but we all know it's not common to come out on the other side OK. And I think that's a good enough goal for right now."

Five other women spoke after me. We took turns standing in front of the mantel, sharing our stories and being open about what we hoped would come true. One woman took the week we had to do the assignment to get the ball rolling on a small business loan to start her own day-care center. Another woman was just like me. She had no idea what she wanted to do with her career. But she'd always wanted to take a hot air balloon ride. She got up one morning and did it.

The biggest shock of the five was when the old Star Jones, who was always quiet and sending text messages during the meeting and refusing to switch her name tag with me, got up and volunteered.

"I tried to kill my husband. I almost did."

The ringleader got up to go and stand beside Star Jones to hold her hand, but she refused.

"I don't regret it. I've always believed that people should pay for the crimes they commit. An eye for an eye. A life for a life. He gave me HIV. I slit his throat."

"Oh God!" some in the circle shrieked.

"I don't expect anyone in here to feel sorry for me. In fact, please don't. I don't need sorries; I need prayers. This has rocked my soul. And if HIV doesn't kill me in ten months or ten years, my anger will." She went into her pocketbook and pulled out a piece of paper. "I was a high school principal. That's what this paper will tell you." She held the résumé up. "I spent thirteen years in the same school system. Worked my way up alongside my husband. He taught math. I taught science. We were at the same school. He didn't want to go into administration, but I wanted the thrill, the power. Soon, I was driving the ship and my husband was still a mate. I felt guilty. He started fucking my entire staff. He kept fucking me. I was angry about what was going on in closets and back rooms and offices, but I let him fuck me because I was afraid to lose him. I got HIV. He got a slash over the whole of his throat. There was blood everywhere." She was crying, but still standing with the paper. "If you look above my job as a principal, you'll see that my eventual goal was to be superintendent of Fulton County Schools. I'd never written that down before, but it was my dream. I thought I'd get there in ten more years. But now, I know that'll never happen."

"Don't count yourself out, sister," the old Madonna said.

"No, I'm pretty sure that's not going to happen for me." She paused. "I've decided to change my plea to guilty. My lawyer first suggested that I plead not guilty. I'm stopping that. I know what the truth is. And I figure that if I can just stand there and tell those people who I am and what happened, I don't care about the result. I'm pretty sure I won't be superintendent in Fulton County, but I'm also sure I won't be a liar and that's how I got into this situation—because of someone's lies."

"See, I don't know," the woman next to me said after we sat

there looking at Star for a few minutes in silence. "I don't think I would plead guilty. Even if I did it. And I know some of you all think that's crazy, but I can't take seeing another sister go down for some bullshit a brother put her through. It's stupid. And this down-low, gay shit, infecting us black women with HIV has got to stop. I commend you for taking a stand."

A few people actually clapped. Star didn't even blink.

"I thank you for your support, but I assure you, this is no courageous mission," she said. "And I'm sorry, but my husband is white. And I know he's never slept with a man. He got this from my best friend."

We walked like sheep to slaughter out of that meeting. Eyes forward. Hands at our sides. Silent. Sober and somber. There was nothing to say. I think it was because so much of Star's story reminded us of the possibilities of scornful courses of action had we not found the Hell Hath No Fury House and been faced with the demons of our own hell. You know, I don't think Star was talking about her husband when she said someone's lies had gotten her into her situation. I think she was talking about herself.

I couldn't see my mother's car when I walked outside, so I took a seat in one of the rocking chairs and prayed for Star. She was right. She didn't need more people feeling sorry for her. Only her God could help her now.

A white Range Rover pulled up in front of the house. Most of the women had already come out. The ringleader was inside counseling a woman privately, so I was sure the ride was for one of them.

The driver honked the horn several times, but no one came out.

"Are you going to act like you don't see me forever?" I heard this clearly, but didn't look up, knowing the driver was speaking to someone else. "OK, Dawn. This is your last chance for romance."

"Last what?" I looked up.

A. J. was standing in front of the car in jeans and a buttoned-up shirt. He waved at me.

"What do you mean my last chance?"

"Come down off that porch and I'll tell you," he hollered.

A. J. was very proud to tell me how he'd broken down one of my lines of defense. He'd seen my mother sitting outside of the HHNFH with the twins in the backseat. He could tell from across the street they were getting on her nerves and got out of his car to offer my mother twenty dollars to take the twins out for ice cream. He said he was a friend of mine and he could drive me home.

"And she went for that?" I asked, surprised.

"She was pretty cool, actually. It was the little girl in the backseat that had the evil eyes routine locked down," he said. "If looks could kill, I'd be having this conversation with you at my funeral."

'That's my daughter," I said.

"Oh, that was easy to discern. She's adorable. Looks just like you and your mother."

I laughed at this.

"What? I'm funny?" A. J.'s dimples smiled at me. We were standing at the side of the car.

"No. You just seem to have all of the right lines. Know what to say to a woman."

"Lines?"

"It's fine. It's you," I said. "The smooth-operator type."

"Whoa! That's a new one! You're judging me?" he laughed.

"I'm not judging you. I'm saying what I see."

"Maybe I'm saying what I see, too."

I let what he said set in and then we both laughed.

"So, that was a line, too?" he said. "I see what you're saying."

"You're good, though."

"How about we just spend a little time together, so you can see that I'm not just all lines?"

"A. J., I told you, I'm not seeing anyone right now. I'm trying to do something and it's not a good time."

"All right, I guess I'll take my second beatdown like a man." He jingled his keys. "I'll be on my way." He started walking to the other side of the car to leave. "But there's only one thing I'm worried about."

"What?"

"How are you going to get home?"

A. J. wasn't lying. He was more than his lines. He was funny. And smart. And after a while of being with him, you forgot how fine he was and even who he was.

I know you're probably waiting for an explanation of how I got into his car; in a minute you'll probably wonder why in God's name I was at that man's house. I'll sum it all up by asking a question and giving an answer. First, what would you do? Second, I was tired of saying no. Not just "no" to A. J. and his odd campaign to date me or whatever he was thinking, but "no" to fun. To life. To doing something I thought I wasn't supposed to do. I wanted to experience something different. Something not me. Something mad. Jump right in, knowing it might hurt and resort to having fun the whole time. I know some of you are on my side. You were probably wondering how long it would take for me to accept A. J.'s offer, but to the rest of you, I offer you this: go outside and make angels in the snow. Wear a bikini with your gut hanging low. Get blond bangs because you like them—it doesn't matter how dark you are. Date a man half your age and kiss him until the sun comes up. Then, you tell me if this wasn't worth it.

A. J.'s house was a bachelor's pad. I'd never been in one, had only seen one in those "Ladies' Man" skits on *Saturday Night Live,* but there I was in a gargantuan house decorated in so much leather and chrome it nearly looked like a sports bar. There was a red leather chaise longue in the middle of the living room floor. It was big enough to seat at least six people. A fish tank stretched from the living room, through the kitchen and into the dining room and pool room. A. J. showed me a trick he'd taught one of his sharks and raced him on foot from side to side in the house. At first, I thought it was a different shark in each room, but then, sure enough, I noticed it was the same shark following him from room to room.

"He's just greedy," A. J. said, laughing like he was R. J. working on one of his science projects. He'd taken off his shoes and was sliding around on the freshly waxed marble floors in his socks.

When I'd gotten in the car at HHNFH, I'd said again that I wasn't going out with him and I'd be happy if he'd just take me home. He asked what all I had to do at home for the evening. I, of course, had nothing to say. The kids were getting tired of me following behind their every move in my mother's house and I knew she'd love having some time alone with them to make them read the Bible and show Cheyenne how to cook; she was surprised Cheyenne was ten and couldn't cook anything. A. J. saw the weakness in my plans and asked if coming to his place to help him cook something for his church's annual men's day potluck was considered a date. I said I wasn't sure. He asked if I knew how to make macaroni and cheese.

"So how did you get involved in this thing at your church?" I asked, sitting on the big red chaise with a wineglass filled with Sprite in my hand. Part of my agreement with the judge to fulfill my DUI probation was participating in a drug and alcohol abuse program. I agreed to stop drinking until it was over.

"It's a group for men at the church. We meet once a month and discuss issues Christian men deal with in their faith," he said.

"So you're a Christian?"

"Born and bred. What about you?"

"I don't know right now. Religion and I haven't gotten along in a while. Guess I'm trying to find what works for me."

"I get that," he said. "It's better to figure that out than to be a believer not knowing what you're believing in."

A. J. had a way of saying things like that. He made everything sound so simple, so easy.

"And the potluck? Why would you volunteer to make something? You know what most men do—"

"Go out and purchase the nearest store-roasted chicken?" he said, leading me into his kitchen. We were both in our socks and sliding across the floor.

"Yes!"

"I did that last year and my pastor pointed it out the next week at church. This year I have to go hard. No more Kroger chicken for me."

"But you don't know how to make macaroni and cheese."

"That's why you're here!"

That man didn't know how to grate cheese or boil pasta. And it was a good thing I'd insisted we stop at the grocery story to get all of my ingredients because he originally had a box of Kraft Macaroni and Cheese on the counter ready to go.

I stood by his six-burner, gas range stove top, listening to A. J. explain how he decided to go into journalism, and I imagined all of the women who were in love with him. He was perfection. And he didn't know it. He seemed to have everything in his life figured out. And his kitchen. It looked like something out of a catalog, a mall display. There was a bread warmer. Two ovens. A hidden refrigerator. But he admitted that he lived on nacho chips and salsa.

I had to drain the pasta in a paper towel and he watched me like I was a superhero. He kept saying he couldn't have done any of "this" and "that" without me and one time he pinched me on the cheek.

"All right, smooth operator," I said, handing him the bowl of cooked pasta. "My work here is done. Your turn."

"My turn?"

"Yes. You need to put it all together. It's *your* macaroni and cheese."

A. J. stepped up like he was being called to battle. He dipped his hand into the butter and spread two war streaks under his eyes.

"What do I do?" he asked gravely.

"OK, Rambo, just pour the pasta into the casserole dish," I said.

"Oh!"

I handed him the eggs to crack and a cup of milk. Butter. And salt.

"Mix it all together," I instructed.

He stepped away from our spot at the counter.

"Where are you going?" I asked.

"I know I have a drawer with some spoons in it," he said, opening a drawer. "My mother bought some the last time she was visiting."

"A spoon? No. I said mix it up."

"I know. I need a spoon."

"I meant with your hands." I grabbed his hand on the knob of one of the drawers and a firecracker sparked in my gut. I couldn't let go. It was just a touch, but I felt him touch me back. He didn't move his hand from the drawer until I moved mine.

"My hands? In that?" He pointed to the clumsy mixture in the casserole dish.

"Yes. They're clean, right?"

He bent over the dish like it was a dead alien.

"You can't be serious," I said. "You're afraid to put your hands in that?"

"There are eggs in there," he said nervously. "And milk."

"All of which are things I'm sure you've eaten before. You have to mix it with your hands. It's the best way. That way you know you have everything all mixed in right all the way to the bottom. Trust me."

"You sure?" He squinted at the dish.

"Yes."

"But it's so squishy!"

"Just put your hands in it!" I pushed his hand into the dish and he felt around for a second. "That's right. Put them all the way down. Move the eggs around. Break them up."

He squinted and squirmed. I pushed his hands in deeper and soon my hands were in the dish, too. We felt around and mixed the concoction together.

His eyes widened soon and watched.

"You feel that?" I asked. "Mix the pasta and cheese together like a soup. It should run right through your fingers. It's soft. Imagine everyone eating it. Enjoying it. You want it to be tasty until the last serving is done."

He smiled and looked at me.

"This is sexy!" he declared. "Cooking is sexy."

"Yeah, right," I said. "You try doing it three times a day and I'll see what you say then."

He hooked pinkies with me in the bottom of the pan and caught my eye when I looked at him to see what was going on.

"I'll cook three times a day if you're there," he said.

I snatched my pinky away and giggled.

"What?" he asked. "Was that another line? Come on! Give a guy a break!"

After the macaroni and cheese cooled, we sat on the red chaise in our socks and ate half of a second pan we'd made just for us right out of the dish.

First, A. J. said he had to taste it to approve of my culinary skills. And then I had to taste it to be sure the people at the church wouldn't laugh him right out of the door.

"Yeah, you're wifey material," he said, taking a spoonful of the top layer into his mouth.

"Wifey material?"

"Yeah. Confident. Strong. Beautiful. Can cook. You're the type who makes a man get down on one knee."

"I'm sure you have plenty of options in that area," I said.

"How many women do you know who would die to be here making macaroni and cheese with you?"

A. J. sat back and pretended to count, as he massaged his chin.

"Exactly," I chuckled. "Too many to name."

"Sure. There are a lot," he said. "But a wise man doesn't take what's given to him. He wants to know what's behind door number three."

"Hum . . ." I nodded. "That sounds smart. I wish someone had told me that a long time ago."

"So what about you? You're always getting on me. What's your situation, Miss Lady?"

My head quickly filled with anxiety. I realized that this was the first time someone I didn't really know was asking me directly about what was happening in my life. I hadn't decided yet how I would respond.

"The situation?" I stalled.

"Yes, your situation. What you keep saying you're working through. Your marriage, right?"

"He's filed for divorce. He cheated on me." I dropped my spoon into the dish.

"Tough break, eh?"

"It's definitely tough. But it's getting easier," I said. "I can't believe I said that, but it is getting easier."

"He's the father of your two children?"

"Yeah. He's not the worst father, and that's really been the hardest part—trying to figure out what to do with our children. We've been going back and forth about them all summer. They're back in school in two weeks and we now need to decide if we're going to enroll them in school in Atlanta or Augusta. It's a whole big mess."

"My parents got a divorce when I was nine," A. J. said.

"Really? What was it like?"

"I think it hurt them more than it hurt me. My dad cheated and when my mother found out, she packed up me and my two older sisters and we moved into a motel. I hated it for a little while—the motel and living in one room with three women—but the older I got, the more I understood what she did. I was proud of her for being so strong. I only wondered why it took her so long to leave."

"And what about your dad? What's your relationship like with him?" I asked.

"It's great." He shrugged his shoulders. "My father was wrong for what he did, but the fact that he did it was just proof that he wasn't supposed to be with my mother. It didn't make him less of a father or a bad human being. His relationship with my mother was over, but neither one of them really knew how to let it go. I think maybe that when you lose something that you really liked, you have to consider that maybe you were supposed to lose that thing and stop looking for it so you can find something else."

"There you go again," I said.

"No, that wasn't a line!"

"No. I mean, sometimes you have this way with words—with saying things in a way that makes it sound so simple. Like it was the perfect thing for me to hear at the perfect time. Just what I needed." I picked my spoon back up and took a huge helping of the macaroni and cheese.

"Hold up, Cookie Monster," A. J. said, pretending to karate chop my hand that was holding the fork filled with macaroni and cheese. "Unless you plan to come back here tomorrow morning, I need you to back away from the cheese."

He jumped up and snatched the dish.

"Oh, one more," I chided, pointing my spoon at him and the dish as I got up to chase him into the kitchen.

"No! This is mine! Control yourself, woman!"

He slid through the living room, nearly falling two times before I cornered him in the kitchen.

"You wouldn't take food from a poor man . . . would you?" he asked.

"There's still another pan," I said.

"That pan is for Jesus."

"If you don't give me more food, you'll see Jesus!" I joked.

He nervously set the dish on the counter and started laughing as I dug in.

Soon we were both laughing almost hysterically.

"You're fun," I said to A. J., standing behind him as he dropped the empty pan in the sink.

"Thank you," he said. "You're fun, too."

He turned to me.

"I have a confession," he said.

"Oh, no. Here it goes. You need a kidney? You're part of some freaky Atlanta sex ring? You're gay?"

"What?" he asked. "And hell no."

"Your confession . . ."

"Why would it be any of those things?"

"I don't know. What is it?"

He took a deep breath and sighed.

"I heard you and Sasha fighting at the office," he said. "I know your husband's living with her."

"Oh no," I said, feeling as if I suddenly shrank to a nickel.

"I didn't want to say anything. I wasn't going to say anything. I didn't think I'd ever see you again, but—"

"So you knew this whole time? Who I've been talking about? What I've been going through?" I don't know why, but this, the idea of him knowing something so personal about me, was humiliating. I knew he'd know soon or that it would come out at some point, especially if we were to continue being friends—I mean, he's Sasha's coworker. He sees her every day. But I thought I'd have a chance to do it on my own terms.

"Yeah. CNN isn't the Pentagon. Those walls are paper thin. I'm sorry."

"Sorry about what?"

"That she did that to you. That she took him."

"She didn't take anything from me. And really that's none of your business," I said, walking out of the kitchen.

"Where are you going?" He chased behind me. "I'm sorry I didn't tell you sooner. I didn't think it would be this big of a deal."

"I knew I shouldn't have come here." I bent down and reached under the chaise to get one of my shoes.

"Wait, Dawn. Let me explain. I wasn't trying to trick you or whatever you're thinking. I just wanted to get to know you."

"What am I, some kind of charity case? Hum?" I sat on the chaise and put my shoes on. "You felt sorry for me and you wanted to save me? Help me? Have sex with me?"

"No! No! You're taking that too far," he said. "None of that. I'm not like that. I keep telling you. Look, all I wanted to do was get to know you. I knew that the first time I saw you."

He sat beside me on the chaise.

"And I'm supposed to believe that? You wanted to date me, and then you found out my marriage is a disaster and your coworker is having an affair with my husband. And you still thought it was a good idea to date me? Highly unlikely."

"I didn't think of it like that."

"So how did you think of it? You wanted to get me into your home so you could romance me? Hum? Get me to cry on your shoulder? Maybe sleep with you? Kiss you? Is that what you wanted? To kiss me? To make out with me like we're some kind of pubescent teens? Or a—"

A. J. grabbed my arm, turned me to him, and kissed me. I was still talking, but my words stopped immediately. And as I felt the heat from his lips on mine, I knew this was something I'd have to do again and again. I think my shoes shot right off my feet. Or did I kick them off? Or did he take them off?

We sat there and kissed forever. And I loved it.

But I had to stop it. Sex was far from my radar. Feeling that kind of intimacy was probably the last thing I wanted. The kiss was enough.

I thought A. J. would be annoyed or upset by my limitations, but he just smiled and kissed the palm of my right hand.

"When you're ready," he said, "I'll be here."

A. J. drove me to my mother's house with the windows down and the music up high. We listened to those old romantic songs they play at night on the radio, sneaking looks at each other and smiling at whatever we saw for no apparent reason.

It was so late that it was almost early and although I hadn't been anywhere but to his house, I felt like I had been on a date. And that feeling was exhilarating. I felt new. Or maybe not as old as I had that morning when I woke up. I wanted to go and buy some new perfume. High-heeled shoes. I thought of Mrs. Harris.

Before we left the house, A. J. explained that he'd always been a sucker for brown skin and when he saw me in Sasha's office, he'd thought, *she's cute*. Then, when I spoke, he'd thought, *she's smart*. Then he'd noticed my wedding band and thought, *she's taken*. He'd given up the idea of trying to talk to me, but when he got to his office and heard the fight with Sasha, he couldn't get me out of his mind. The attraction had nothing to do with my being vulnerable, and everything to do with the prospect of me being free.

"Next week?" A. J. said, pulling in front of the house.

"What about it?"

"Can we hang out again next week? Maybe we could make lasagna next time!"

"Oh no. Please don't mention lasagna," I said, remembering Sasha slipping her recipe into my hand. "And why would I want to come to your house next week to cook? We did that tonight!"

"I know, but I had so much fun just sitting in the house and talking to you," A. J. said, rolling up the windows as the breeze we'd gotten while driving had stopped and the late July heat was sneaking into the car. "I get so bored with dating sometimes. It's like the same old thing. And I never really get to know the women—well, I know what they like to eat."

I laughed, but A. J. kept a serious frown.

"No. Really. I know Lisa likes steak at Chops; Deena likes the anchovies on the salad at Maggianos; Michelle likes the mussels at Après . . . I could go on and on."

"It can't be that bad," I said.

"It is. Trust me. Women see me and they think of money and being able to say their man is on television. I'm not stupid. I know if I was any other broke brother out here working at the bus station, 95 percent of the women in my phone wouldn't call me."

"That can't be true," I said. "You're a cool guy. And you have to take the good with the bad. You had to expect that you would be chased by these women when you made your career choice. Just accept it and make the best of it."

"You're right. I do. I just know I have to look for something special," he said. "And speaking of the job, I don't know if you know it, but CNN isn't renewing Sasha's contract next season. They're canceling her show."

"What?" I looked at him. "I mean, why? Are you serious?"

"Unfortunately, I am. Ratings are down and she's not attracting any new groups. It's a numbers game," he explained. "Plus, she's not exactly nice to producers. Always has that chip on her shoulder."

"Does she know?"

"She was pulled into a meeting yesterday. She knows."

"Wow. That's awful. What's she going to do now?"

"It's media, so she'll probably stumble around for a little while, but she should be OK in the long run," A. J. predicted.

"But what about that house? It must be so expensive. How's she going to pay the bills?"

"The house? Oh, that's not her house. She's renting it," A. J. said. "You didn't know that? It belongs to one of the producers. You thought she could afford that on her salary?"

I remembered the maid, the chandeliers, Sasha walking around the house like a diva in her dark shades.

"But what about the pool? She has her initials in the bottom of the pool," I said.

"What? S.B.? The producer's name is Scott Barnes."

"But it's pink!"

"And he's gay!" A. J. laughed. "What's the deal with all of the questions and concern? I didn't think you'd be so mature about this. I kind of thought you'd be happy. You know, with everything she's done to you."

"I think I thought the same thing," I said. "I know I did. I wished for it. But right now, I'm just in shock. Who's taking her place? Are they going to create another show?"

A. J. smiled faintly.

"I got pulled into a meeting, too. They're moving me to her slot."

"Oh my God! That's a good thing. Right?"

"A very good thing." A. J.'s smile grew.

I reached over and hugged him.

"You must be so excited. I can't believe you kept that inside all night. Why didn't you tell me?" I asked, pinching his chest playfully.

"I didn't want tonight to be about me," he said. "I wanted to get to know you."

"When did you find out?"

"Today."

"And you came all the way to the HHNFH and didn't tell me?"

"You were the first person I wanted to see."

* * *

I was doing the funky chicken dance through my mother's doorway. I hadn't been able to feel my excitement about Sasha's dismissal in the car with A. J.—I'd been stunned and had too many questions—but once I got in the door and he waved before driving off, I felt my arms springing up and my legs kicking out. And somewhere in my head Kool and the Gang were singing "Celebration." It was a petty party in my body, but I let it loose.

"What you dancing around down here for?" my mother asked, tiptoeing down the steps to see me walk into the house.

"Oh, nothing. Just doing what I was told to do in therapy! *'Celebrate good times, come on!'* " I sang and pulled my mother into a two step.

"They told you to dance?" she asked, stepping back from me.

"They told me to accept my emotions. And right now, I'm glad the wicked witch is going down, so I'm going to dance. *'Celebrate good times, come on!'* "

"You are so crazy, girl," my mother said, laughing, and I could tell she was a little excited to see me so happy. "I thought this was about that man. You sure it's not about him?" She grinned and went to sit on the couch.

"Is that why you're still up, Mama?" I asked. "About a man." I stopped dancing and looked at my mother sitting on the couch. It was 3:00 a.m. and she was still fully clothed. Her eyes were wide open. "You've been waiting for me? Waiting up for me to come home?"

"No . . ." She hesitated. "OK. I was. Who is he? Where'd you two go?"

"He's A. J. and that's none of your business," I said, sitting down next to her. "Why do you care anyway? I thought you would be all upset about me making new friends. I am still married. And the church looks down on that."

"You can't live your life by all of those old rules those fuddy-duddies make up," she said. "This is *your* life. As long as you check in with *your* God, I am all right with that."

"Mama!" I looked at her surprised. "I can't believe I'm hearing all of this. From you? I'm so proud."

"There's a lot about me you wouldn't believe. Spare me the drama, little girl," she said, getting up from the couch. "Now, let's go in the kitchen. I got you some ice cream and I want to hear all about this man. And who's the wicked witch?"

12

"We deserve love. We give love. We offer it freely. We open our arms and we love everyone, but we must continue to be open to getting it, to receiving it, because we deserve it," we all read from cards in a circle at the HHNFH. We were dressed in white. Had taken off our shoes and gone into the backyard of the house. Lit torches gathered us into a circle. We had no name tags.

"You have to believe this," the ringleader said. "To know that you are worthy. You've always been worthy of an infinite love. The kind you dreamed of. The kind you deserve."

We read the cards again aloud. It was love day. What the ringleader said was us making a sincere decision that we wouldn't let our fury, our anger at our current situations bar us from accepting love into our lives.

Some women cried. Some hadn't yet responded to the idea of opening themselves to loving again. There was still a lot of anger and resentment.

I'd gone out with A. J. a few times and even held his hand once, but I knew I was closer in my feelings to these weeping women than I was to fully opening up myself to him. I still saw Reginald in my dreams. Still wondered what he was doing and how he was doing. And although I hadn't said more than, "When are you coming to get the twins?" and "Don't be late," I still loved him. What I needed, A. J. couldn't offer me. I had to find it myself.

But I agreed. Or rather, I knew that love wasn't something I'd never see again. It would all come in time. I was focusing on understanding and embracing the new love I'd discovered in my life. My relationship with my mother was blooming so independently and effortlessly I wondered where she'd been all of my life. She was amazing. An open heart that bled for me after I'd left her for so long. And I had to make up for that lost time.

We enrolled R. J. and Cheyenne in a school a few blocks away from my parents' house. I was surprised that there was more classroom support and assistance available for R. J. He loved his new school. There was a special bus that came and picked him up from my mother's doorstep every morning and while I was ready for him to cry and hold my hand, he ran off proudly down the walkway every morning. He had friends. A group of boys his age, who took guard at the back of the bus and even started knocking on our door every day after school. I tried to follow behind him. Tried to take him to find a new park to play at. A new sandbox. But he laughed at me. "I'm too old for that now, Mama," he said. And I'd forgotten that, but he was right.

Cheyenne wasn't so easy about the transition. She wanted her old friends. She wanted her old room and seemed nervous about every little move I made. She was still watching me and I knew she was afraid of whatever was to come. I tried every day to connect with her. But I couldn't give her certainty about something I was so uncertain about.

The dissolution of my marriage, of our lives was something I never saw coming. And although I saw myself as the mother who had to have all of the answers for my little girl, I couldn't answer her, because I wasn't able to answer why myself.

"Big day coming up," the ringleader said, sitting beside me in one of the rocking chairs outside of the house when the meeting was over.

"Yeah, we have our mediation next week."

"Nervous?"

"Numb is more like it," I said. "I don't know what to feel right now. I'm so tired of fighting. I was so blind about everything." Reginald and I were set to meet with our attorneys to discuss the possibility of dividing our only asset. "The house was in his name; I never bothered to mention having myself added on after his parents died. I didn't think I needed to watch my back like that."

"A lot of women think that way. Don't feel guilty about that. You just have to put measures in place now to change that."

"I don't want anything from him. I just want to make sure my children get what they're owed. You know?" I said. "He's not the kind of father who'd stop taking care of them, but if anything happened to him, I need to know they'll be OK."

"Have you told them about the divorce?" she asked.

"I can't even say it to them. I don't think I can say it at all. I keep calling it, 'the situation,' " I admitted. "I can't even think it. And I know it's coming, but it just seems so ugly. Such an ugly word. I never thought I'd be the type of woman who had to say that word."

"Who does?"

"I was a good wife to him and I expected him to be good to me."

"And you had every right to expect that. You certainly did," she said.

The next week, A. J. and I were in his truck on our way back from my meeting. He'd been my scheduled weekly chauffeur for the last months as I waited to get my license back from the DUI conviction and my mother was now saddled with the task of shuttling the twins everywhere.

A. J. and I were debating about whether or not wildlife activists should let the panda population die when he pulled in front of my mother's house and I noticed Reginald's new blue pickup truck parked in my mother's driveway.

"Pandas wouldn't even survive in the wild. They don't mate naturally," A. J. was saying. "All they do is eat and sleep all day. Pandas don't even like other pandas. They avoid each other."

"But they're cute, so we should save them." I repeated the stance I'd taken since we'd started the debate.

"But why? Everything in nature is set up for them to fail. Survival of the fittest? Come on!" A. J. laughed and I felt him looking at me. He'd stopped the truck right behind Reginald's truck and I was looking to see if Reginald was inside. I was trying to consider any reason Reginald's truck would be at the house. I had my cell phone on and in my hand, so I knew there wasn't anything wrong with the children. My mother would've called me.

"So we should continue to support this dying species just because they're cute and cuddly?" A. J. asked.

"Yes," I said distractedly.

A. J. must've noticed how I was distancing myself from the conversation. He finally looked out of the window to discover the blue truck.

We sat there looking for a second. I'd made out Reginald's head and shoulders in the driver's seat.

"That's not your uncle, is it?" A. J. asked.

"No."

"Hum. Is he supposed to be here?"

"I don't think so. Maybe my mother called him."

Reginald got out of the truck and looked at me and A. J. He put his hands in his pockets and leaned against the truck.

I could feel A. J.'s alarm. I picked up my purse from the floor and looked at him.

"Don't feel any kind of way," I said. "I know what you're thinking—here you are in a car with this man's soon-to-be ex-wife."

"I'm not concerned about that," he said. "I'm wondering if I need to walk you to the door."

"No. That'll just make things more awkward. I don't want to get you involved."

"Are you sure?"

"Completely," I said. "And he's not the violent type." I looked at Reginald. "He probably just wants to talk about the mediation tomorrow." I opened the door.

"Maybe I could sit here and wait for you to go inside."

"A. J., you don't need to do anything. I'm fine. I'll call you tomorrow." I kissed my fingertips and brushed them against his cheek.

"You'd better. I have these tickets to the zoo this weekend," he said. "I'm not walking around there alone, looking like the new black Tarzan."

"Is that what this whole panda conversation was about?" I said, laughing. "I was beginning to think you were crazy."

"No, crazy is spending a billion dollars every year to save a species that clearly wants to commit mass suicide—"

"Yeah, you're crazy."

I got out of the truck, keeping my eyes on Reginald.

"Do your research," A. J. joked. "Do you think the twins would like to go?" he asked. I still hadn't introduced him to them formally.

"We'll see," I said. "That might be a good idea."

I waited for A. J. to take off and get clear down the street before I walked over to Reginald. I didn't know if something could happen out there, but I knew I didn't want it to happen in front of A. J. He had no stake in my private life and getting him involved would only put a cloud over something that had become so bright in life.

"Something happen?" I asked Reginald. We were far from "hello" and "good-bye."

"Hello," he said cheerfully. "How are you?" He smiled and nodded to me.

I didn't recognize anything about him. Not his clothes or his shoes. Not the truck. Even his hair was cut differently.

I saw a light flash from the living room as someone moved the curtains.

"Did my mother call you?" I asked, ignoring his small talk.

"No, I was just around here—Hey, who was that man?"

"What?"

"Are you dating him?"

"I don't think that's any of your business." I folded my arms.

"I wasn't asking like that. I was just wondering, you know, if you're seeing anyone."

"Why would you wonder that? You're seeing someone. Look, just cut to it. Why are you here? You don't get R. J. and Cheyenne until Friday. What do you want?"

He pushed his hands deeper into his pockets and a look of seriousness came over him.

"The mediation is tomorrow," he said.

"I know. What about it?"

"I was just thinking . . ." His voice trailed off and I could tell that he wanted me to try to pick it up and ask what he was thinking about, but I stood with my arms folded and my mouth closed. "Remember when we moved to Augusta?"

"Yes. I was twenty-one and had never been anywhere else outside of Atlanta. Did you and Sasha enjoy Cabo? That is where you two went so she could clear her head and think about what's next for her career. How's she handling getting fired?"

"She's fine. But why did you bring her up? We're talking about us. About when we moved to Augusta."

"No, you're talking about when you and I were married and you took a vow before God to remain faithful to me. And then we went to Augusta. And then you cheated with Sasha. So, I think it's all very relevant to bring her up." Months ago, if you told me that I'd ever know how to speak to anyone like this, I would've called you a fool. But every discussion I had with Reginald was making me better at the art of argument.

"When we moved into my parents' house, we lived in Cheyenne's room. We had to share that one bathroom in the hallway." He laughed. "Remember that?"

"Yes."

"You used to wash your underwear in the middle of the night and hang them in our bedroom because you didn't want my mother to know you wore colored underwear."

"She said they caused cancer."

"Right. But you loved the little pink ones," he said. "And when we had the twins. The house is so small, but we couldn't keep up with them. Remember when they started walking and Cheyenne discovered how to push the front door open?"

"She almost made it to the sidewalk," I recalled, laughing with Reginald.

"We haven't been able to keep her in the house since."

I smiled, remembering Cheyenne sitting at the screen door, just wailing when we got a latch put at the top of the door to keep her in. She looked up at the latch and hollered so loud the neighbors could hear her.

"What do you want, Reginald?" I asked.

"I don't know if we should be moving so fast with this divorce," he said straightforwardly.

"What? But you—"

"No. No. No. Listen to me," he said. "I've been thinking about us and our family. I don't know if I'm ready to just let it all die like that. What we had, it wasn't perfect, but we had something. We were together."

"Don't you think you should've thought about this before you slept with my best friend? No. No. Before you so obviously chose my best friend right in front of me?"

"I'd prefer not to talk about that. Sasha and I aren't exactly happy. There's a lot going on."

" 'I'd prefer'?" I repeated, laughing at the insanity in his statement. "I don't care—no, I don't give a damn what you prefer. Is this because things aren't going so well for Ms. Bellamy? Now you realize what a crazy, psycho bitch she is? Or is it because things aren't going well for you?" I stepped closer to him. "I heard about how you've been losing clients. Canceling calls. All to be with your sweetheart. In her rented house. And I know you didn't get the Landon contract."

He looked at me.

"You've got this big fancy truck and nowhere to drive it."

"Dawn, I'm just—"

"I don't want to hear anything you have to say," I said, turning to walk to the house. I stopped. "You know, I can't believe you had the freaking unmitigated gall to bring your black ass over here talking about what you prefer. I'd prefer not to be living in my mother's house and living off of her life savings. I'd prefer not to have to uproot my children from their home and their school and their friends. I'd prefer not to be humiliated by the experience of knowing that everyone I know knows that my husband was dumb enough to run away with an insane lunatic."

"I love you," Reginald said.

"Don't you dare!" I cried, feeling my heart breaking again. I turned to the house and started walking up the path.

"I don't want this divorce," he said, grabbing my arm.

I trembled.

"You started this," I said. "You'll finish."

"Tell me you don't love me, too. Tell me you don't miss our family. Miss us being together."

I wouldn't turn around, so he walked in front of me.

"Tell me you don't love me and I'll let it go. Just say it."

"I don't have to say it; I know it," I said. "Get out of my way."

The front door opened and my mother turned on the outside light.

"Everything OK out there?" she asked.

"Yes, Mama," I said. "I'm coming in." I looked back at Reginald. "I'll see you at the mediation tomorrow."

"He was out there all night," my mother said, opening the door for me. "I didn't know what to do."

"You could've called me."

"I didn't want to scare you."

"Did the kids see him?"

"No. I've had them in bed since 8:30. He got here at nine," she said. "What did he say?"

"Nothing worth repeating."

After eating a plate of food my mother left on the kitchen table for me, I went upstairs to a hot shower and cold bed. I couldn't stop thinking about what Reginald had said. He'd written our memories in my mind and every time I tried to think of something new, an image of Cheyenne gripping his fingers to stand up or R. J. figuring out how to pick up Cheerios flashed. I could feel the memory of my family like it was hours ago since I was in Augusta. I could smell Reginald's work boots in the front hallway. I could hear him singing in the shower. See him sitting on the couch with the kids watching basketball. I missed the confidence I'd had in my life when I had all of those feelings on a daily basis. A twin-sized bed in my mother's house hardly made up for it. Now, I was in fragments.

The call from Sasha must've come after 2:00 a.m. That was the last time I remembered seeing on my alarm clock before I dipped into a dream of chasing a toddling Cheyenne around the house. At first the ring was in my dream, disguised as the house phone. But then I opened my eyes and saw Sasha's name on my cell phone.

I let it ring three times. And then a fourth. It stopped. And then it started again.

"What do you want?" I asked after she called back the third time.

"Where is he?" she snapped.

"He? Who?"

"Don't play fucking stupid with me. Where is he?"

"Tell me who he is and maybe I can help you."

"Reginald. Where is Reginald?"

There's no sentence I can write to describe the irony I felt deep in my soul at hearing this question. It was pleasurable. Almost like the first night of A. J.'s show on CNN, which marked the end of Sasha's. Almost like the afternoon R. J. told me that Sasha had to sell her fast car. I wasn't riding high on these tidbits of information, but they gave a little pleasure. Just enough to make me giggle in knowing that true revenge comes from the universe.

"Have you called him?" I asked, faking concern.

"Bitch, spare me. Have you seen him?"

"No, I haven't," I lied. I figured it would be more interesting to tell her the truth later—see what I mean about becoming a better arguer (hint: play offense and defense)?

"God damnit," Sasha cursed. "I thought he was going there."

"What would make you think that?"

"He's gotten all fucking emotional now. Was talking about his 'family' and said he missed you."

"He said he missed me?" I don't know why, but this mattered to me.

"Don't get excited. He was probably drunk," she snarled.

"Sasha, when did you become the devil?" I asked wryly. "I mean, I knew you in undergrad and you weren't anything like this shell of a human you are now. What happened to you?"

"Well, if you're really concerned, I'll tell you, life happened," she said. "This kind of shit happened. And in order to make sure I came out on top, I had to get smarter than everyone else. Follow me? Great."

"So because of that, you're angry at the world? Angry enough at me to come into my home and break up my family? Angry enough to have an affair with Landon?"

"Landon was a joke. A crackpot."

"I'm sorry to tell you, but the way things turned out, it seems like you were the joke."

"A joke! Are you trying to be funny, Dawnie? Was that your attempt at comedy?" Sasha laughed wildly. "The last thing I remember was you lying in your bed alone and your husband carrying me down a hallway. Now, that was a joke. I laughed at that shit for days. You begging and shit. That was a joke. You should take that pathetic shit on the road."

"Poison any more of your friends lately?" I asked rather casually.

"I don't know. You should ask Reginald. He's taken a liking to my expensive wine. Just like you did."

I felt like coming through the phone and cutting Sasha somewhere. Hurting her.

"All this time, I was actually feeling sorry for you," I said. "I know about your fibroids and wanting to get pregnant."

"Who told you about that?"

"I know about Landon leaving you high and dry in a hotel. There really was no conference. You'd come to Augusta with garbage in your heart. And I even know about how guys used to treat you in college. How they'd run over you and pretend they loved you until things got serious and then they'd leave you. Didn't they?"

"They were fools," she yelled.

"All of them? You think all of them were fools? They can't all be fools. Most of them are married. Almost all of them. They found someone else to settle down with. Just not you. That has to hurt you."

"Fuck you and fuck them," she shouted and I heard tears in her voice. "Reginald doesn't mean shit to me. You don't mean shit to me. None of you mean shit to me! I'm Sasha Bellamy! Do you hear me? I saw your marriage breaking up the moment I walked into your house. You were easy. So fucking stupid. Just like all of those other wives. You couldn't keep your husband if you tried. I did you a favor. Reginald wasn't staying with you. He was bored. I'm the best thing that ever happened to him."

"But now you're calling me to find out where he's at," I said softly.

"Fuck you!" she yelled. "Fuck you! Fuck you! Fuck you! Fuck you! I don't need you. I don't need any of you."

"I'm sorry to hear that."

"I'll pay you back!"

"I'll have the last word. I promise you."

13

I left my mother praying in the lobby of the building where Reginald and I were supposed to meet with our attorneys. We weren't going before a judge. The mediation meant that we would try to sit and come to a compromise about the house before it got to a point where we needed a decision from a judge. I wasn't contesting the divorce. Reginald didn't have any money. I didn't have any money. So the only thing we had to figure out was what would happen with the house. I'd lived there so long and we didn't have a prenuptial agreement, so I had some rights. And after we made an agreement, the divorce would be finalized.

It's interesting how people in buildings and public places look when you have something so heavy hanging over you. You've put on your best business clothes and fixed your mind on your problem. But there they are, walking around in their everyday lives. Going on lunch breaks and laughing with friends at their desks. They might stop and compliment your shoes or ask for the time. Very casually. Very friendly. You smile. You use some robot inside of you to say the time, but you're not connecting. It's all a blur. The entire world.

Mama and I had trouble finding parking, so I was a little late and I expected Reginald to be sitting in the waiting area of the meeting room, but our attorneys were sitting there alone.

We waited for him a while. The attorneys chatted about some local bill that was going into effect.

When Reginald was thirty minutes late, his attorney called him and then Sasha, but got no response.

My attorney suggested that we go wait in the conference room. She joked that the chairs were more comfortable and there was actually a window.

"Did he call you this morning?" his attorney asked me as we sat at the table. "Did he mention he'd be late?"

"I haven't spoken to him today," I said.

Our eyes all floated to the window. We were on the thirty-fifth floor and there was nothing but blue sky.

"I'm sorry I'm late." We turned to see Reginald standing in the doorway in a sweat suit. He came to the table and did an awkward dance with the extra chairs until his attorney motioned for him to come sit near him.

My attorney started by restating the necessity of us meeting, adding what we hoped to gain in the discussion. His attorney did the same and then they began having this delicate conversation between the two of them. They flipped through papers and compared notes.

My attorney submitted a breakdown of my salary and how much I contributed financially to the household each month. There was also a discussion of the money I gave to Reginald over the years when his business was sagging.

I listened, but I watched Reginald. He was slumped over in his seat, looking distantly at the pages. He hadn't shaved, probably in two days, and he looked nervous. Every few seconds, he looked up at me.

"So, what is your client willing to offer in the compromise?" my attorney asked.

"He'll put the house in trust for the children. If anything ever happens to him, they'll get it."

My attorney nodded and checked something on her notepad.

"And in the meantime? Can my client have access to the home?"

"Well, in this matter we're hoping to—"

"Excuse me," Reginald interrupted. He looked at me. "Can I talk to you outside?"

"No," I said.

"Dawn, just talk to me. That's all I'm asking."

I looked at my attorney.

"It's your call," she said. "It's just a mediation. It can't hurt."

"What do you want?" I asked, standing out in the hallway with Reginald.

"I want you back."

"Don't do that," I said. "Don't say that."

"I want you back and you couldn't say you don't love me, so you must want the same."

"Stop it!"

"Do you love me?" he asked. "Do you still love me?"

"Just stop it."

"Tell me you love me!"

"Yes, I love you, but that doesn't mean anything," I said.

"Yes, it does. It means we still have a chance."

"A chance for what?"

He touched my chin.

"To have our life back. To have our family back," he said. "We can do that."

"But you're with Sasha."

"That's a mistake and you know it. You told me. See? You're my better half. You're my eyes. She doesn't compare to you. It's over between us. She knows that."

"But you left me." I started crying. "You left us."

"It was the worst mistake of my life. But in all these years we've been married, it was the first. I never cheated on you. You know that. This was just a bad situation. We can't lose our family because of it."

"I don't know, Reginald," I said as he wiped my tears. "I'm just getting over this. I can't turn back. You hurt me too much."

"I want to make it better," he said, pulling me into his arms. "I want to make it up to you."

"But everything is different now."

"We can change it right back. Right now. We can call off these lawyers and get out of this freaking building. We can go home. To our house tonight. Me and you. We can have it all back," he said and he was crying, too. "Don't you want that?"

"Yes. But I don't know. Maybe it's too late."

"We can change everything back. Let's just do it. I promise I won't let you down. If you give me a chance to hold you again, I promise I won't let you down. I'm your husband."

I fell into Reginald's arms and all of the pain and hurt I'd felt after all of those months away just funneled out of me. I cried "no" until my heart said "yes." I had to try. I had to give my life one more try.

"What happened up there?" my mother begged when I found her. I saw in her eyes what I saw the night before when I came in the house—a fear of what was going on. Of what she already knew, but I was blind to.

"I'm going to Augusta later," I said like a stone. I was walking quickly out of the building with her jogging to stay at my side.

"Augusta? For what?"

I stopped.

"Mama, he's sorry," I said.

"No." She sounded broken somehow.

"He still loves me. I love him."

"No, baby."

"We're meeting at the house later to talk."

"No. You can't go back there. Not after everything you've been through. You can't go back."

"He's my husband. He made a mistake and he said he's sorry. I believe him. He may have made a bad decision, but he's not a liar."

"And what about you? What about what you've started here? Your new life? You're just going to walk away from that?" she asked.

"What life? I live in a house with you. I can hardly pay any bills. I don't have a career. I'm just floating. At least I had something there."

"Well, how are you going to get there? You can't drive," she said.

"Mama, you can't stop me. I'm doing this."

"But what if you get caught?"

"I'm doing this."

My mother repeated herself again and again as we drove home. She threatened to call Kerry. To call the police. Said she wouldn't watch the twins for me. Cried.

I couldn't be broken though. Being back in Reginald's arms had already taken me halfway home and I wasn't turning back. He was my love. Not the greatest. But mine. I was happy, and I wanted her to be happy with me. To trust me and support me.

Once I'd packed a few things and was moving them out to my car, she came out of the house wiping her tears.

"If you do this, you'll see yourself back," she said.

"Mama, you've said that."

"I don't want you to take the children. They can stay here with me for as long as they need. I don't want your mistake to be their burden. Not like I did with you."

"This isn't like that. I promise you. It's going to be good."

14

If someone saw me walking around downtown Augusta that day I was supposed to meet Reginald back at the house, they'd say I was skipping or prancing, maybe bouncing like a ball. I couldn't contain my happiness. It was all over me. The farther I got from Atlanta, the closer I got to Augusta, I was returned to myself. I had to have my husband back. I knew it when he touched me. He was a part of my whole and I couldn't live without him. When you have someone in your life for that long, the idea of moving forward without them, especially when they make it clear they don't want to do that, is impossible. It took my breath away.

I decided to make Reginald and me a big dinner. A romantic night, a meal to claim our new start. I'd bought and planned to cook everything he loved. I proudly put these gifts into my car and looked at them through the eyes I'd had for Reginald when I was 19. I wanted to make him happy. To see him happy. I just needed to get a few more things. One more stop.

As I walked into Target, the sun in the sky had little feathery clouds around it. I know, because I looked. I stopped and looked at the sun and smiled before I walked inside.

"Dinner . . . flowers . . . my baby's favorite cut of steak," I listed slowly to myself, passing a galley of red shopping carts as I walked into the superstore. "I've got everything we need. Even my old Luther CD."

I just needed to get his favorite almond-scented candles. I thought that would be a nice touch.

I got the candles, put a few in a basket I was carrying, and went to get in line to pay. But when I got near the front, I looked over at the Customer Service station and remembered that I still hadn't gotten the pictures from our spring camping trip to the mountains. Reginald had kept begging me to get them, but I was too busy. I headed toward the counter, thinking how cute it would be to have the pictures of us camping with the twins in DeSoto Falls spread out on the dining room table when he walked in the door.

"Ma'am, you picking up?" one of the women in the red vests behind the counter asked.

"Yes, I ordered prints a long time ago. I wonder if they're still here."

"You have your stub?"

"No. I'm sorry," I said.

She took my information and said the prints were done. It would take her a minute to go in the back and find them.

"Can you wait?"

"I'll be right out here," I said, putting my basket on the floor.

"Only be a minute. I'm sure."

The woman disappeared into the back room.

I stepped out of line and looked at the woman behind me.

"Twins?" I said, looking at her bulging belly.

"Twins," the woman confirmed, smiling.

"I have twins, too," I said. "A girl and a boy."

"I'm having a girl and boy, too!"

"Oh, Lord, get ready! The drama will be in full swing from day one," I said. "The key is to keep good people around you."

"Why thanks," the woman said. "I think we're off to a good start."

"Wait," I said, noticing that her stomach was so big, there was no way she wasn't at least in her eighth month. "What are you doing outside? You don't need to be in anyone's Target! You should be on bed rest. Trust me, it's the last real rest you'll ever get."

She laughed.

"I know. I know. I'm taking it easy," she said. "We just had our baby shower last weekend and people kept showing up with gifts we hadn't ordered."

"What a shame."

"Yeah. Target's baby registry got our names confused with a couple in Atlanta. Can you imagine, a couple with the same first and last names living in the same state?"

"That's crazy!"

"I'm here to try to get Target to come and pick up these gifts. It was their computer error."

"Yeah, you shouldn't have to deal with that," I said. I heard the woman who was helping me call for a representative to come to the back to help her.

Someone else called for the next person in line and the woman I was talking to stepped up to explain her situation. I watched as she spoke and pointed at the baby registry machines behind the waiting area.

The line grew longer, so I picked up my basket and went to stand by the machines until the woman who was helping me came back out front.

I looked at the registry machines thinking what an awful predicament the new mother was in.

"They really need to fix these machines. It's a mess," I said affectedly, as I tried to recall every instance of error I'd experienced with a Target registry machine. There were none. But then, out of nowhere, I remembered the conversation I'd had with Sharika at the library about that woman who killed herself. She found out while snooping at the Target baby registry her ex-husband was having a baby with someone else. *"Why did she look up his name?"* I remembered asking Sharika. I couldn't remember if she answered or if the woman was real or from one of the books she'd read.

I looked at my watch. A manager had come out to talk to the pregnant woman. They pointed to the machines.

My voice played again: *"Why did she look up his name?"*

No. That's ridiculous, I thought to myself about what I was thinking. It was ridiculous. I couldn't look up Reginald's name. Then I remembered all of the information from Landon. What Sasha had said about wanting a baby so bad.

No, I told myself. It was ludicrous. Ridiculous. But if it was so ridiculous, why wouldn't I try it? I could try it. Just to prove myself correct. And just to prove that it was ridiculous. There was no way Reginald could've been having a baby with Sasha. He was still married to me! He'd wear protection when he slept with her. Right? Then I remembered that he hadn't used any protection that night in our bedroom.

I clicked the little mouse. I had to prove myself wrong.

The first hit was Reginald and Sasha Johnson in Snellville, GA. And according to the shower date, their baby was probably sitting up by now.

The second was Reginald Johnson and Sasha Tolliver in Athens, GA. Their baby shower was in a few hours.

I decided to try Sasha's last name.

Sasha Bellamy was expecting a little boy in five months. She had no husband listed.

I laughed at my detective strategy. This witch hunt was sad. There had to be at least four or five women in the city with the same name.

I waved at one of the representatives and asked where the woman helping me had gone. He said she'd be right out.

I turned back to the machine and decided I'd kill time by being nosy. I entered Sasha Bellamy's registry to see what kinds of things she was ordering—bottles, nipple cream, a baby bag, bibs, the necessities. I smiled, remembering getting those things at my shower. I'd used maybe half of them.

I kept reading and saw a note the mother had posted for her guests:

> Reginald and I are so happy to share with the world the coming birth of our son. We know it's early for a shower, but we were hoping to say good-bye to all of our friends before we move to my hometown in North Carolina to start our lives. See you all in September. —Love, Sasha and Reginald

"Mrs. Johnson, I have your pictures here," I heard behind me, but my eyes were glued on that screen. I felt my mind shut off. I couldn't think. I couldn't see.

I left the candles on the ground and ran out of the store.

"Do you want the pictures?" I heard the woman call after me.

When I got outside, it was raining. Coming down in buckets. It was late afternoon, but the sky was black. The sun was gone. As I ran to the car, water came up onto my legs.

My face was wet. I wasn't crying though. I was erased. Void. Empty. Emotion couldn't ride me. I just couldn't believe it.

I drove home with the windows down. I let the rain come in and wet everything. It was all I could do to stop from driving right off the road. I had to feel something. To let the fury grow inside of me until I saw Reginald. I'd wield it and twist it into his gut like a samurai sword.

By the time I got to the gate leading into our neighborhood, the prime rib and fingerling potatoes were swimming in a pool in the paper bags in the seat beside me. My bra was showing through my shirt. My hair was soaked. I still wasn't crying.

Reginald's new truck was pulled into his old spot in the driveway. He'd moved it up far enough so I could pull in behind him, but fury drove me right onto the lawn. I smashed into the flowers and bushes and stopped the car right at the front steps.

Reginald opened the door smiling, but when he saw the mess, he rushed out.

"Babe, what happened?" he asked, meeting me as I jumped out of the car. "You slid? Was it the rain?"

I looked at my husband. At his mess. At my life in that two thousand-square-foot box behind him. I was shaking. But I wasn't cold.

"Babe?" Reginald said again. "What happen—"

"I know! I know! I know! You fucking bastard!" I rammed into Reginald's gut, pushing him to the grass.

"What the hell?"

"Don't talk. Don't you dare fucking talk to me." I was on top of him swinging.

"Dawn, what's wrong with you?" He tried to grab my arms.

"The baby. I know. I know about the baby."

"How? Who told—" He pushed me off him and I landed beside him in the grass.

"Does it matter? Does it really matter how I know?" I started getting up.

"Let me explain," Reginald said, getting up on his knees in front of me. "I can explain. I didn't mean to do it. She said she was on the pill—"

I slapped him hard.

"What didn't I do? What?" I asked.

"You did—"

"What?" I hollered. "You tell me. You make sense of this right now. You tell me what I did to deserve such a shitty life. Oh God! Oh my God!" I cried and looked up at the sky through the rain. Vacant of anything to keep me up, I fell into Reginald and he wrapped his arms around me.

"Babe, I can fix it. I can fix it," he said and I swear I almost believed him. Needing to hear anything, I almost believed that this, a child, could be fixed. That's what Reginald did. It was who he was. "That's why I'm here," he went on, "to tell you that I'm going to make everything OK. Make everything like it was."

I started hearing voices. Words splitting my ears. Screaming. Ms. Juanita Jordan's voice saying, "Nothing can ever be like it was." My ringleader holding my hand and whispering in my ear, "No matter what he says, and no matter what you want to believe, it can never be like it was. There's either today and tomorrow or no day and never. The past, dear Ms. Aniston, is prologue." My mother telling me to have hope. Praying over me as I slept on the floor.

I pushed away from Reginald.

"What?" he asked still on his knees.

"We can never go back to the way things were," I said defiantly. "I almost forgot that, but now I know." I started walking back to the car.

"But she said I don't even have to be there for the baby. That I can sign my rights away if I want to."

"And you considered it, didn't you? Signing away your unborn child just like you signed away your whole family," I said without turning around. Reginald tried to grab me, but he fell down in the muck. "You can keep this house. I want a divorce."

I opened the car door and was about to get inside when I heard a familiar ring. It was Reginald's cell phone.

I had the key in my hand, but I stopped myself from getting into the car. The way that ring sounded—there was just something about it. And somehow I knew instantly, in the way that any woman who's ever given birth does, that something was wrong.

"It's your mother. She's called five times. Now it's a text. She said she's been trying to reach you, too. She's at the hospital, at Grady. Something happened with one of the twins."

We ran to my car and got on the road without so much as a comment. I had to get to my child. I didn't care who was in the car. I kept calling my mother, but her phone was off and Reginald said it was probably because she was in the hospital.

"I never should've left him alone," I said.

"He's fine. I'm sure your mother's handling it," Reginald said.

"If something happens to him, I'll never forgive myself."

I kicked off my shoes and ran up the pavement toward the emergency room doors at the hospital in my bare feet. I stopped right out front and left Reginald to park the car. In my mind, I could hear my baby crying. His cries from his crib when he was a baby. I was always there. Would sit there with him, rock him to sleep, and let him know I'd never leave him alone and he was safe.

I had to know that he really was safe now. That his world, unlike mine hadn't come crashing in.

Reginald caught up with me and we followed a zigzag of little rooms and hallways, closets, and staircases to find my mother. The front desk didn't have a patient registered named Reginald Johnson Jr., but we knew he was there.

I saw my mother's purple jacket hanging out of one of the rooms and Reginald and I rushed to the door.

"R. J.? Where's R. J.?" I asked immediately as I walked into the room.

But inside there was a doctor standing beside the bed, helping Cheyenne up. They were laughing. R. J. was actually standing beside my mother, eating a chocolate-covered pretzel.

"Me?" R. J. asked, making his way to me. "I'm fine. Cheyenne fell down." He pointed to Cheyenne.

"Cheyenne? Is it you? What happened?" I went and stood in front of the doctor. "Are you OK?" The doctor and my mother explained everything to Reginald as I pressed and patted Cheyenne's arms and legs.

"We came as soon as we could." Reginald reached over and patted Cheyenne's head.

"Your daughter is fine," the doctor reassured Reginald. "She just sprained her pinky." He pointed at a little silver sling holding Cheyenne's pinky just as I made my way to it.

"A sprain?" I held the little swollen fingers.

"What happened?" Reginald asked.

"I climbed a tree," Cheyenne said matter-of-factly.

"I told her to stay out of that tree in the backyard," my mother said.

"A tree? What were you doing climbing a tree?" I asked.

"We were playing in Grandma's backyard and R. J. said he wanted to see me fly."

"Fly? But you know you can't fly? You know that's not for real," I said.

"She knows now," my mother said. "Cried the whole time on the way over here. They had to give us a room, she was so loud."

"I wanted to climb the tree in the backyard like a boy," Cheyenne admitted.

"But you can't just do whatever you want, baby," Reginald said. "You know right from wrong and you know you shouldn't be climbing trees. You can hurt yourself. You could've really hurt yourself and your brother."

I listened as the doctor explained how the sprain would affect Cheyenne: the swelling would go down in about a week, but until then there was no reason to limit her activities. Maybe no tree climbing.

"Ice cream is the best remedy," he joked. "My prescription is an immediate trip to the nearest ice cream parlor."

"Ice cream? Really?" R. J. said excitedly. "I want to sprain my finger, too. Can I?"

"No! No! No!" we all said.

As we attempted to retrace our steps to exit the hospital, Reginald and I naturally took sides around the twins and held their hands. My mother, who'd been silent and trying to avoid talking to Reginald walked a few steps ahead. Cheyenne held her pinky to her chest and walked closest to her father.

"We going home, Daddy?" R. J. asked.

"Yes, son," Reginald answered.

"Yes," Cheyenne cheered. "We're a family again."

Reginald looked at me.

"Mama, did you drive?" I asked.

My mother turned around.

"No, I couldn't," she said. "That child was hollering like somebody was killing her. I had to call an ambulance."

"Reginald and I are in my car," I said. "I guess we can all fit in."

"It's OK; we're all going home," R. J. said and then I realized that he was talking about Augusta.

I looked at Cheyenne holding Reginald's hand.

"No, I think we're going to have to drop Daddy off," I said.

"Drop him off?" Cheyenne looked at me and dropped Reginald's hand. "But I thought you said we were going home together. That we were going back to Augusta with Daddy. Isn't that why you went there?" She stopped walking.

I looked at my mother.

"I didn't say anything," she said.

"I know what I said, pumpkin, but"—I tried to reach for Cheyenne, but she stepped back—"Daddy and Mommy aren't getting back together. Not right now. Reginald, could you explain this to her?"

"But you said that if we were all happy, we could go. We could go home!"

"I know, but—" I tried, looking at Reginald.

"Baby, what your mother's trying to say is—" Reginald started.

"You're liars!" Cheyenne hollered so loud it seemed as if everything in the hospital stopped. "You're both liars." She pushed away from us and ran back down the hallway toward her room.

"Chey!" Reginald called, turning to follow her.

"Where did she go?" my mother asked.

"I'll get her," I said. "You all wait here."

* * *

There was a nurse in front of the room where Cheyenne had been earlier.

"She's in the corner," the woman said, as I rushed around to the door.

"Thank you." I went inside and saw Cheyenne scrunched up in the corner, her legs pushed into her chest just enough to cover her arm. Her eyes were red with tears and she stared straight ahead.

I walked over and sat beside her on the cold tile.

"I'm sorry," I said. "I'm sorry this didn't work. And I don't think you'll ever know or understand how sorry Mama is. But I am. There's nothing more that I wanted for you guys than for our family to work. But . . . what Mommy wants and what Mommy knows is right are two different things right now."

Cheyenne wiped one of her tears but said nothing.

"But you know what will never change?" I pulled at Cheyenne's face and made her turn and face me. "That I love you. And no matter what else happens, that's never going to change. And your father loves you, too. Even if he doesn't live with us. He'll always be in your life. He'll never leave you."

"Then why can't he live with us?" she mumbled behind tears.

"You're a little too young to understand that. But what happened between me and your dad had been going on for a while," I said. "It's no one's fault. It's just how it is."

"Doesn't he love us anymore?"

"Of course he does. Our relationship has nothing to do with you. I bet your daddy loves you more than any other woman in the world."

"You think so?"

"I know so."

Three hours and a few scoops of ice cream later, it was as if Cheyenne had never had an accident at the foot of the tree. This was really the best prescription ever. The twins were upstairs getting ready for bed and I was sitting in the living room watching television with my mother.

She hadn't asked what happened with Reginald yet and I really didn't want her to.

The incident with Cheyenne brought me right to where I needed to be. What happened in Augusta was going to stay there as far as I was concerned. There was no reason to fight it or talk about it. It was over. And now I could move on, knowing I tried to make it OK.

It wasn't my job to hate Sasha or Reginald or seek vengeance. They were bringing a new life into the world and they had plenty to handle. I was thinking about what all I had to handle.

I heard feet pattering against the wooden floor upstairs, wrestling, a wince, and then a holler. Someone screamed, "No"; someone shouted, "No" back.

I just sat there and listened to the noise. I reached into a little red bowl sitting between my mother and me on the couch and retrieved a salty boiled peanut.

"You aren't going to say nothing to them?" she asked.

I looked up at the ceiling. There was a clump and then silence.

"They'll be OK," I said. "Kids need to be rough." I laughed and reached for another peanut.

My mother reached for one, too.

She popped it into her mouth and looked at me.

"You think you're staying here for a little while?" she asked.

"I hope so," I said. "Why?"

"Oh, it's nothing, I just thought that maybe this weekend I could start cleaning out my garden. Pull some weeds. I can't do it myself. It's hard to get on my knees. And I figured maybe with my grands here, I could have some new knees."

"Say no more, Mama," I said, reaching into the bowl with her. "We'll stay."

"That's good, baby."

"And, Mama, thanks for being honest with me," I said. "When it really mattered, your advice helped pull me through."

Ignoring the red bowl between us and the remote control that was sitting on my lap, I reached over and embraced my mother wholly.

15

I had been standing in front of A. J.'s door for thirty minutes—well, the total waiting time was actually forty minutes if you count the time I spent sitting in the car looking at the door—before I finally got the courage to ring his bell. I raised my hand and was about to push the little lighted button, but then my nerve left me and I decided to go with the first plan I'd come up with in the car.

I looked in my purse and found a pen. I didn't have my writing pad, so I took out an empty envelope and started writing a note.

A. J., I wrote and then scribbled over it. It looked too friendly. Like I was a neighbor. *Hey A. J.*, I wrote and then scribbled over it. It looked like I was trying to be friendly.

I ripped the sheet in half and tried to put the part I wrote on in my pocket.

"What am I trying to say?" I said. "Hello A. J.! How are you? I was in the neighborhood and I wanted to stop by to apologize for standing you up," I said, imagining that saying the note first and then writing it would make it sound better.

A neighborhood security vehicle rolled past slowly.

"It's eleven o'clock at night; I'm gonna get arrested out here," I scolded myself, thinking that I probably had no business coming over to his home so late at night in the first place. What was I thinking? What if he had company? A woman? Of course he had company! Of course there would be a woman there.

I balled up the torn piece of envelope and put it into my pocket. I turned to go back to my car, but light caught my footsteps in the darkness as the door behind me opened. I didn't turn back around though. I was too embarrassed and thought that maybe if I stood still enough, whoever was holding the door open behind me wouldn't be able to see me and just go back into the house. I closed my eyes tightly and wished I was invisible.

"Dawn?"

I peeked through one eye.

"Is that you?"

"Yes," I answered, clenching my teeth.

"Are you leaving? Did you ring the bell?"

I turned around like I was facing a firing squad, but what I saw was much more attractive. A.J. was standing square in the doorway wearing only a pair of thin beige night pants. Sleep was streaked all over his face. He rubbed his eyes like a little boy.

"Oh, you were asleep? I was just stopping by, but then I figured you were busy," I said, hoping he wouldn't think I was a complete stalker—which would prove to be true if he had video surveillance. I looked up for cameras over the doorway.

"Yeah, I was asleep, but my neighbor called. Said someone was sitting in a car in front of my house," he said, yawning.

"Oh no! I'm sorry."

"It's cool. They look out for me. We've had some funny situations."

"I won't do that again. I just . . . I wasn't sure if you were having company."

He straightened up and looked at me with a grin.

"It's fine." He backed up into the house. "We can talk about it inside—"

"No," I said.

"No?"

"Look, you told me to come here, to come see you when I was ready."

"Yes, and . . ." A. J. moved back a little more, using his hand to direct me into the house.

"No, that's not why I'm here," I said. "I'm here to apologize for standing you up and to tell you that I'm not ready. And I don't know when and if I ever will be. I know that sounds a little crazy with everything that's happened. But I'm a long way from starting anything. I have a lot on my plate. And you; for a minute, you were a bright and promising thing for me. You reminded me that I'm beautiful. That I'm worth chasing. And I'll forever be grateful to you for that. You're an amazing example of a man. And when and if I'm ever ready for what you're ready for, I pray that some amazing example of a woman wasn't ready first."

A. J. came down one step and was nose to nose with me.

"Well, I accept your apology and I respect you sharing all of this with me, but you came all the way over here at eleven o'clock to tell me you're not ready?" he asked.

I nodded.

"You know this is officially booty-call hour? Especially if I have on nightclothes."

We looked at his night pants.

"Well, I'm fully clothed," I said.

He took a deep breath.

"What am I going to do with you?" A. J. said. He kissed me softly on the forehead. "Why don't you come in and just chill for a while?" he asked. "I can't have a young lady out on the roads this late at night, now."

I laughed at him. It was such a line. A bad line.

"What?" he asked, faking surprise. "I'm not trying anything. I'm just being nice. A good, upstanding guy. You just said I'm a 'great example of a man.' "

"I don't sound like that!" I protested his mocking nasal voice.

"Yes, you do!" he said, laughing. "Look, why don't you just

come in and relax. No pressure. We can make macaroni and cheese!"

"It's too late to make macaroni and cheese," I said.

"Not if you want to eat it at sunrise."

"No funny stuff?" I asked.

"Not if you grate the cheese!"

He put his hand out to me and I took it.

I saw the curtain in the living room window moving when I pulled into my mother's driveway. There was a little brown hand against the glass. It disappeared when I stopped the car.

I got out and trudged up the walkway with the keys in my hand, ready to open the front door.

The sun was rising, but our Indian Summer was wrapping up and the cold blew right through my clothes. I felt a chill and hustled to the door, but right when I got to the steps, I stopped and turned around to look at the street.

It was so quiet out there and nothing was moving. It looked like a picture. Houses and cars. Trees and fences. Flowers. Grass. I unfolded my arms from a protective embrace over my chest and inhaled the crisp morning air. I felt a rush vibrate through my body and thanked God that I was there to feel the world. To see it. And in my clear mind, I imagined that it was fresh and new and I was the first person to pull it all in. It was the start of a new day. It was my start of a new life.

"God," I said. "Thanks for helping me."

When I walked into the house, I heard a creak on the stairs and looked up quickly to see a brown foot hanging from pink pajama pants turning onto the upstairs landing.

"Cheyenne Loren," I called softy.

The movement stopped. I imagined that she was standing at the top of the steps against the wall.

"Cheyenne Loren," I called again. "I know you're up there."

I sat on the couch and pulled off my shoes quietly. Seconds

went by. I sat back and watched the steps. There was no movement.

And then the pink pajama pants came from around the corner.

"I was just waiting for you to come home," she said softly.

"Come down here," I said. "I can't see you."

She came down the steps slowly like they were covered in ice and stood at the bottom.

"Come sit down next to me," I said, patting the cushion beside me.

She looked at me and I could tell that she hadn't slept all night. Her eyes were completely red.

"I'm not mad at you. You can sit down. It's fine." I patted the cushion again.

She sat down.

"Where were you?" she asked.

"I was out," I said carefully. "But now I'm home."

"Were you driving?"

"Yes," I answered, putting my arm up on the couch around her shoulders. "Were you afraid that I was driving?"

She nodded and looked away into the living room.

"Chey, I'm not going to mess up again. Look at me."

She turned back to me.

"You don't have to worry about me," I said. "You don't have to sit up at this window and ever worry about me not coming home, or driving drunk or putting you in a bad situation like I did that night. That will never happen again. Do you understand me?"

"Yes."

I leaned over and started playing with her hair.

"Now, things are about to start changing for us. For you and me."

"How?"

"Well, for starters, we're going to start spending a lot more time together."

"Really?" She pulled her legs up onto the couch.

"Yeah. I was thinking, you know how I read to R. J. every morning?"

"Yes, his *Goodnight Moon*," she said mockingly. "But he gave that book away."

"Well, we'll get him a new one. But, in the meantime, I was thinking, maybe you and I could do something together in the morning."

"Read a book?" she asked, frowning. "I can read already. Those are kiddie books."

"There are plenty of other books we can read." I put my arm over her shoulder and she rested her head against my chest. "We can even read poems."

"You know any poems?"

"Oh, I meant we need to get some books to read poems," I said, laughing. "I memorized some poems . . . when I was about your age, but I don't remember any of them anymore."

"None of them?"

I looked up and rested my head on the top of the couch.

"Hum . . . There was this one by Maya Angelou that I memorized for a talent show I was in. I don't know if I remember the whole thing. It was called 'Phenomenal Woman.' "

"Phenom—?"

"Phenomenal."

"Phenomenal. What does that mean?"

"I means someone who's special. Not common. Not like everyone else," I said. "Kind of like you."

"Really?" She looked up at me. "You think I'm special?"

"You're strong, Cheyenne. You're strong and smart. You don't take any mess. Not from me. Not from your brother. Not from your father. Not from anyone."

Cheyenne and I started laughing.

"You don't remember it, Mama? Come on, say it! You can try!"

"Oh . . . it was so long ago," I started. "It opened kind of like—'Pretty women wonder where my secret lies . . . I'm not cute or built to suit a fashion model's size . . ." I tickled Cheyenne's stomach and looked at the ceiling trying to remember the rest of the poem. I got through a good bit of it. I know I left out a line somewhere, but the last, I could never forget the last lines: " 'It's in the click of my heels/The bend of my hair/the palm of my hand/The need of my care,/'Cause I'm a woman/Phenomenally./Phenomenal woman,/That's me.' "

I smiled at my half-baked sunrise performance and I looked down at Cheyenne expecting a round of applause or a smile, but she was fast asleep. Nestled under my arm and fast asleep.

I watched her and thought to carry her upstairs, but my baby girl, who was soon going to be a young woman, was growing so fast, and even with her lanky arms and legs, I knew we wouldn't make it past the first step.

I rested my head on top of hers and went to sleep, too.

Discussion Questions

1. Because of RJ's autism, Dawn spends lots of time brooding over him and hardly pays the other twin, Cheyenne, any attention unless she's being unruly. While it's understandable that she focuses on the more needy child, what effect did this have on Cheyenne? How might Dawn have better handled their relationship to avoid issues? Do you believe the old saying that mothers tend to love their sons and raise their daughters?

2. By marrying Reginald and moving to Augusta right after college, Dawn seldom sees her mother or any of her friends. What effect has this had on her life? Is Dawn's separation from her mother about distance or a desire to detach herself from a past filled with pain?

3. Before Sasha arrives in Augusta, it's made clear that Dawn hasn't seen her college roommate in years and she knows how conniving Sasha was in the past and how attractive she is in the present. While her attention seems to be focused on making sure her former best friend gets along with her husband, maybe it should have been elsewhere. In other words, should she have let this woman stay in her home? At what point should she have said NO? How do you feel about women staying in your home or hanging around your husband? How do you handle it if a long-lost friend (who happens to be very attractive) asks to stay with you and your husband for a weekend?

4. Dawn feels anxiety about Sasha visiting her home because she knows many of her sorority sisters felt she married down by marrying a country boy who was mowing the lawns at their college to make a living. While she claims she's happy, she isn't as successful as she thought she would be, she's far from her family and friends, and struggling to make ends

meet. Were her sorority sisters essentially correct in their prediction? Was she wrong to marry for love? In this time of financial rule where less money can often equal less access for one's entire family, is it wise to marry for love? Or should one marry for fortune? Maybe a bit of both?

5. At the Hell Hath No Fury House it is suggested that the women feel free to express violent desires and plots of revenge. Do you think this helps the women? How so? If you've ever been through a breakup, what's the worst sad fate you've ever secretly wished upon the dearly departed? Do you feel bad about it?

6. Reginald isn't the only one ogling Sasha in this book. A close reading shows that Dawn is painfully aware of everything Sasha wears, how she smells, and the exact shade of her lipstick. Is Dawn attracted to Sasha or just plain envious? How does this play out in the scene where the women kiss? Do you think Dawn wanted to be intimate with Sasha or maybe she was just seeking any kind of intimacy in her life? Did Sasha use this against her? In this age of sexual exploration, it seems like everyone is trying Sasha's suggested *menage á trois*. What affect do you believe this can have on a marriage? Do kissing or making out with a woman make another woman a lesbian? Would you ever do something like that with one of your friends?

7. Sharika may be a smart cookie, but in Dawn's eyes, she's less intelligent when it comes to selecting appropriate business attire and conducting business in general. To Dawn, Sharika is all passion and no poise. In fact, Sharika seems to agree when she admits that she is afraid to enroll in a prestigious doctoral program because she won't be accepted by fellow classmates. She doesn't want to be the butt of the jokes.

Should Sharika change her style and/or change herself to fit in? How far should one go to fit into a particular business or social setting? How far have you gone? Have you ever felt a need to share such advice with a coworker or friend?

8. Reginald was the first person in the marriage to break his vow of fidelity when he slept with Sasha. When Dawn meets AJ, she is attracted to him, but she's still dealing with the emotional baggage of her pending divorce, and when he makes a move, she pushes him away. Should she have slept with AJ to "get her groove back"? Was she right to continue to support vows though her husband had clearly moved on? Have you ever had sex simply because you wanted to get over something? How did that turn out?

9. While Dawn turned her back on her friends and sorority for many good reasons, it's actually a former college acquaintance who steps up to support Dawn financially during her divorce, as she suspects Kerry paid for the attorney through the Hell Hath No Fury House. When was the last time someone paid little attention to did something like this for you? When was the last time you did something nice for someone you hardly know?

10. Like many women dealing with cheating men in divorce, Dawn goes back with her husband to try to patch things up. She believes she can make it work. She's never known how to love any other man and she wants to keep her family together. Was it right for her to do this—to at least try? Have you ever begged a man to stay with you the way Dawn did?

If you enjoyed *Should Have Known Better*,
don't miss Trice Hickman's

Keeping Secrets & Telling Lies

Available in February 2012 at your local bookstore

1

Still Going Strong . . .

"Listen," Victoria whispered. "Did you hear that?"

"V, it was nothing," Ted whispered back in a low moan, breathing hard into his wife's ear as he pressed his hard body against her soft curves.

"No . . . listen. I think she's up."

Knock, knock, knock.

There was no mistaking the faint sound of small knuckles rapping on the door. Victoria quickly adjusted the spaghetti straps of her silk teddy as she sat up in bed. She could still feel Ted's warm body next to hers as she gathered the sateen sheet around her waist.

"Mommy, Daddy . . . it's morning time!" Alexandria called out in a high-pitched squeal, peering into her parents' bedroom through the crack in the door. "Are you up?"

Ted sat up beside Victoria and sighed. As much as he loved his precious little daughter, he also cherished his alone time with his wife, especially since it was something they seemed to have very little of lately.

Over the last several months he'd been spending extra-long hours at the office in preparation for taking his company public next year. ViaTech had survived the telecom industry's downturn several years back, and was now poised to make a strong initial public offering next spring. And Victoria's days were just as long and hectic because her business kept her equally on the go. Divine Occasions, her event planning and catering company, was in its sixth year of full-time operation, and had established her as one of Atlanta's most sought-after event coordinators.

But despite Ted and Victoria's jam-packed work schedules, they always made sure to carve out time for their daughter. She was the single most important part of their lives. On evenings when Victoria didn't have an event to oversee she was diligent about spending quality time with Alexandria, making sure that she prepared dinner so they could eat together. And most nights when Ted wasn't out of town on business, he managed to return home from the office just in time to tuck her in and read her a bedtime story. After their professional and parental duties ended for the day, they'd steal a few treasured moments together before falling off to sleep.

"Yes, we're up, sweetie," Victoria answered.

With that, Alexandria came barreling into the room, ponytails flying, and a grin on her face as big as the sky. She ran up to her parents' large four-poster bed, using the antique mahogany footstool as a springboard to hop in between them. She giggled hard as she made an indention in the soft, jacquard-print comforter where she landed. "It's morning time, Mommy and Daddy!" she shouted again, full of all the excitement that a combination of Saturday morning cartoons and the promise of an afternoon playdate could bring for a five-year-old.

Ted put his hand to his chest and fell back onto the bed, pretending to suffer an imaginary attack. "You yelled so loud, I think you gave me a heart attack," he teased.

Alexandria stopped grinning and stared at her father. Her face carried an odd, serious look. "Daddy, are you all right," she said softly, putting her small hand on his broad chest. "Don't have a heart attack," she whispered, peering into his deep blue eyes.

Ted couldn't help but let out a laugh. Alexandria Elizabeth Thornton was the joy of her parents' hearts, and as they had both come to agree, was one of the most serious five-year-olds to ever own a pack of Crayolas. She was playful and exuberant, yet incredibly mature and cerebral for someone who could only claim graduating from preschool as her highest level of academic achievement to date.

She was what her Nana Elizabeth called an old soul. "That child has been here before. Any child who has that much common sense has walked this earth and seen things in another lifetime," Victoria's mother often said.

"No, sweetie, your father's fine," Victoria reassured. "You just startled us. What have I told you about using your inside voice?" she lightly scolded.

Alexandria didn't answer right away. "Daddy, your heart's not right?" she said, tilting her head to the side, making it sound more like a pronouncement than a question.

Victoria didn't know why, but something in her daughter's tone put a chill on her arm.

"Daddy's fine, princess," Ted smiled, grabbing Alexandria and tickling her until she dropped her frown and began smiling along with him.

Victoria tried to smile, too, but she felt unsettled by Alexandria's comment and reaction to what should have been a playful moment. She looked into her daughter's eyes, wanting to reassure her again. "Sweetie, your father's fine, he was just playing around, okay?"

Alexandria nodded in compliance, but still didn't look completely convinced. "Can I watch *Big Bird*?" she asked in her small, high-pitched voice.

"Sure, princess. I'll set it up for you downstairs." Ted reached under the comforter, pulled his pajama bottoms up to his waist, then leaned over and whispered into Victoria's ear. "When I get back we'll pick up where we left off," he winked, then scooped Alexandria off the bed and headed downstairs.

Victoria watched her husband and daughter as their heads disappeared down the long hallway. She marveled at the way Alexandria had Ted wrapped around her finger. It reminded her of the relationship she'd shared with her own father when she was growing up. Alexandria was Ted's little princess, just as she'd been her father's little queen.

Victoria stretched her arms high above her head and thought about the busy day that lay before her. First on her list was dropping off Alexandria at her first Jack and Jill playdate, then making a quick trip to her office to go over the remaining details for a large celebrity wedding she was coordinating next weekend. After that, she planned to head back over to pick up Alexandria, drive across town to pick up Ted's dry cleaning, and then swing by the grocery store before she took Alexandria to their neighbor's house for a sleepover.

At times, Victoria felt as though she didn't have time to think, let alone breathe. She always seemed to be going to this, hurrying to there, or coming from that. Running her business required her to put on a good face for the public, even when she felt crappy. Motherhood demanded that she appear eager and attentive, even when she felt exhausted. And being a wife meant she had to master the delicate art of compromise, even when she wanted to do her own thing.

But she knew there were worse things than having a busy life, and she knew that a lot of women would gladly trade places with her in a heartbeat. She was blessed to have a happy, healthy daughter who was smart as a whip, and whose loving spirit made her a joy to raise. And even though she wished her husband spent more time at home and less time away on business and late nights at the office, she knew that he loved and adored her. She lived in a custom-built home in an exclusive, gated community. Her child-care service was reliable and trusted, and she was fortunate to have neighbors and friends who gladly pitched in to help. She had quit her corporate job several years ago to pursue the passion she'd loved since childhood, and to top it all off, she was in good physical health. Yes, she knew she was blessed, and she knew there were worse things than busy days.

After Ted secured Alexandria in front of the TV with her juice box in one hand, the remote control in the other, and her favorite DVD playing, he hurried back upstairs, taking them two at a time. When he walked into the bedroom a smile slid across his face.

Victoria was waiting for him, perched on her knees in the middle of their king-size bed. Her silk teddy and lacy thong were tossed to the side, and the look on her face said she remembered his parting words. She was ready to pick up exactly where they'd left off.

Ted was struck by the fact that even though he had seen his wife's naked body a million times, her sensuous allure and striking beauty never failed to stir him. He loved the velvety smoothness of her deep, chocolate-brown skin that always felt soft to the touch. He took pleasure in running his fingers through the silky thickness of her long black hair that draped the slender elegance of her neck. And he felt he could lose himself in the gentle curve of her lower back that gave way to the seductive pull of her soft, round behind. Motherhood had given her slim figure slightly more weight, and an added sexiness that he loved.

"Damn, you're beautiful," he said, removing his pajama bottoms. He pushed the door closed behind him and walked toward the bed.

Victoria smiled, enjoying the look that always came over Ted's face when they were about to make love. It let her know that he wanted her. He climbed into bed, covering her naked body with his. She embraced the feel of her husband's tall, muscular frame as she prepared herself for the pleasure to come.

He kissed her slowly and deeply, gently tweaking her hardening nipples with his fingers before moving down, alternating between his hands and mouth as he suckled her soft mounds of flesh. He eased his way farther down her body, dotting small kisses along a man-made trail until his head rested between her legs.

"I love it when you're this wet," Ted breathed, gently rolling his tongue over her throbbing tenderness. Victoria threw her head back, digging her heels deep into the mattress as she clenched the bedsheet between her fists. He placed one hand under her hips and the other at the center of her warm middle. He worked with diligence, licking, sucking, and gently kissing her glistening folds. He took his time, devouring every inch of her sweet spot until she shuddered into a creamy orgasm that made her tremble. She released a deep, ecstasy-filled moan that rumbled in the back of her throat.

After a brief moment, Victoria regained her senses, ready to give Ted the same intense pleasure she'd just received. She secured her hands around him, holding him in her firm but gentle grip as she stroked his hardness, massaging him with care. A long, slow, *"Uuummmmm,"* escaped his lips as Victoria worked her magic. She opened her mouth wide and swallowed him, sucking and licking with controlled precision. When she squeezed the tip of his head deep into her tightening jaws, he could barely hold on any longer.

"Oooohhhhh, V," Ted moaned, perspiration dampening his skin. He shifted position, gently laying Victoria on her back as she wrapped her long legs around his waist, arching her pelvis into the air to meet his. He slipped inside her with smooth, even strokes. Her body received him as he moved in and out, delighting and electrifying her all at once. Their rhythm was a slow and easy grind that flowed into a growing and heated frenzy as Ted went deeper, increasing the speed of his thrusts. Victoria moaned, clinging to the sex-drenched sweat pouring from his body while she worked her hips at an equally hungry pace. Finally, they both surrendered to a second wave of pleasure.

Victoria reveled in her husband's ability to fulfill her sexual desires. He knew exactly how to please her; anticipating her wants and knowing her most intimate needs. Over the course of their six-year marriage, even though the frequency of their lovemaking had slowed, he had never left her wanting. This was yet another one of her many blessings, and again, she knew there were a multitude of women who would kill to be in her shoes.

She had heard more than a few of her friends and clients complain about their dead sex lives, citing disgruntled husbands, overactive children, and underactive libidos as major culprits. One of her best friends, Debbie Long, who was like the sister she never had, had recently confided that since the birth of her son seven years ago, her love life with her husband had dwindled to a state of near nonexistence. "We're like roommates," Debbie had told Victoria a few months ago. "We love each other, but the passion is gone. We're just going through the motions. As a matter of fact, I can't remember the last time Rob and I made love," she'd complained.

Victoria had been shocked to learn that Debbie and Rob's marriage had shriveled into the dull, sexless picture her friend had painted, especially since she and Rob had always been romantic and affectionate with each other. Aside from her own parents' strong and lasting union, Victoria had held Debbie and Rob's relationship as the gold standard by which marriage could be measured.

But as Victoria would come to learn in the weeks ahead, time and circumstance were instruments that could change the tune of one's life in shocking and unexpected ways.

Looking at her own relationship made Victoria feel grateful that she and Ted were still going strong. She knew their marriage wasn't perfect, but they had love and trust as their anchors. The sex was hot, and he made sure that he pleased her. He was in excellent physical health and his age-defying good looks made him appear a decade younger than his fifty-two years. His vanilla-hued skin was taut and supple with a hint of olive undertone that carried hardly a trace of any wrinkles, and the small hints of gray that now peppered his thick black hair added to his outrageous sex appeal. He kept his muscles strong and well toned with regular workouts, and jogged several times a week to round out his physical fitness regimen. Having a mate like Ted was what Victoria had always dreamed of, and again, she knew she was blessed.

After making love, Victoria lay next to her husband, running her fingers across the faint, dark hairs on his broad chest. "Alexandria's movie is probably half over by now," she said.

"Um-hm," Ted answered in a dreamy, after-sex voice.

"I'm gonna take a shower and go downstairs to make Alexandria's breakfast. We have a busy day ahead and I need to run a few errands before I drop her off at Susan's later this afternoon."

"Another sleepover?"

"Yep."

Ted pulled Victoria on top of him and grinned. "That means we'll have tonight all to ourselves."

"*Mmmm,* we sure will," she nodded.

They enjoyed another long kiss before Victoria rolled out of bed.